# AND THERE I'LL BE A SOLDIER

## A WESTERN STORY

# AND THERE I'LL BE A SOLDIER

## A WESTERN STORY

JOHNNY D. BOGGS

Copyright © 2012 by Johnny D. Boggs
Published in 2017 by Blackstone Publishing
Cover design by Alenka Vdovič Linaschke

Printed in the United States of America

ISBN: 978-1-4708-6144-5

1 3 5 7 9 10 8 6 4 2

CIP data for this book is available
from the Library of Congress

Blackstone Publishing
31 Mistletoe Rd.
Ashland, OR 97520

www.BlackstonePublishing.com

For Mark McGee

# FOREWORD

My ancestors fought on both sides of the Civil War, a fact my deeply Southern relatives never bragged about when I was a kid. Come to think of it, many still don't own up to that "Yankee" bit of family lore. Maybe that's why I started out with the idea of writing a novel told from Northern and Southern viewpoints about the Battle of Shiloh, which, of course, is no stranger to novelists (Will Henry, G. Clifton Wisler, and Shelby Foote, for example). Yet when a research trip brought me to Corinth, Mississippi, I decided to include the Second Corinth battle in this narrative, as well. Shiloh is Shiloh, with countless historians analyzing it, while Corinth is often overlooked. Corinth also was a direct contrast to Shiloh; Shiloh was fought in fields and woods, while Corinth took place in a town.

Walking around Corinth, a wonderful town with well-preserved history, I was struck with the need to add a third voice to the mix, that of a noncombatant Southern citizen. After all, the war certainly affected civilians and not just soldiers. Thus, Grace Dehner was born. Grace Dehner, Texian Ryan McCalla, and Missourian Caleb Cole are products of my imagination, but many other figures in this novel did fight for the North and South, and many of those died or carried the scars earned at Shiloh and Corinth in 1862.

# CHAPTER ONE

He stood ankle-deep in pig dung, slogging through a pen filled with squealing Durocs and snorting Poland Chinas. Even with his rubber boots and thick gloves, he knew he'd stink for the rest of the week since one of those ill-tempered big red hogs had charged and knocked him onto his hindquarters. Probably would carry the stench the rest of his life. So when Jimmy Crawford came riding up the road, Caleb welcomed the chance to climb out of the muck and sit on the top rail, maybe catch a breeze in the sweltering heat but at the least escape the stink for a while.

"What you doing?" Jimmy called out after reining to a stop. In lieu of a saddle, the lanky teen sat on a worn woolen blanket, and instead of a bridle he used a horsehair-hitched hackamore.

"What's it look like?" Caleb Cole shook his head.

Jimmy shot a worried glance at the house. "Your pa around?"

Caleb shook his head. "He went off this morning to Bryant Station to haggle with Mister Metzger." *Haggle*, Caleb thought with disgust, *over another big red Duroc. As if we don't have enough already.*

"Bessy? Your ma?"

He didn't bother to answer. "Why aren't you working at the sawmill?"

Jimmy Crawford sat up straighter, blue eyes straining first toward the cabin and then across the Cole farm. He wore duck trousers, a sweat-stained blue shirt, and no hat. He wiped sweat off his brow, and lowered his voice.

"Ezra Meachem says some Rebs are recruiting and drilling at Unionville."

The mule snorted.

"Your pa's been preaching Abolition and the Union forever since you moved here," Caleb reminded his friend and neighbor.

"I know that." Another quick look to make sure nobody could overhear him, which irked Caleb. These hogs, sows, and piglets wouldn't tell anyone what Jimmy Crawford had planned. "But I figured it couldn't hurt to go watch them. Be fun and downright interesting. Thought you might like to tag along with me and see for yourself."

Now it was Caleb's turn to look at the house. Smoke wafted from the cook shack's chimney, chickens pecked the ground in front of the porch, but he couldn't see his mother or sister. He looked down the path that led to the Putnam County Pike and scanned the rolling prairie. That would be just like his father, to come home right now. Although he saw nobody, at length Caleb sighed.

"I can't go."

"You got something better to do today?" Jimmy grinned, and pointed his jaw at the sea of red, black, and black and white swine crowding the pen.

Caleb dropped to the ground, but kept his left hand on the top rail. Like it would anchor him to his chores.

"Ezra said they were drilling right on the courthouse lawn," Jimmy said.

"That takes gumption." Putnam County was spitting distance from the Iowa border, and residents had changed the name of the county seat to Unionville from Harmony a few years back. Maybe the Rebels wanted to rub Secession in everybody's face.

Jimmy's head bobbed. "Yeah, but Ezra up and joined the Southern cause. Says so did Parker Pruitt and a couple other boys he didn't know."

Caleb lifted his left hand from the fence, using the bottom cedar rail to scrape mud and manure off his boots. "You planning on joining?"

A rough laugh caused Jimmy to lean back on the mule. When he straightened, he said: "Are you joshing me, Caleb? My pa would skin me alive if I turned Secesh. I just figured it sure had to be funner than sawing logs. Or slopping hogs." He prodded on. "Bet we could even stop at Whit's mercantile for some sassafras tea after watching the Rebs." Looking at the clear blue sky, Jimmy added thoughtfully: "I imagine Maryanne's working there today."

Caleb had taken a couple steps away from the pen. His lips parted, and he wet them with his tongue. Then his head shook. "I'm not fit to see Maryanne. Or anybody in Unionville."

Jimmy countered. "You can wash off at the creek. Clothes will be dry by the time you walk to Unionville."

By then Caleb already knew that he was going. He stood six-foot-one and weighed better than one hundred ninety pounds. Too big for a whipping from his father, and his mother wouldn't mind. Bessy would give him grief, but, no matter what he did, she'd find some excuse to needle him. Besides, he reasoned, his parents and sister would like to hear his report. Most likely Pa would be perturbed that he hadn't gotten to see a Rebel militia in Unionville rather than just another red stud hog in Bryant Station.

Likewise, Jimmy Crawford knew that Caleb would tag along. Smiling, he lifted the hackamore and clucked his tongue, heading the mule back toward the pike. Caleb dropped to the dirt, pulled off his rubber boots, shucked his gloves, tugged off his socks, and, barefoot, followed his friend. With his long stride, it took him little time to catch up.

* * * * *

A lot of people lived in Putnam County, Caleb Cole always thought, but, then, he had never been out of Putnam County. There were tons of farmers, something like eighteen sawmills, and more pigs than trees, and Parker Pruitt's family ran one of three flour mills in the county. Yet for all those people living in the county—right around nine thousand, his father had told him that spring—Union-ville never struck Caleb as much of a town.

You would expect the rarity of a traitorous militia drilling and recruiting right dab in the middle of town would have drawn a crowd, yet, even around the square, Unionville was quiet. Of course, it was Tuesday afternoon, and a blistering one at that. Besides, Caleb reasoned, it was Unionville. It was always quiet.

Jimmy Crawford had no trouble finding a place to tether his mule in front of Whit Corneilison's mercantile.

Only two or three years old, the red-brick courthouse anchored the square. It was two stories, but the upper story was vacant. Typical for Unionville.

The town had no newspaper. Caleb's father often said Union-ville had no need of a newspaper, not with the combined mouths of the Meachem family.

Ezra Meachem had been right. On the square, between the elm trees, Caleb saw a flag popping in the wind. Three large stripes, two red ones sandwiching a white one, and a blue square in the upper left corner with one white star circled by ten more. About twenty or so soldiers, dressed in everything from butternut to duck to wool to one moth-eaten uniform of a dragoon, marched across the grass as some black-bearded gent in a wide-brimmed straw hat sang out orders and a barefoot kid wearing mismatched brogans tapped a drum.

"Let's slake our thirst with some tea!" Jimmy called out, hooking a thumb toward the Corneilison store.

That was just like Jimmy Crawford. Work up a sweat and talk so much about the Rebs in Unionville, then chicken out at the last minute. If they went into Mr. Whit's store—especially if Maryanne were there—they might miss the whole show.

"No," Caleb said. "Let's watch the Secesh." Besides, Caleb didn't have money to spend on sassafras tea.

He crossed the street, not knowing if Jimmy Crawford would follow him or not, and found a shady spot underneath one of the thick elms.

The Rebs had stopped, and the straw-hat leader stepped in front of the line and said: "Let's show these Yanks the way real Missouri fightin' boys soldier. Let's teach 'em the School of the Soldier. *Eyes right! Left and front!*"

Caleb looked around. *Show these Yanks. What Yanks?* The only person watching the parade was Caleb. Typical Unionville. Maybe everybody in town was scared.

"No, no, no. That's not the way. Listen … 'Heels on the same line, as near each other as the conformation of the main will permit … The feet turned out equally, and forming with each other something less than a right angle …'"

Straw Hat spoke in a dull monotone. Caleb stifled a laugh and shook his head. The Rebel leader was reading from a book.

"'The knees straight without stiffness …'"

"What are they doing?"

Jimmy Crawford had joined him.

Caleb glanced at his friend, who, apparently, had decided that tea and Maryanne could wait.

"I don't know," Caleb answered honestly.

"Lordy, they don't even have any muskets."

Caleb pointed. "Sure they do. See them stacked in that circle. They're just practicing without their long guns."

"Practicing what?"

"How to stand in a line, near as I can tell."

"'The palm of the hand turned a little to the front, the little finger behind the seam of the pantaloons ...'"

Jimmy shrugged. "I thought for sure they'd have a cannon."

"They only have one horse."

"One horse? Ezra said they came up all the way from Chariton County."

Caleb shrugged. He had heard of the Chariton River, but not any Chariton County. It could be as far away as Washington City or as close as Iowa for all he knew.

"Soldier, what in thunder's name are you doing?"

Straw Hat gripped the hilt of his saber and strode toward a red-headed boy who was sitting at the end of the line, rubbing his right foot with both hands.

"This is the 'School of the Soldier,' boy!" Straw Hat bellowed. "You don't sit down."

"But my feet hurt, Gen'ral."

"I'll chop off your feet if you don't stand up and get back into formation!"

"But, Gen'ral!"

"I'm not a general, boy, but a duly elected captain. Now stand up!" He unsheathed the saber, and the soldier quickly shot to his feet, bumped into the nearest Reb, and sent him tumbling into the grass.

Caleb shook his head and, with a grin, faced Jimmy Crawford. "Well, we've found Parker Pruitt."

Jimmy chortled. "Don't reckon this war'll last very long."

"That's certain sure."

When the line of soldiers had reassembled into something like a formation, Straw Hat barked out a command to march. The drum began again, and Straw Hat resumed his grunts. They marched right past Jimmy and Caleb, and Caleb felt intense pleasure about how red Parker Pruitt's face got as he limped along, a few rods behind the rest of the Secessionist parade.

"You want some tea?" Jimmy asked.

"Nah."

"My treat."

*No, you'll just put it on your father's bill.* But his throat felt parched, and it was a long walk back to the farm, so his head bobbed.

"I'll fetch us a couple of bottles," Jimmy said. "You stay here and watch. Let me know if that general chops off Parker's feet."

"He's not a general!" Caleb called out to Jimmy's back as the gangling boy sprinted back toward the store. "He's a captain."

Caleb watched his friend bound up the steps and through the open doors to the mercantile. *Little sneak.* He'd probably spend the rest of the day inside, sipping tea and conversing with Maryanne Corneilison, and forgetting all about Caleb Cole.

The wind picked up, and the flag popped. Caleb looked up, and tilted his head. He hadn't noticed before, but red letters were stenciled onto the center white stripe: EQUALITY AND UNION.

That made him chuckle, and he said to himself: "That's a good joke."

"What's so funny about our flag, boy?"

Startled, Caleb took two steps backward and swallowed. Straw Hat stood in front of him, flanked by Parker Pruitt and three lean, bearded men with tobacco pushing against their cheeks.

"Answer me, boy," Straw Hat repeated. "What amuses you about the flag of the Keytesville Methodist Rangers?"

"No offense intended, Captain." Caleb chose his words carefully. "It's just that the word 'Union' on your flag struck me as peculiar. Since you want to dissolve the Union."

One of the bigger men spit brown juice between Caleb's bare feet. "What about the other word, boy. 'Equality'? That amuse you, too?"

It had, but Caleb shook his head.

"Mister Pruitt, here," said another tobacco chewer, "says you're a black Republican."

"That's not true," Caleb stammered. And it wasn't. He had

often wondered what it would be like to have slaves tend to those pigs all the time. He'd sure smell a lot better. He said: "I'm not old enough to vote."

"But you're old enough to make a choice, lad." Straw Hat had changed his tone. "Mister Pruitt enlisted in our regiment yesterday. We will free Missouri from Yankee tyrants and Abolitionist scoundrels."

Caleb looked back at the mercantile, hoping to find Jimmy Crawford, but, by thunder, now the door was shut.

Straw Hat kept talking: "We return to Keytesville tomorrow and await our orders from General Sterling Price."

He had never heard of Keytesville or Sterling Price.

"Mister Pruitt says you are a good fighter."

Caleb thought: *He ought to know. I've whipped him five times.* He said: "Parker's a good fighter himself." That was a lie. "And a real good shot." That wasn't.

"Mister Pruitt shall have ample opportunity to prove that as we drive the Yankees out of our great state. We came to Unionville all the way from Keytesville … nigh one hundred miles … to increase the ranks for Southern liberty."

"And because we don't like the name of your town," the third tobacco chewer said, and spat. The others chuckled.

"The pay is ten dollars a month and the glory of the Confederate cause," Straw Hat said. "The Methodist ladies of Keytesville are, at this very moment, sewing gray blouses and green pantaloons for our guards. You must provide your own musket."

"I don't own one." Whenever he went hunting, he always had to borrow his father's, and that was an ancient flintlock that his Grandpa Pinnix had used back in Ohio.

"That's all right, boy," said one of the tobacco chewers, "you can take one off a dead Yank."

Straw Hat pulled off the gauntlet, and extended his right hand. "I am Captain Benedict Crane, son, and I offer you my hand in the name of the Confederacy and offer you a chance for glory in the most glorious cause."

"Or you can go back to your pigs, pig farmer," Parker Pruitt said with a snigger.

"What say you, Mister Cole?"

Now Caleb's throat felt really dry. He wiped his sweaty palms on the sides of his britches, and shook his head. "Captain Crane, I just came to watch the show."

"There will be better shows, Mister Crane, when we engage the enemy."

"I'm not so inclined for that."

"He's yellow," Parker Pruitt said.

Caleb's fingers balled into fists, and he almost took a step toward Pruitt. "I'm no coward, Parker, and you know that."

"Then what are you?" Captain Crane asked.

The flag fluttered. Behind him, Jimmy Crawford's mule brayed.

"Caleb."

His fingers unclenched, and he turned, face flushing, catching Captain Crane sweep the straw hat from his head, and bow.

"Maryanne!" Caleb said. "What in tarnation are you doing here?"

"I brought you a bottle of sassafras tea." She held it out, and the Rebels sniggered.

One of them said: "We can give you something stronger than that, boy, if you've got enough sand in your belly."

Caleb wished he were back home with the Poland Chinas and Durocs. He took the brown bottle from Maryanne, and said: "Let me walk you back to the store."

She smiled, and briefly Caleb forgot all about the Secesh in the town square. He had taken only three or four steps when Captain Crane's voice stopped him.

"Ma'am, with your kind permission, will you allow Mister Cole and me to finish our conversation?"

Carefully Caleb looked back at the Rebels.

"You say you are not a coward," the captain said, "yet you will not join our cause. So I ask you again … what are you?'"

Maryanne gave him courage.

"I'm just a pig farmer," he said with a smile. And remembered something he had heard his father tell the Reverend McLintock a year or so ago. "A by-grab Andy Jackson Democrat pig farmer who's not about to leave the Union and join a bunch of Secessionist rabble."

# CHAPTER TWO

AUGUST 10, 1861
CEDAR BAYOU, TEXAS

His mother's bright soprano voice filled the parlor, her high D notes bouncing off the walls, almost drowning out the cord on Ryan McCalla's violin.

*I sigh for Jeannie with the light brown hair,*
*Floating like a vapor on the soft summer air.*

Ryan concentrated on the music in front of him, and as his mother's voice faded—she sounded as strong and youthful as always when she sang—he closed the song's final notes, squeezing the strings, feeling the bow glide. It felt like poetry.

It sounded, Ryan thought, pretty good. Applause led him to believe that his mother's guests agreed, although they could have been clapping for his mother's beautiful voice, or just to be polite.

Lowering the violin, Ryan turned to face the crowded parlor, seeking out Matt Bryson standing in the corner by the window curtains, but having to look at Mrs. Tennebaum when she began to speak. After all, she was president of the Ladies Auxiliary Club of Harris County, and her husband a representative of the State Legislature.

"That was wonderful," Mrs. Tennebaum said, dabbing a silk

handkerchief under her eyes. "Utterly delightful. You have given Mister Foster's music such rhapsodical legerdemain. Master Ryan, your accompaniment was prodigious, and, Reine, you sound as if you were twenty, not forty …"

"Thank you, Beatrice," his mother interrupted, and she quickly rang the silver bell, summoning Fionala for refreshments.

His mother's blue silk taffeta skirts rustled as she crossed the rug and, smiling ever so sweetly, extended her hand. "I shall take the violin," she said, her Southern drawl rich and musical even when she spoke, "while you study Mister Foster's music so that at our next tea, you shall be able to play without relying on this. Why don't you and Matthew step outside while we ladies …"—she winked—"gossip. I shall send Fionala outside with a pitcher of lemonade and some lemon cookies."

He knew what she meant, and it had nothing to do with music lessons or Saturday afternoon recitals for the Ladies Auxiliary Club of Harris County. It had to do with Ryan's father, who at any moment would likely be coming home from the brick kiln and tannery he owned. Although the man who made the violin was a Frenchman named Miremont, his father had bought it at the New York Crystal Palace at Reservoir Square during the Exhibition of the Industry of All Nations in 1853. "It sounds as sweet as one made in the fourteen hundreds," his father had said when he had given it to Ryan on his eighth birthday. Those times and feelings had long since faded. For the past two years, Josiah McCalla had refused to have anything "Yankee" in his home. Thankfully he had forgotten about the violin. So if he happened to find his only son and Matt Bryson sipping lemonade and munching on cookies on the front porch and his mother surrounded by a dozen chatting ladies in the formal parlor, he would not suspect that his home housed rough-scuff traitors to the Confederate States of America.

Outside, Ryan settled into one of the oak rocking chairs on the north corner of the porch. The house was two-story brick—bricks, naturally, from his father's kiln—with a hipped roof and double galleries, supported by columns, that spanned the entire home. The kind of house, his father said, you'd find in New Orleans, although Ryan would have to take his word for it. Josiah McCalla had never taken Ryan or his mother to New Orleans, or New York, not even Austin or Indianola. The house had been built in 1848. A white picket fence surrounded the lush green lawn, and phaetons, stanhopes, and barouches lined the street beyond the gate, their drivers waiting patiently to return the women of the Ladies Auxiliary Club of Harris County to their own homes.

Matt sat beside Ryan, staring at the cover of Foster's Melodies sheet music.

"Man, that's one beautiful girl." Matt held up the portrait of the woman, as if Ryan had never seen it. The woman sat, gracefully poised, hands clasped, head tilted, a cross necklace on her throat. To Ryan, her hair seemed darker than light brown.

"Mother says Foster wrote the song for his wife," Ryan said.

"What a lucky duck."

"Is that the only thing you think about, Matt?" He took the music and slid it inside his satchel. The music was published by Firth, Pond & Company. Of New York. His father would roar like a gale if he found such Yankee propaganda on his porch. From the satchel, Ryan withdrew a copy of *A Tale of Two Cities*. Published by Bradbury and Evans in London, it was safe from Josiah McCalla's wrath—at least, for now. If England ever refused to recognize the Confederacy, however …

"No," Matt answered in a solemn voice that grabbed Ryan's attention. "I've been thinking of …" He looked toward the windows and door, then withdrew a folded piece of parchment he had stuck inside his shirt. "*This!*"

Before he could pass the paper, the door opened, and the parchment disappeared. The two boys smiled as Fionala set a silver tray topped with two glasses of lemonade, a pitcher, a tray of sugar cubes, and a China plate of lemon cookies on the wicker table between the two rockers.

"Is there anything else y'all needs?" the slim Negress asked.

Ryan smiled. "No. Thank you."

"Yeah," Matt echoed, reaching for the nearest glass and snatching up a handful of cookies. "These look great."

"Well?" Ryan demanded impatiently after the front door had closed behind Fionala.

Mouth full of cookies, Matt stared at him blankly, then quickly remembered, wiped his lips with the back of his arm, set the glass on the porch floor, and found the parchment.

To Arms! To Arms! To Arms!
WANTED!

Underneath that banner was a drawing of the Goddess of Liberty waving a blue flag with a single star in her left hand, toting a musket in her right, and grinding the American flag into the mud. Somehow, the goddess reminded Ryan of the girl on the cover of Stephen Foster's sheet music. Under that:

Able-Bodied Texian Patriots
To Form a Company of Militia
To Protect Us from the Yankee Hordes
The Bayland Guards
call You to Duty
Enlistment applications to be addressed to
Dr. Ashbel Smith,
Evergreen Farm, Harris County
Long Live Texas and the Confederacy!

And in smaller script:

Muskets Needed to Provision Troops
Cannon Sought
Glory Forever!

With a tired smile, Ryan shook his head and returned the poster. He picked up his own glass of lemonade, leaving the cookies for his best friend's disposal, and sipped the refreshing if tart juice in his left hand while thumbing through Charles Dickens' book with his right.

"You considering joining the cause?" he asked.

"I already have."

His glass shattered on the porch floor. Ryan looked up, mouth agape, incredulous.

Matt Bryson was only a month older than Ryan, but Ryan stood a good three inches taller and weighed fifteen more pounds. Sandy-haired and fair-skinned despite living on the Texas coast, Matt's blue eyes rivaled the bay. His father's shipping line practically ruled Galveston Bay, and his father had sailed to just about every port in the Atlantic Ocean and Gulf of Mexico, so, if Ryan had been one for gambling, he would have wagered that Matt Bryson would have joined the Confederate Navy and not some army being assembled by Harris County's most famous doctor.

"Bunch of us have," Matt said. "Harry Cravey. Anson Jones' son. And Little Sam."

"Little Sam?"

"That's right."

Ryan shook his hand. Anson Jones Jr. was the son of the last president of the Republic of Texas. That was big, but Little Sam? That was leviathan. Sam Houston Jr. was two years older than Ryan and Matt. His father was the hero of the Battle of San Jacinto, just a few miles away where Ryan and Matt often went to gig frogs. Just down the road, the town of Houston had been named after Little Sam's dad. The elder Sam Houston had been general of the Texas army, president of the Republic, senator from Texas. He had known Andrew Jackson, Jim Bowie, Davy Crockett. Sam Houston had been, Ryan always believed, the biggest hero ever to stride mortal steps across the Lone Star State. Or had been, until, as governor of

Texas, he had refused to recognize the Confederacy even after Texas voted to secede, and had been kicked out of office and banished to his home up in Huntsville.

You couldn't speak Sam Houston's name any more in the McCalla household. Not when Josiah McCalla was home.

Little Sam had defied his father. Ryan shook his head, amazed that any son had such courage.

"Well?" Matt asked.

"Well, what?"

"Doc Smith asked me if you'd enlist, too."

Ryan leaned so far back in the rocker, he almost toppled over. He had to catch his breath. When he straightened, Ryan shook his head.

"Ashbel Smith's Yankee born," he had heard his father say, "but Texas bred. Unlike that swine Sam Houston."

Sam Houston had appointed Smith surgeon general of the Republic's army back in 1837. He had fought in the Mexican War, been secretary of state in the Republic years, negotiated a treaty with the Comanches, and served in the state Congress. Everybody around Cedar Bayou had expected him to take some big office in Austin. To serve the Confederate, and Texas, cause in government. Not form a militia. After all, Dr. Smith was well into his fifties, and the Mexican War had ended when Ryan and Matt had been toddlers.

"I'm not cut out to be a soldier." Ryan tried to laugh, but kept hearing his father tell his mother: "You've seen to that, Reine. I've tried to raise a son worthy of the McCalla name, but you've brought him up so that he's likely to squat to pee."

Matt leaned forward. "It's not like we're going to do any fighting, Ryan. The guards will just protect the coast, and even Abe Lincoln's Yankees aren't foolish enough to try to invade Texas. Especially on Galveston Bay." He drained his lemonade, popped the last cookie into his mouth, and resumed rocking. "Besides," he said while chewing, "Doc Smith … asked for … you … personal."

"Why?"

"It's not just all soldiering, marching and shooting and glorious stuff like that. My dad says that according to the Confederate Army regulations, a company needs to have two musicians."

"Musicians?"

"Yeah. You've seen those parades before. Beating drums, blowing that whistle …"

"Fife," Ryan corrected.

"Trumpets and things."

"Not a violin."

Matt shrugged. "Ryan, everybody in Cedar Bayou knows you can play anything you set your mind to. You play piano at the Methodist church every Sunday. You tooted that horn …"

"Flute," he corrected.

"… at that meeting of the Ladies Auxiliary Club of Harris County two months back. I remember that. You played real well, too."

"Well …" He couldn't make up his mind.

"But …"—Matt lowered his voice into a conspiratorial whisper—"don't think you'd just be blowing that trumpet or tapping out something on a drum. Doc Smith says you'll train like the rest of us soldier boys. You'll fire a musket. And if we can lay our hands on a cannon!" He slapped his thigh excitedly. "Anyway, we'll get to dress up in real fancy uniforms. Some seamstresses are already making uniforms for us guards. We'll be parading about every weekend for Texas dignitaries, and I bet every girl in the county will be wanting us to dance with them."

Ryan's smile returned. "So that's why you enlisted!"

Shrugging, Matt refilled his tumbler of lemonade and saw the shards of glass beside Ryan's rocker. "You want me to fetch your girl, have her clean up this mess, and get you a new …?"

"No!" Having Fionala, not to mention his father's two manservants and two other slaves, always made Ryan uncomfortable. He looked at the open page in his book and read: It was the best of times, it was the worst of times, it was the age of wisdom, it was the age of foolishness …

Matt sipped the lemonade. "Your father won't mind. It would make him prouder of you than he's ever been."

That was something Ryan couldn't deny. He closed *A Tale of Two Cities*.

"And your mother, she won't raise any stink because it's not like we'll be marching off to old Virginy to fight those Abolitionist zealots. Unfortunately we'll just be hanging around Galveston Bay, and you'll be playing music most of the time. Or so Missus Reine'll think. Besides, my father says the whole war will be over in six months. If that. You heard about the thrashing our boys gave the Yanks some place in Virginia, didn't you?"

Ryan nodded. His father had brought home news of the Confederate rout at Manassas last night. To hear Josiah McCalla talk, the war would be over in six weeks, not six months.

"At least talk to Doc Smith," Matt pleaded.

Before Ryan could argue, Matt was standing, pointing to the phaeton that had brought him to his house. "Gibb Gideon's been driving me and my folks for ten years now. He joined up, too. He can drive us to Tabbs Bay right now, and he'll attest to everything you just heard from me, if you don't believe me. Plus, you can talk to Doc Smith. He'll tell you exactly how things will be. Then you can sign the papers and tell your parents. Once you've signed, it's not like anybody can do anything about it. And your father, he won't want to do anything. It can't hurt to talk to Doc Smith. Can it?"

The front door opened again, and Ryan feared the auxiliary club had finished its business. Instead, Fionala stepped onto the porch.

"I …" She stopped as she saw the shattered glass.

"I'm sorry, Fionala," Ryan said. "It slipped from my hand."

"I'll cleans it up, Master Ryan," she said. "Missus Reine wants to know if y'all wants more lemonade or more cookies."

Ryan shot to his feet. "No. We're fine. But could you tell Mother that Matt and I are going to drive out into the county? Just to pay our respects to Doctor Smith. We'll be back. Real soon. I promise."

"That's right," Matt echoed. "Tell my mama that Gibb's taking us out there, and I know how much she likes visiting with Missus Reine. If she doesn't want to wait, I bet Missus Tennebaum would be delighted to take her home. And I'll be home before supper. Tell her that, please."

They didn't wait for the slave's reply.

Grabbing the satchel, Ryan bounded down the steps and on the path toward the gate, Matt at his heels. Ryan didn't need to hear any of Ashbel Smith's persuasive speeches. He had already made up his mind.

# CHAPTER THREE

AUGUST 7, 1861
PUTNAM COUNTY, MISSOURI

"Caleb, wake up."

Someone nudged his shoulder, and he tried to roll over, to pull the pillow over his head, but his mother's voice said urgently, though in a hoarse whisper, "Now, Caleb. Now!"

That was just like his mother. Waking him up from a perfectly divine dream. He had been dancing with Maryanne on the town square. He had been about to …

"Caleb. There are men outside."

His eyes opened, but he saw only blackness. His mother hadn't even lit a candle.

Another voice: "What did you tell those Rebels in town?"

"Hush, Bessy," his mother snapped. "Caleb, *get up!*"

He rubbed his eyes. "What time is it? What are you talking about?"

"There are a dozen men outside, Son. Your father's talking to them now. They call themselves the K-something Methodist Rangers, and they are demanding to see you."

For the first time, he heard fear in his mother's voice. Quickly he sat up as his mother rose from the bed. Pants dropped in his lap. "Dress quickly," she told him. "Then you need to go outside. Hide in the broodmare pen."

"In the pen? Ma!"

"Do as I say!"

Socks, boots, shirt, and hat landed beside him. He fumbled in the darkness, not knowing why he had to go to all this trouble getting dressed to run and hide in a pile of …

A gunshot ripped through the night. Outside, pigs squealed. His mother and sister sucked in deep breaths.

He was standing, starting for the front door, but his mother's hand pressed flat against his chest. He felt her breath as she whispered: "No."

Then, his father's voice sang out: "I tell you men, my son is not here. He left this evening to visit his cousin in Centerville, Iowa."

Caleb's brain felt dulled with cobwebs. As far as he knew, he had no cousin anywhere in Iowa.

"No offense, sir, but a bunch of Secessionist rabble is not likely to take the word of a family of by-grab Andy Jackson Democrat pig farmers."

That voice, Caleb recognized, and fear jolted his spine. Captain Crane, the straw-hatted fellow with the saber, commander of the Keytesville Methodist Rangers. He couldn't recollect the soldier's first name. Benjamin. No. Wait. *Benedict.* Like that traitor from the American Revolution. Now he remembered everything that had happened at Unionville that afternoon. He wondered if Parker Pruitt had tagged along with them.

"I do take offense," his father said. "It is three in the morning, an unfit hour for Christians to come calling."

"I care not. I will search your house, sir."

"Hurry!" This time, it was Bessy who spoke.

He pulled his shirt over his nightshirt, pulled the hat on his head, and grabbed boots and pants, not bothering to put them on. The socks he had misplaced in the dark. His mother and sister didn't give him time. They led him not to the back door, but the west-facing window.

"They are certain to have someone at the back door," his mother explained, "but I dare say they might not have noticed this window."

"I can't fit through that."

"Do it! And, confound it, be quick."

Bessy must have opened the window, because he felt the breeze. Caleb reached up, pulled himself through the tight opening. He remembered the greased pig contest at the Independence Day celebration two years back, and wished someone had swabbed his body with bacon grease. Twisting his shoulders, grimacing, he felt his skin tear. The boots dropped to the earth, along with his pants. He dangled, felt his mother and sister pushing him, shoving him. His pants ripped. Then, he landed on his head, flipped over, and lay spread-eagled in the darkness.

Above him, someone pulled the window shut.

It was a new moon. In the depth of blackness, he rose, rubbing the top of his head, hearing the snorts of horses from the front of the house, the rising voices of men.

*God*, he prayed, *don't let them harm my family.*

Crouching, he ran.

He didn't need to see. Sixteen years on this farm, he knew how to find his way to the chicken coop, the barn, the pigpens, the big elm tree in the front yard where he used to push Bessy in a rope swing. He cut a wide arc around the front of the house, pausing beside one of the smaller trees to catch his breath. He could see the torches the Confederate ranging militiamen held, and could make out the shadowy outline of his father on the porch. Another musket spat flame, and he jumped, almost cried out in terror.

"I know not which you Methodists are better at," his father said, "shooting off your muskets or shooting off your mouths."

"The next ball goes into your stomach." Captain Crane's voice displayed an icy venom.

Caleb looked around to the back of the house. Something glowed red near the privy. Cigar. And another. His mother had been right.

The front door squeaked, and a candle appeared.

"Let them in, Nicholas," his mother said. "They can see for them-selves that Caleb is not home. Shall I put some coffee on, gentlemen?"

He hadn't realized that he had been holding his breath. Now he ran, hoping he didn't happen to step on a snake, rat, or 'coon. The stench greeted him, and he slowed, hearing the grunts of sows, the screeches of piglets. He put his foot on the bottom rail, started to climb over the fence into the filth.

"My clothes!"

Caleb froze. His boots and pants. He'd left them by the window, and his hat had fallen off. If Benedict Crane's Secesh found those …

He started back down, but, as he turned, torches glowed from that side of the house.

An oath escaped his lips, and he dropped into the muck. A sow rasped angrily, but he ignored her. Blindly he slogged through the filth, and tripped over a Duroc pig, splashing into the manure as the pig ran screaming for its mother.

"Over yonder!" a voice cried out. "I hears somethin'!"

Caleb swore again, and crawled. He found the pile of hay he had forked inside the pen that evening, and burrowed his way inside, pulling the scratchy hay around him, and sinking deeper into the wretchedness.

Holding his breath once more, Caleb peered through the Strands of hay. He could make out the flames from two torches, no three, could see the Durocs running back and forth, screaming. One torch rose higher, and moved left, then right. Another torch poked through the rails, lower, making a slow sweep just above the ground.

"This reeks," a voice said.

"Smells better'n you, Vern."

Someone laughed.

"C'mon," the first voice said. "Ain't nobody in his right mind be hidin' in there."

Caleb wanted to let out a sigh of relief, but feared they would hear him. Unmoving, he watched the torches grow smaller.

How long he stayed, he didn't know. Probably minutes, but it seemed an eternity.

Someone called from the house. "We should burn them out, Captain! And kill every last one of their pigs."

Caleb ground his teeth, and clenched his hands in the mud, forming fists that left both arms shaking.

"Mister Pruitt," Captain Benedict Crane told the Putnam County miller's son. "We are good Christian soldiers and citizens of the Confederate state of Missouri. We do not wage war on civilians. We are not Kansas trash, boy. Remember that."

Horses hoofs clopped on the ground. The Keytesville commander spoke again to Caleb's father. "But your son, Mister Cole, is someone we consider a traitor and a conspirator and a braggart and a brigand. We will not trifle with the likes of him, so he had better find a home in Iowa. Do you understand, sir?"

He imagined he could hear his father spit tobacco juice as a reply.

"Missus Cole. Ma'am. I bid you good night."

The ground shook as the rangers rode into the blackness. Letting out a deep breath, Caleb unclenched his fists, filled his lungs, and gagged. He almost vomited as he pushed his way out of the hay pile, and stood, scooping off globs of muck as he fumbled through the darkness until he reached the fence rails.

He could see the candle approaching, could hear his mother's sobs, and his sister's prayers.

* * * * *

"Never thought the war would come to us." A heavy sigh escaped his father's throat as he fumbled with the cork and took a pull from the brown jug.

"You brought it to us, Caleb," his sister snapped. "This is your fault. I swear, Brother, the next time you're …"

"I tell you what I'm not going to do!" His voice rocked the room, and his mother stepped back, her eyes filled with fear. Bessy flinched, fearing he might strike her. His father set the jug on the table, and waited. "I'm never going to hide in a lake of crap …"—his mother gasped, his sister's eyes widened, but Caleb didn't care—"from the doggery like just paid us a visit. Never again, by thunder!"

He had cleaned up as best he could, found the clothes he had dropped by the window, had dressed, and now sat at the table with his parents and sister. His mother recovered to pour coffee, and slide the jug away from his father.

"I'm joining the Army. The Union Army!"

"Caleb …" His mother sounded so tired.

"You're too young to go about soldiering," Bessy chimed in.

"No." His father's head bobbed, surprising Caleb. "Caleb's right. He sure can't stay here. Those Rebs might come back. That's why I told those men you'd gone up to Iowa. In case they ride up that way. You pack up some extra clothes. Bessy, fetch my long rifle and horn. Caleb, you know how to get to Milan?"

Milan? That was down in Sullivan County, south of Unionville. He'd never been outside of Putnam County.

"Head southeast, cross the creek, and right beyond Garner's farm you'll come to the road. Just follow that south and it'll take you directly to Milan. About twenty miles or thereabouts. Don't stop. And if you see strangers on the road, you hide, Son, you hide, till you're certain they're not Rebels."

His father sipped coffee. Bessy handed Caleb the Kentucky rifle, and put the powder horn and shot pouch by a coffee cup on the table.

"Jacob Clark," his father went on, "has been forming a company of soldiers betwixt Milan and Unionville. I served with Jacob in the Mexican War, and he's a good man. Good soldier. The Union runs through his blood. You find Jacob. Tell him you're my son."

His mother had started crying. Lordy, so had Bessy. Caleb just sat there, struck dumb, couldn't even move. The rifle in his right hand, the stock butted on the floor, felt like a reaper. His father pushed the coffee cup away, and reached again for the jug of corn liquor.

It was still dark when Caleb stepped outside, carrying the rifle in his arms, a gourd canteen strung over his left shoulder, and spare drawers, socks, and an extra shirt in a haversack that his mother had filled also with biscuits, cheese, and a jar of apples.

"Southeast," his father said, pointing. "Cross the creek, and you'll be on Garner's farm. When you hit the road, head south to Milan. Jacob L. Clark. Tell him you're my son." He held out his hand, and Caleb shook it. It must have been the poor light, because he could have sworn he saw tears streaming down his father's face.

His mother kissed him gently on the cheek, and straightened his hat. "Goodness," she said, "I should have packed you a razor."

He touched his face, but felt no whiskers.

"The Bible!" his mother shouted. "You should take it."

"No, Ma," he said. "It's too heavy. And you'll need it the next time the Reverend McLintock comes through."

"But …"

"I'll get a Bible, Ma. I promise."

She kissed him again, choking back sobs, and hurried inside.

He shook his father's hand again, and his sister said: "I'll tell Maryanne."

"Thanks." His legs would not move. "I'll write. Let you know where I am."

His father's head bobbed. Bessy sniffled.

Past his father and sister, he saw his mother inside the house, collapsed in the chair, her head lying on the table, her body shuddering, though he could not hear her cries.

It remained dark, but he could see the skies lightening into a rich gray in the east. He had best get moving, at least be off the farm and past the creek before dawn broke. There was a fair to middling chance the Keytesville Methodist Rangers might be patrolling the road to Milan.

"Good bye, Son," his father said. "God be with you."

Somehow, he managed to turn, put one long leg out in front of him, then the next. He did not look back. He heard nothing. Even the Poland Chinas remained quiet as Caleb walked past the pens and left the Cole farm.

# CHAPTER FOUR

AUGUST 23, 1861
GALVESTON, TEXAS

Wearily, eyes still filled with sleep, they filed out of the warehouse that still smelled of cotton and into the dawn, tasting the morning mist and salt air on tongues parched from baking inside the musky, wooden furnace that night. Matt Bryson carried the Mississippi rifle his father had fired with distinction while fighting Mexicans alongside Jefferson Davis at Buena Vista. Gibb Gideon toted a shotgun. Sam Houston Jr. shouldered a fancy British-made Enfield rifle musket. Harry Cravey lugged an axe. All Ryan McCalla had, for now, was his violin, which he sawed as he fell into the line forming on the shell-paved street.

"Can't you play something else?" someone mumbled.

Others offered more profane comments.

Despite promises, the Bayland Guards had no uniforms. Well, Sam Houston Jr. wore one: fancy black boots, blue trousers, and a tailored, gray shell jacket with brass buttons stamped with Texas stars. Captain Smith donned the uniform from his Republic of Texas years, and some volunteers—including an old coot named Mills—had moth-eaten uniforms from the Mexican War. Currently the guards had to provide their own weapons, too. They had no cannon. Neither fife, drum, nor bugle, so Ryan had been ordered to supply the music. It came with a promotion. Much to Matt Bryson's disgust, he was now *Corporal* Ryan McCalla.

Finishing "Old Dan Tucker," Ryan stepped into line beside Little Sam Houston. Next to Houston, Matt offered his own rude comment about McCalla's fiddling.

Quietly a giant of a man stepped into line beside Ryan, and Sam Jr. sucked in a lungful of breath. Before Ryan could chance a glance at the newcomer, Captain Smith bellowed: "Attention!" Straightening his shoulders, bringing bow and violin to his sides, Ryan stared ahead.

They had been mustered into the Bayland Guards on the thirteenth—the fifty-sixth birthday of Captain Ashbel Smith—and had drilled first at Smith's Evergreen plantation before moving to Galveston Island, finding their billets in a warehouse. Once filled with Texas cotton, the wooden building now housed seventy-two privates, four sergeants, and four corporals. They slept on bedrolls rolled out on the floor. Captain Smith and his three lieutenants fared better, sleeping, the story around the warehouse went, in four-poster beds in a nearby mansion. Well, Harry Cravey didn't sleep on the warehouse floor, either. He would start out atop his bedroll between Gibb and Little Sam, but, before long, he'd stand up, announce that he was going home, and he'd walk out. Just like that.

"You're going to land in the stocks or hang by your thumbs, Harry," Sam Jr. would warn him, but Harry never listened. At twenty-two, Harry was older than any of the others, excepting thirty-one-year-old Gibb Gideon, but he never acted that way. Behind his back, Matt called him Baby Cravey. Harry's mother had a home on the island, and that's where Harry would sleep. And eat breakfast. Yet every morning, before Ryan's violin began to wail, Harry would be back, refreshed and ready for another day of drills. He brought home-cooked food, too, so Ryan prayed Harry Cravey never heard Matt Bryson's insults.

"Well, well, well." Captain Smith stopped in front of Ryan's line. He was a small man, gray-streaked hair thinning on top, but his salt-and-pepper mustache and goatee thick and well groomed. His face had been bronzed by the Texas sun, and he sported a prominent nose, but it was his eyes that stood out. They blazed with an intensity, and his voice was powerful, a stunning contrast to his diminutiveness. Ryan had not been able to catch a trace of any Connecticut accent. Then again, he didn't really know what a Connecticut Yankee was supposed to sound like.

The old doctor moved closer and, instead of saluting, gave a slight bow to the man standing beside Ryan. "Are you not too hoary and impuissant for military service, Mister President?"

Ryan's mouth dropped open. He wanted to look at the leviathan towering just inches from him, but dared not incur Dr.—er, *Captain*—Smith's wrath. After all that drilling, Ryan was just becoming comfortable with being at attention, and he had seen how sergeants and officers humiliated the Bayland Guards who didn't, or couldn't, come to terms with all this discipline.

"I can," the big man said in a deep drawl, "at least stand at the right of the line and be counted, sir."

"Indeed." Captain Smith bowed again. "Yet I find your presence here rather odd, given your feelings toward our cause."

"My feelings toward my son," the legendary Sam Houston said, "have not changed, Captain Smith. Nor, sir, will they ever."

Captain Smith's eyes gleamed. "Well spoken, my old friend. Sam, it would honor me and my men if you would inspect the troops with me this fine morning."

"Ashbel," Sam Houston said, "fine comrade, the honor would be mine."

He was old, pushing seventy years, white hair receding, and his face shockingly gaunt on his massive six-foot-six frame. He sure didn't look like a legend—black coat disheveled, cravat loose, tan-and-blue checked vest unbuttoned, and one woolen pant leg stuck halfway inside his boot top, the other covering the uppers. He walked with a gold-handled mahogany cane, grimacing with every step. Ryan McCalla, however, couldn't stop staring at the Texas celebrity.

"I thought your pa was a Union man," Matt Bryson whispered.

"He is," Little Sam said softly.

"You heard what he said," Gibb Gideon said. "He's here for Little Sam."

"He had this uniform made for me," Sam Jr. whispered. "But he said … 'I condemn your cause,'"—lowering his voice into a scratchy bass tremolo—"'but I shall not have anyone saddle my views on your back.'"

"Bayland Guards! Eyes right!" There was nothing hoary or impuissant about Sam Houston's voice.

"Do you see Louis T. Wigfall?" the old soldier and statesman thundered.

"No!" Ryan couldn't hear his own reply from the yells of his fellow soldiers.

He began: "Who is Louis …?"—but Houston's next command cut off the question.

"Eyes left!"

Still at attention, he looked in that direction.

"Do you see Williamson S. Oldham?"

Answering as one, the Bayland Guards shouted: "No!"

Ryan had heard of Williamson S. Oldham. He recalled his father talking about him with admiration, and knew him to be one of those fire-eating Secessionists from some town up north. In fact, he thought he had heard that Texas Secessionists had sent Oldham to Arkansas, where he had helped lead that state to join the Confederacy, as well.

"Eyes front!"

He looked ahead, found Sam Houston dwarfing Captain Smith and every other officer standing underneath the Bonnie Blue Flag. "Do you see either of them in front?"

"No!" Ryan roared with the others.

Sam Houston smiled. "No," he said flatly. "Nor will you."

The Bayland Guards applauded and cheered. Ryan cringed. They were still supposed to be at attention, but Captain Smith didn't seem to mind. With a wide grin, the short doctor extended his hand to Sam Houston.

"Who is Louis T. Wigfall?" Ryan asked at the same time Harry Cravey inquired about Williamson S. Oldham.

"They're both fire-eaters," Gibb Gideon answered.

"Wigfall called my father a coward and a traitor," Little Sam said. "He's a senator now, and the biggest blow-hard this side of the Red River."

"Your father's no coward," Gibb said.

"Well," Harry said, "what did he mean, saying that we'd never see those two gents?"

"I warrant he means that they are all talk," Gibb said.

"Attention!" Sergeants and officers ran about the assembly, trying to get the soldiers back into formation.

"Play!" Sergeant Rutherford ordered. "Play!"

Ryan stared, then realized the sergeant was talking to him. He brought up the bow, settled the violin on his shoulder, and began "Dixie."

* * * * *

Dismissed for breakfast, Ryan gathered with his friends on the sand behind the warehouse where they had made their fire pit. Other groups of men did the same, and soon the morning air was filled with the pleasant aromas of chicory, bacon, grits, even biscuits browning in Dutch ovens. Gibb fried salt pork, Matt made the coffee, and Harry Cravey passed out scones and sourdough bread his mother had made for him that morning.

"Man," Ryan said as he washed down a cherry scone with water from his canteen, "I hope we never leave Galveston Island. Not as long as Harry's mom's around."

"I don't want to stay here," Matt Bryson said, closing the lid on the coffee pot. "Nor do most of the boys. We want to see some real fighting."

"We will," Little Sam said solemnly.

"Here?" Harry's voice trembled. "You think the Yankees will invade us here?"

"No," Little Sam said. "But from what Sergeant Jardine and Lieutenant Hawthorne say, we won't stay in Texas."

"But …" Harry Cravey sank to his knees.

Matt filled the first tin cup with coffee for himself. "How come you get to converse with sergeants and officers, Sam?"

The young Houston grinned. "My name does have certain privileges."

"Where would we go?" Ryan couldn't hide his own nerves. His mother had bawled after he came home that Saturday afternoon to tell his parents that he had joined the Bayland Guards, and that was even after he had to soothe her by saying they were just to guard the Texas coast. His father had snorted: "It's not like he joined up with Hood's brigade, Reine," adding with contempt, "enlisted in a real outfit that will fight real battles and help win this war."

Little Sam shrugged. "Virginia? New Orleans? Mississippi? I don't know. But somewhere."

"That's great!" Matt set his cup down long enough to fill those of the others. "I didn't join this army just to shoulder arms and say, yes, sir, no, sir, and march to Ryan's fiddling. I want to fight some Yankees. See some real glory."

"Scones, coffee, and salt pork."

Ryan shot to attention, and fired off a salute. He didn't know what else to do, but Sam Houston, the hero of San Jacinto, shook his head, and said: "There is no need to salute me, young man. I am just an old, deposed … or should I rather say decapitated? … Texas statesman." His eyes showed pain as he gripped the walking cane and forced himself to sit on the ground in front of the fire. "Might I trouble you men for some coffee and grub?"

Ryan handed the hero of San Jacinto his own cup. Harry Cravey filled a plate with the last chunk of bread and two scones. Gibb Gideon speared the first piece of cooked salt pork and handed the meat, knife and all, to General Houston.

For a few minutes, they ate in silence before Harry Cravey could no longer hold his tongue.

"General ... I mean, Governor ... er, *Senator*, I mean, Mister President ..."

"The name, son"—Sam Houston's blue eyes, so often cold, twinkled—"is Sam."

"Uh, yes. Mister Houston, why don't you believe in the Confederacy?"

The old man sipped his coffee, then passed the empty mug back to Ryan. "Thank you, son. Now you'd best fill your belly with some of that warmth."

Ryan couldn't take his eyes off Sam Houston. He held out the empty mug in the direction of the fire, and moments later heard coffee filling the cup, feeling the warmth in his fingers.

"I believe, young man, in Texas," Sam Houston finally answered.

"Yes, sir." Harry didn't seem to know anything else to say.

"Boys, I made Texas." Sam Houston nodded, his voice strong, his eyes, no longer twinkling, reinforcing that strength. "I don't think it's immodest of me to say that, do you?"

"No, sir," everyone sang out in reply, even Little Sam.

"I think the citizens of Texas have prospered when they have listened to my counsel," the statesman continued. "Would you not agree?"

Heads bobbed all around to echoes of "Yes, sir," and "Of course, sir." For the first time, Ryan realized he wasn't alone with his mess. Other soldiers from other messes, including Sergeant Jardine, Sergeant Rutherford, Lieutenant Hawthorne, even old Private Mills, and Captain Smith himself, stood in a semicircle.

Sam Houston fingered a scone and pointed it at Matt Bryson.

"You want to fight, isn't that right?"

Matt's voice was barely audible. He dropped his eyes and muttered something that might have been affirmative.

"Any particular reason?"

"States rights!" Harry Cravey shouted, and a few heads in the ever-growing circle around them bobbed in agreement.

"Yeah." Matt had found his own voice. "Those Northerners can't push us around. We're tired of it."

Houston's head shook. He looked at Gibb. "And you?"

Gideon grinned. "The glory."

"Amen!" someone behind him shouted.

"Glory." Houston sighed. "You think war is glory?" He didn't seem to be addressing Gibb Gideon, for his eyes stared at the tip of his cane, but Gibb answered.

"You won more glory than just about anyone in Texas, General Houston."

"I have wounds that will never heal," he said, still staring at the cane. "Some physical. My son here can attest to that. And others …" His massive head shook.

The salt pork sizzled in the cast-iron skillet, but no one noticed. Silently Sam Houston finished his scone, and started to rise, straining against the pain, as he relied on the cane to push himself up and rise to his immense height.

"And what of you?" Houston asked. "Why do you join this cause?"

Those piercing eyes bored into Ryan, and Ryan felt the entire company of Bayland Guards staring at him.

"It just …" He started, trying to find the right words. "It just seemed the right thing to do."

Immediately Ryan regretted that answer. He didn't know what it meant, and wasn't even sure that was why he had signed up with Doc Smith. Maybe he had joined to prove something to his father. Or to escape the teas and brunches of the Ladies Auxiliary Club of Harris County. Or perhaps it was just like Gibb Gideon had answered. For the glory. He remembered Scott's *Ivanhoe* and *Rob Roy*. Cooper's *Last of the Mohicans* and Prescott's *History of the Conquest of Mexico*. Mostly, right now, he recalled stories he had heard all his life about San Jacinto, the Runaway Scrape, and the Alamo. And Sam Houston.

Glory.

Houston's response surprised him. "That is as honest an answer as I have yet heard."

The old man leaned on his cane, and his eyes swept across the gathering of the Bayland Guards. Smiling, he motioned at his oldest son and said: "Sam here came home one night up in Huntsville. Margaret nods to me, then points to this pretty little thing pinned on his lapel. So I ask ... 'Sam, by thunder what is that on your coat?' And he answers, with pride ... 'Father, it is a Confederate rosette.' And I tell him ... 'Son, you're wearing that in the wrong place. You should wear that on the tail of your coat.'" Only Houston chuckled, and he shook his head, straightening. "Sam was angry, but I was only joshing him. You men are not cowards. You are Texians, and those of you who fight for what you believe in, I respect you. I don't agree with you, nor do you agree with me, but we Texians are not easy to change our minds when we know we are in the right. And when is a Texian ever wrong? Even when they don't agree with each other?"

The Bayland Guards chuckled. Even nigh seventy years, the old man hadn't forgot how to stump.

"But there is an hysteria enflaming these Southern states. An hysteria fueled by numskulls like Oldham and Wigfall and William Gilmore Simms who are more ignorant than that late, great, cantankerous old reprobate, John C. Calhoun. At least, I could respect Calhoun. But Oldham ... Wigfall ... Simms?"

Simms. Ryan had heard of him. He enjoyed his books, *The Partisan* and *The Life of Francis Marion*, although he had not much liked *The Sword and the Distaff*, the novel his father claimed "would teach that Abolitionist harlot, Harriett Beecher Stowe, what slavery is really all about."

Sam Houston stood like a bronze statue. "But those of you who seek only glory, or who join a great Texian leader like Captain Ashbel Smith because of the rhetoric of idiots like Wigfall, I bid you warning. You will find no glory. None of you will, no matter your beliefs. Those stripes on the flag … the flag I support and love, the flag of the Stars and Stripes … they have been forged in fires hotter than the hinges of hell into the hardest steel, and will neither bend nor break."

Ryan expected hisses and boos, but no one spoke. They all listened as Sam Houston concluded his speech.

"You think the Union is weak, but I know better, and I leave you with this warning … you are about to sink in fire and rivers of blood."

# CHAPTER FIVE

Colonel W. James Morgan paced back and forth, waiting for his new recruits to line up as the drummer—an immensely nettling private named Young—pounded out "Reveille." A small sword in a nickel scabbard, suspended by thongs attached to a red sash, dragged across the dirt as the commanding officer of the Missouri Rangers walked, shredding a soggy cigar in his teeth.

"Get a move on, boy!" Harold Masterson bellowed.

Squatting by the smoky fire, Caleb Cole gave the former Pennville barber a quizzical look. "I haven't finished my coffee yet."

Morgan wasn't the only soldier with a sword. Harold Masterson drew his from a shining scabbard and, using the broad side, sent the tin cup spinning into the hot coals, which sizzled from the coffee that had not drenched Caleb's left hand.

The next thing Caleb knew, he was sitting on his bottom, hand almost numb. Seb Woolard, a farm boy from near Milan a few years older than Caleb, tossed his cup aside, and hurriedly helped pull Caleb to his feet.

"Fall in!" Masterson roared. "Fall in! Fall in, you worthless petticoats! You're in this man's army now, girls. When that drum beats, *you move!*"

Shaking the feeling back into his hand, Caleb followed Woolard as they hurried away from their tent, trying to find Captain Clark and the rest of Company E, Woolard cursing Harold Masterson, and Caleb agreeing with every word.

"Give a barber three stripes to sew on his sleeve, and he thinks he's George Washington."

"More like Napoleon," Caleb grumbled.

"Who?"

They fell in line beside the Ehrenreich twins—Caleb still couldn't tell Ewald and Rémy apart—and waited as other sergeants from other companies rushed their farmer's and clerk's and merchant's and mason's and carpenter's and preacher's sons into lines.

Caleb wasn't sure about this man's army.

He thought he had been joining his father's friend, Captain Jacob L. Clark, who he had met on the Milan pike late on the morning that Caleb had left the farm. He remembered seeing the dust, and thought about hiding in the bar ditch, but something came over him. He had hidden from those Secesh brigands in a pigpen, and after such ignominy he wasn't going to hide from any Rebel again. So he had dropped his sack at his feet and, fumbling with his Kentucky rifle, pushed the frissen forward, put powder in the flash pan, pulled the frissen back, and stood in the center of the road, brandishing that long, heavy weapon.

Later, he had realized how foolish that had been, yet fortune had been with him. Riding a black horse, Captain Jacob L. Clark led his fifty-seven men up the road.

"We are bound for Unionville," Clark had told him, after introductions and explanations had been made. "Word reached us that treasonous fiends dared show their face there."

Caleb had filled in Clark and his men on all that had transpired, and when the volunteers marched back to Milan, Captain Clark had fifty-eight men.

Fifty-eight men, Irish-born, English-born, Scottish-born,

German-born, but most of them with roots from the Ohio Valley, and many of the youngest ones, including Caleb, Missourians by birth. They would join a new regiment of mounted infantry, the Missouri Rangers, commanded by one W. James Morgan.

Morgan was about the same age as Clark, and, if Caleb could believe what he heard around camp, was a New Yorker who had settled and farmed in Chariton County before opening a grocery store in Brunswick. Before that, he had served in the militia in Ohio and Indiana. Harold Masterson, however, had whispered that Morgan had never even fired a shot or had ever been shot at, and, Harold Masterson believed, Captain Jacob Clark should be commanding the regiment.

That, of course, was before Harold Masterson had been appointed sergeant, and those stripes had gone straight to his thick head.

Others around camp said Captain Isaac Pratt should be commander.

Pratt, a rich farmer from Linn County who hailed from Maryland or Massachusetts or Rhode Island or one of those Northern states, had also been forming his own Union regiment, but he and his men soon joined Morgan. Morgan's Missouri Rangers came from Linn, Chariton, Sullivan, Grundy, Carroll, Livingston, and Putnam Counties, many of which Caleb had never even heard of, much less walked across. Now Caleb found himself in Laclede, way down in Linn County, more than fifty miles south of Unionville. The way Caleb's feet ached, that distance might have been more like one hundred rocky miles.

Sergeant Masterson huffed and coughed, wiping his sweaty brow with his left hand, as he herded the last of Clark's Company E into line. He had sheathed his saber, and back-pedaled his way toward Captain Clark.

"All present and accounted for, Captain," Masterson said.

"And hungry," Seb Woolard whispered.

Masterson and Clark snapped to attention, and sharply saluted Colonel Morgan, who did not bother to return the address, and instead turned to face the rows of rangers.

"Attention, soldiers!" the colonel barked. Caleb and everyone from Company E knew that order, although Seb constantly complained that there was no reason to stand like that.

"Look to the left and right, and dress!"

Blinking back confusion, Caleb turned to Seb, whose face, likewise, went blank. He looked the other way, expecting to find Ewald or Rémy Ehrenreich, whichever one was closest, but the twins had broken out of the line and started footing it back toward their bedrolls.

"My shoes!" Seb shouted, and followed the two Germans.

Caleb had his boots on, and shirt, but knew he had left his hat and the flintlock back in the tent. When one of the Company E boys came running back with his shotgun, Caleb decided he had better get his, too. And his hat. That had to be what *dress* meant.

He started forward, but Sergeant Masterson stopped him with the flat of his thick, right hand. "Stay! Stay!"

Someone blew a whistle, and, above the commotion, Caleb heard Morgan shouting at his adjutant. Other sergeants, corporals, and lieutenants ran about trying to collect their men. Caleb fell back into line, saw Captain Clark smiling and shaking his head, heard curses and grunts. Seb Woolard came hobbling back, one brogan on, the other in his left hand. The Ehrenreich twins fell back into place, one of them holding a musket, the other lamenting that his remained by the elm tree. The drummer rapped out something. More curses. More shouts. That screeching whistle kept blasting. Seb Woolard squatted, and managed to pull on his other brogan, which would certainly blister his feet since he hadn't gotten on his socks. By the time Woolard was standing, the regiment had fallen, relatively, back into a line.

"I am not commenting on your attire, boys," Colonel Morgan explained. "What I meant, my fine comrades, is for you to line up in a straight row. We will work on military etiquette. Mister Godfrey."

Godfrey, the adjutant, shouted an order, and here came Sergeant

Masterson, prodded along by that carpenter named Ault and some fellow from Pennville, both of whom had been elected lieutenants. Masterson's huge hands straightened, twisted, and pulled Company E's soldiers into proper position. Caleb leaned forward, saw how the men were standing, and tried to copy that stance. He must have succeeded because Masterson kept his paws off Caleb. Seb Woolard and one of the Ehrenreichs did not have that much luck.

"Brave soldiers of Missouri," the colonel eventually said, "thanks to Mister Pratt." Here, Morgan nodded at the rich Linn County farmer who had merged his men into Morgan's Rangers. "The department has awarded us with a new designation. Instead of being called the Missouri Rangers, we are now the Eighteenth Missouri Volunteer Infantry, and that is a name that will reap untold glory and help restore our precious and glorious Union."

As men up and down the line cheered, Sergeant Masterson glared, so Caleb kept his lips tight.

When the din quieted, Morgan called the Reverend John Garner to lead the regiment in prayer, and that tall, rangy Tennessean strode to the center of the line, removing his wide-brimmed black hat. Caleb grinned. He had heard that Methodist circuit rider preach on occasion, and never minded going to meeting when he knew that the Carroll County sky pilot would be leading the congregation.

"Boys," he drawled, "about the only qualifications I have to lead you are ignorance, impudence, and a couple of strong lungs."

Caleb couldn't stop from laughing at that one, and felt relief to see Sergeant Masterson chuckling, too.

"Back in Tennessee, my kinfolk consider me the blackest-hearted gent to disgrace the Garner name. Why, they'd hang me if I were to return to the hills. They hate me, but I tell you what, I hate them more. I'm an Andy Jackson Democrat, and I'm not only right with God, but I stand in the right. Let us pray."

In all his years, Caleb had heard some blood-and-thunder sermons in his time, but never had Caleb heard a preacher calling for blood and thunder, for destruction and desolation, for the rivers in the South to overflow with blood. Instead of glory, Garner besought gore. Caleb drew in a deep breath and shook his head, amazed, after Garner said amen.

The speechifying continued after Garner saluted Colonel Morgan and fell back into line behind the company commanders.

"Battalion," Colonel Morgan said, and he drew the tiny sword from its scabbard.

Chuckles from the ranks were quickly squashed by sergeants as vehement as Harold Masterson.

Morgan held the sword up toward his face, and Caleb thought that the colonel's hat was as small as his sword. After clicking his heels, the colonel returned the small weapon into its sheath.

"I've seen pocket knives bigger than that thing," someone whispered, prompting Sergeant Masterson's growl.

Standing in the center of the field, W. James Morgan seemed not to notice the commotion his diminutive sword had caused.

"Your colonel congratulates himself on being at the head of a regiment that would have done honor to Julius Cæsar. I must also congratulate you on the fine progress you continue to make. Many regiments I have had the honor to command, in Indiana and Ohio, but never have I found your equal."

He gave a slight bow and, turning to his adjutant, gave a quick nod.

"Eyes front!" the adjutant shouted.

Easy enough.

"Shoulder arms!"

One of the German twins brought his musket up. Caleb cringed. His rifle remained in the tent. Seb Woolard slapped his shoulder with the palm of his right hand. When the other Ehrenreich did the same, Caleb followed suit, and soon he could hear the slapping of hands on shoulders.

"By thunder!" Morgan's voice carried over the laughter seeping out of the line of soldiers. "The issue of guns did not cross my mind." He looked again at the adjutant.

"Parade, rest!" Godfrey shouted.

Seb Woolard squatted, but the anger in Sergeant Masterson's eyes warned Caleb that his new friend had made another mistake. The barber's hands roughly jerked Woolard to his feet, then shoved him roughly to the ground.

"Sergeant."

It was Captain Clark who spoke in a surprisingly calm voice.

Woolard quickly climbed to his feet, and tried to approximate the stance of other soldiers.

Clark strode to the line. "A gentle hand is sometimes in order, Sergeant."

Masterson's lips tightened. His fists clenched.

"You didn't cut everyone's hair the same way, did you?" Clark asked.

"No, sir."

Clark tilted his head. "You disagree with me, Sergeant?"

Masterson stood mute.

"You may speak freely, Sergeant."

The sergeant remained rigid.

"You fought in Mexico, didn't you, Sergeant?"

"Yes, sir."

"So did I."

"I know that, Captain."

"I saw the elephant more than anyone should, Sergeant."

No response.

"This war will be over shortly, Sergeant. And our regiment will only protect Missouri. A rough hand ..."

"Does the captain still give the sergeant the right to say his piece?" Masterson interrupted.

Surprised, Clark slowly nodded.

"What you saw, what I saw in Mexico, Captain, will bear little resemblance to what we are going to observe, sir. Even if we never leave Missouri, sir, because of Sam Jones and Lawrence, and John Brown and Pottawatomie. Because of Black Jack and John Reid's raid on Osawatomie ..."

Names. Caleb knew of John Brown. Bessy used to sing "John Brown's Body," and he could vaguely recall hearing something about Osawatomie, but Sam Jones, Lawrence, Black Jack, Pottawatomie ... those meant nothing to him, about as much as Laclede and Milan and, gee willikins, even Keytesville, had just a few weeks earlier.

"The Rebels will fight, sir," Masterson continue, "and put up quite a row before peace ever returns to Missouri, or our United States." He looked to be about to continue, but instead merely concluded: "Sir."

Clark nodded respectfully and stepped aside, now addressing his men. "How many of you men have arms? Muskets. Shotguns. Rifles."

The Ehrenreichs and Caleb raised their arms, but a surprising number of men, Seb Woolard included, merely dropped their heads in shame.

"Heads up, men," Clark said. "I see your musket, er ...?"

The German said: "Ewald Ehrenreich."

"I don't recognize it."

"It was made by our grandfather," the German boy said. "He made one for Rémy, my brother, too."

Clark turned to Rémy, and Caleb tried to find something that would separate the twins, help him identify them, but other than the fact that, for the moment, Ewald held a musket and Rémy looked jealous, he could find no difference.

"Your musket?" Clark asked Rémy.

"Back yonder," he muttered. "He wouldn't let me fetch it." He nodded at Sergeant Masterson. "Made me come back here to stand at attention."

"Caliber?" Clark had turned back to Ewald. Yet as Ewald answered, "Forty caliber, sir," the captain was staring at the German's bare feet, then at those of his twin's. He wanted to ask. Caleb could tell, but Captain Clark bit his bottom lip. Caleb could have told him that the twins came with weapons, but no shoes. They didn't even have a change of clothes, only the rags they wore morning, noon, and night.

"And you?" Clark stepped in front of Caleb.

"A long rifle, sir," Caleb answered "It's in the tent. I can fetch ..."

"Tent?"

"Yes, sir." He felt a little ashamed. Seb Woolard had joined the Missouri Rangers with a tent, not much of one, and rumored to have been stolen, but it kept the dew off, although it was rather small for Seb, Caleb, and the twins. Had been even smaller, before Harold Masterson became a sergeant. "Umm ..." He couldn't think of anything else to add.

"That's all right, Caleb."

Caleb grinned. Captain Clark remembered his name.

"By long rifle, do you mean a flintlock?"

"Yes, sir. Pa calls it a Kentucky rifle. He's had it ..." He shrugged, and smiled.

His grin faded as Clark sighed heavily, shaking his head. "A flintlock. What caliber, Caleb?"

Caleb opened his mouth, then closed it. His face flushed, and he had to fight to keep his head up. "I ... I ... I don't know, sir."

"That's all right." The captain stepped down the line.

"I got a pitchfork, Capt'n," drawled a freckle-faced kid with auburn hair.

"I see that, soldier."

\* \* \* \* \*

They issued passes that morning to send those soldiers without firearms—Colonel Morgan instructed the men that axes, pitchforks, and hickory sticks did not count as firearms—to go home or into Laclede or Brookville or Meadville and come back with something that would shoot.

Caleb had half a mind to find a new weapon himself, but Ewald Ehrenreich told him, after examining the rifle, that it was a magnificent piece—.52 caliber, the twin guessed after examining the lead balls— and Caleb figured that, if his weapon could impress a German whose grandfather had made two muskets, well, then, maybe he'd just keep the rifle that had been in Caleb's own family as long as he could remember.

The passes were for only two or three days, and Caleb wondered how many soldiers would bother to return to Laclede. This soldiering wasn't anything like Caleb thought it would be. Drilling and marching, drumbeats and sore feet. He had hoped the rangers would have driven the Keytesville Methodist Rangers out of the state by now, after a bloody but glorious battle. After the rough treatment Sergeant Masterson had given Seb Woolard, Caleb was surprised when Seb returned that evening.

"What you think?" Seb thrust out the oddest-looking thing Caleb had ever seen.

"What is it?"

"It's a gun, idiot. Look." He removed the stock, dropped it onto his bedroll, and brandished it like a pistol. A pistol with a fifteen-inch barrel flaked with rust and a tad crooked.

"Where did you get it?"

"There was a peddler set up on the main street right in Laclede," Seb bragged. "He was selling these like hot cakes. Only cost eleven dollars."

"You paid eleven dollars"—Rémy Ehrenreich rolled his eyes—"for that?"

Seb was fiddling with the cheap weapon, trying to affix the stock back onto the weapon. It clicked, and, beaming, Seb Woolard proudly shouldered his new musket.

"How's that?" he asked, and Caleb had to grin.

He wouldn't want to be standing anywhere near Seb when he fired that thing.

# CHAPTER SIX

This man's army proved impossible to figure out.

One minute he was a corporal with the Bayland Guards, then learned that he was part of Company C, First Regiment, Texas Infantry, only later to be told—along with Ashbel Smith and the rest of the guards—that Richmond had already designated a First Texas Infantry, commanded by John Bel Hood, so now Ryan McCalla was fighting in the Second Texas Infantry of the Confederate States of America.

*Fighting?* Ryan snorted and slapped at a mosquito with the copy of the *Galveston Civilian and Weekly Gazette* he had just rolled up.

"Can I see that?" Matt Bryson asked.

Without looking up or rising off his cot, Ryan handed the newspaper to his friend.

"What's happening in the world?" Gibb Gideon asked.

Shrugging, Ryan answered: "Everybody's still celebrating Manassas, and Ben McCulloch and our Texas boys whipped the Yankees last month at some place called Wilson's Creek."

"Where's that?" Harry Cravey asked.

"Missouri," Sam Houston Jr. answered. Sam had already read the newspapers.

"By jacks," Matt said, slapping the newspaper across his thigh, "we're going to miss the whole war."

"Yeah," Harry Cravey said. "I'd like at least to shoot at a Yankee."

"With what?" Gibb Gideon chided. "All you got is an axe."

That resulted in some sniggers in the barracks, echoed by Baby Cravey's objections.

Sluggishly Ryan swung his legs off the cot and sat up, running his fingers through his hair and stifling a yawn. His bunkies were the same—the war was the same—everything was the same.

Oh, the Bayland Guards had merged into the Second Texas Infantry, along with a bunch of other once-independent militias across South Texas: the San Jacinto Guards from Lynchburg; from Harris County, the Confederate Grays; the Texana Guards out of Jackson County; Dr. Belvedere Brooks' recruits from Wheelock Prairie; the city of Houston's own Confederate Guards; the Burleson Guards and Lexington Grays from Burleson County, and the Gonzales Invincibles and Wilson Rifles from Gonzales County, now Company I. Ryan and the Bayland boys still took orders from Captain Ashbel Smith, but Smith these days had to take his orders from a Tennessean colonel named John Creed Moore.

Boy howdy, did Colonel John Creed Moore love giving orders.

Six days a week, the companies filed out of warehouses and cotton compresses and into the summer heat or pounding rain where they would drill and drill and drill.

At first, Ryan had enjoyed his promotion to corporal, and his fiddling, but soon he regretted he had ever learned to play any musical instrument. "Reveille" and roll call began at 6:00 a.m. every morning, but the designated buglers had to assemble at 5:45. Among the ten companies of the Second Texas, only three had bugles, but there were also four drums and two fiddles. Company I, consisting of two militias from Gonzales County, had a kid with a jew's-harp, who probably had not even reached being thirteen years old yet.

"The worst band I ever heard," Matt Bryson frequently complained.

After roll call, the soldiers wolfed down breakfast, then went through fatigue call and sick call before those so-called buglers had to assemble again.

After that the drilling began, and Ryan had to join his friends, filing into line from right to left with Company C, *née* the Bayland Guards, always in the middle, between Company H, formerly the Lexington Grays, and Company K, the Texana Guards. That's another thing Ryan couldn't fathom about this man's army. There were ten companies, but there was no Company J. The brass skipped that letter and made it K.

"To avoid confusion," Captain Smith had explained.

Which left Ryan scratching his head until Sam Jr. had told him: "An I could be mistaken for a J in written orders." Ryan had accepted that until he read over a letter Gibb Gideon was writing his mother, and Gibb's Hs looked more like Ks than anything else. When he tossed that argument to Little Sam, his tall friend merely smiled and said: "I don't think Gibb Gideon will ever be writing any orders, Ryan."

Double-quick steps ... soldier arms ... loading and firing weapons (for those that had weapons) by squad or rank ... bayonet exercise ... more marching ... wheeling ... right turn ... left face ... *company halt!*

He heard those commands in his sleep.

Little Sam still wore the only real uniform in Company C, excepting Captain Smith's moth-eaten blouse, but Colonel Moore kept promising that they would be getting uniforms that Texas had appropriated from Union soldiers after the Secession. He also said they'd be getting captured Yankee weapons as well.

When they weren't repeating the three motions required to fix a bayonet—a silly drill, Ryan declared, since a search would turn up fewer than thirty bayonets in the entire company—or a right or left oblique, the Second Texas dug.

Lengthening ditches—or what the officers called trenches—or shoveling mounds of sand to build fortifications—or what the officers called redoubts—along the coastline or on the outer islands.

Ryan really had to laugh at Colonel Moore's orders to dig those trenches on the barrier islands. "Yeah, he's from Tennessee, all right," he'd say as soon as salt water began seeping into those trenches after only minutes of shoveling. A few of the boys from Burleson County had taken to calling Moore "the king of spades," the same moniker Ryan had read that some Confederates had slapped on this general named Lee up in Virginia.

Still sitting on his cot, listening to the rain pelting the warehouse's roof, Ryan stared at his hands, once smooth but now callused from using the shovels near the beaches, and the long wooden pole they forced him to use during drills until the Second Texas Infantry issued him a real musket.

"This just isn't fair," Matt Bryson said again, and stood, slapping Ryan's knee and saying: "Let's go."

Ryan looked up. "Go where?"

"I don't know. Somewhere."

He pushed himself off the cot, grabbed an India rubber poncho off the wall, and pulled it over his head, then found his hat, and waited, looking at his messmates while Matt Bryson laced his brogans and grabbed a wide-brimmed straw hat, already battered and ruined from recent rains.

Coughs and sneezes echoed throughout the warehouse as they made their way to the big doors. It was late Sunday afternoon, and Colonel Moore did not drill his soldiers on Sundays, although they had held a dress parade that morning. Since the end of September, the squalls had begun pelting the coast with wind and rain, and now it seemed as if half of the regiment had taken sick. Or, rather, half of the regiment had the good sense to report for sick call and get out of the drills and diggings. Sunday afternoons, after worship, the boys had free time. Usually Baby Cravey would head home, but he had pretty much stopped that since the rains began, and since P. M. Woodall, who had been elected the company's second lieutenant, had sternly warned him that Colonel Moore was "by the book"—*Hardee's Rifle and Light Infantry Tactics*, without question—and could have Cravey flogged, shackled, or even shot if he didn't stop his tomfoolery. The weather had stopped the others. Habitually Gibb Gideon would have hit the dram shops along the harbor, Little Sam Houston would go courting or visiting some high society businessman, and Ryan and Matt would either go fishing, shrimping, or frog-gigging if not trying to manage a quick visit with their folks.

It was too late to head to up to Cedar Bayou, and the pattering on the roof told Ryan that the rain had not abated. He didn't know what Matt Bryson had in mind, but he followed his friend out the door, anyway.

Rain pelting their faces, they ran down the shell-paved street and leaped onto the back of a covered wagon, hitching a ride for a few blocks, and leaping off when they reached the Strand. They turned west down the street, staying close to the wooden buildings, slowing down only underneath the awnings. Ryan trailed Matt, who passed a vendor and deftly pocketed two apples, before turning a corner and sprinting toward Galveston Bay.

Despite the rain, the wharf was busy. The two boys wove through a path lined by cotton bales and hogsheads, barrels and boxes, slipping between stevedores and roustabouts—able-bodied men who, Ryan and most of the Second Texas believed, should have been serving in the Confederate Army; "wharf lice," Captain Ashbel Smith called them. Slaves, scantily dressed demimondes, and drunken sailors also roamed about. A calliope whistled, echoed by a deep horn. Black smoke and embers belched out of the stacks of one of the docked steamboats, mixing with the rain, fog, and gloaming.

Finally Matt Bryson stopped. If he hadn't, he would have stepped off the wharf and into the bay. He stared out into the deepening blackness.

"I wish they'd come already," he said, still looking out toward sea.

Ryan had taken off his hat to let rain water run off the brim. He combed his wet hair with his fingers, pulled the soaked hat back on, and asked, shivering: "Who?"

"The Yankees. They're out there, you know."

Of course, Ryan knew that. The Union Navy had already managed to start a blockade, but it had been a quiet war so far. Except for that night when a man-of-war, the USS *South Carolina*—of all names!—had exchanged fire with a Confederate battery at the end of Twentieth Street. That had been back in early August. Captain Smith had dismissed the troops, and Ryan had raced to the beach, joining businessmen in silk hats, women with picnic baskets, and even children and their schoolteachers to watch the show.

The slaves sang, Ryan fiddled "Dixie" with a wharfie clawing a banjo, and Little Sam Houston danced with a beautiful redhead wearing a walking dress with a long jacket. An elderly woman had rewarded Ryan and the banjo picker with heaping servings of pumpkin bread, and they watched the shells explode like fireworks overhead, and the shells from the South Battery sent geysers hundreds of feet into the air out in the bay. It had reminded Ryan of the Independence Day celebrations, which, for a reason he couldn't quite comprehend, saddened him.

After half an hour, the fireworks had ended, Company C and the rest of the Second Texas had returned to drills, and everybody else had gone back to work or home. Except for that poor fellow from Portugal. One shell from the *South Carolina* hadn't exploded in the air, but had landed on the beach, and the foreigner had been blown to pieces. Three others, also civilians, had been wounded.

That had been as close to battle as anyone in the Second Texas Infantry had come.

"We're going to miss the whole blasted war!" Matt smashed a fist into an open palm.

"We'll get our chance," Ryan said.

"Yeah, with a spade. Our boys in Virginia killed ten thousand Yankees at Manassas. Appears we must have slaughtered half that many up in Missouri."

"I wouldn't believe everything you read in the newspapers," Ryan said. "Especially in the *Weekly Civilian and Gazette*." He stepped beside his friend and looked across the black waters. Through the fog, he thought he could make out the flickering light from a ship, a Yankee ship.

"No, we'll miss our chance." Matt's voice sounded a thousand miles away.

Ryan shuddered. Remembering that line from the newspaper's report on the battle at Manassas, Virginia, "The battle was terrible and ended with great slaughter on both sides," he wouldn't mind missing his chance. The Confederates had lost three thousand, according to newspaper accounts.

Yet since then, news had been scarce. The blockade had seen to that. Oh, Galveston had a couple of sleek and slippery ships that kept proving successful at running through that gauntlet, but Ryan kept thinking about General Sam Houston's warning. Most citizens and soldiers dismissed the old war horse, with a handful of fire-eaters calling him a traitor to the South and saying he should be hanged from the highest yardarm in the harbor.

*You are about to sink in fire and rivers of blood.*

Little Sam had whispered rumors he had heard about the Confederates deciding to abandon Galveston Island, that it could not be defended, that it was only a matter of time before the Union captured the port. This afternoon, he had read a story, more vague and mostly innuendo, of a Union naval assault on a couple of Confederate forts—he couldn't remember their names—along North Carolina's Outer Banks.

Newspaper editors and Galveston's leaders proclaimed that the war would be over in six months, if not six weeks, but Colonel Moore said they must prepare to defend Texas, the South, their homes, and their families.

The rain slackened, and, wiping his nose, Ryan turned around. Somewhere along the Strand, a piano player hammered out

"Jeannie with the Light Brown Hair," and he imagined his mother singing along in their parlor, Mrs. Tennebaum and all the other fine members of the Ladies Auxiliary Club of Harris County applauding politely, then Fionala serving tea and cookies.

"You two buckos come here."

The deep-throated call, more snort than sentence, snapped Ryan and Matt out of their daydreams. A massive shadow stood in front of them—a face, dark beard dripping with water, intermittently illuminated by a stinking cigar.

"*Anda logo!*" the man shouted. The words were Portuguese, but his accent was Texian.

Ryan shot Matt a quick glance, but the rough voice snapped out a curse, and the two boys had become used to following orders, especially those punctuated by profanity and threats. They eased down the wharf, brogans sloshing through the dampness, and stopped in front of a blue-coated man who looked larger than some of the wooden barrels they had passed along the dock.

"You boys be with Capt'n Ashbel's Guards, ain't you?"

"Yes, sir," Matt answered first.

"Thought so. Remembered that one sawing 'Dixie' when the *South Carolina* give us a show last month." He jutted the cigar toward Ryan. "Come here, I gots something for you soldier boys."

Again, they shot each other nervous looks, but the big man was moving down the wharf, and they followed him into the darkness until lights from the city guided them again through the cotton bales and hogsheads. The sailor stopped, flicking his cigar into the night, and pointed at a half dozen crates.

"That idiot, Mister Crisp, brung these here by mistake, but that be a land-lovin' freighter for you." He spit out his contempt. "I need one of you to run fetch Capt'n Ashbel. Tell him to bring down some wagons and a score of men. The other one of you needs to stand guard here."

One of the crates had been pried open with crowbars, and the big man shoved the lid off, and, bending over, he reached inside, his hand rustling through greasy, dark paper.

"What is it?" Matt asked.

The big man turned, and shoved something heavy into Ryan's arms.

"Before long, bucko," the sailor said, "you'll declare that this here baby plays as pretty a tune as your fiddle."

Ryan almost dropped the weapon, which must have weighted ten pounds and had to be close to five feet long.

"That's a sixty-nine-caliber musket, boy, and it's just a-itchin' to kill a mess of Yankee tyrants."

# CHAPTER SEVEN

They had gone as far as Brookfield, to protect the Hannibal &
St. Joseph Railroad, only to return to Laclede to be shouted at by
Sergeant Masterson and preached at by sky pilot Garner. To drill
and march. To march and drill.

Colonel Morgan and the other officers were fêted by the society
of Laclede, the Confederate officials, even passers-by. There seemed
to be a ball every other night for the officers of the Eighteenth
Missouri, but for the enlisted men there was only drilling—and
Fort Morgan.

The monotony of learning to be a soldier had been broken
up by shoveling and swinging a pick. Caleb and others of the
Eighteenth Missouri had worked alongside Negroes—conscripts,
Sergeant Masterson had called them—to build an earthworks
fort. It looked like nothing Caleb Cole had ever seen, but it sure
stood out in Laclede.

Colonel W. James Morgan had named the redoubt Fort Morgan.

"Since we're no longer Morgan's Rangers," Caleb had overheard Captain Clark tell Captain Pratt, "he had to have something
named after him."

So here lay Caleb Cole, in a tent surrounded by earthen walls, sweating, itching, dying.

For three days, he had been sick. At first, he thought he had caught cold, coughing, his nose running, his head aching. His eyes seemed bloodshot, and chills made him shiver. Reluctantly he had taken to bed. Ewald Ehrenreich had jokingly told Caleb he just didn't want to risk having Sergeant Masterson order him on privy duty. Now Ewald lay next to him.

Caleb tossed the blanket off himself, rolled over, began scratching his left arm. It felt like a million fleas biting him. A firm hand gripped his right arm, jerked it away, and Caleb swore.

"I itch all over!" he wailed.

"I know," the voice said. The blanket pulled up again.

"I'm burning up," he said. "Don't cover me with that."

"Doctor's orders."

His eyes opened. The face fell slowly into focus. "You aren't Doc Torrey."

"I'm not Doctor Hamlin, either."

"Then what do you know?" He tried to toss the blanket off, to ease that relentless itching that had spread up and down his arm to his back, his side, his neck, and his stomach.

The cover came back up. His hand was pinned to the bunk.

"Come on, Sergeant Masterson!"

"You got the measles, Caleb!" the one-time barber from Pennville snapped. "Doctor Torrey said you must stay warm."

"I am warm. I'm on fire!"

"You don't want this to turn into pneumonia."

"Don't you have somebody to boss around?"

Beside him, Ewald wailed. With a sigh, Sergeant Masterson eased his grip and craned his neck, saying something to the Ehrenreich twin that Caleb couldn't catch.

William Torrey had been the sawbones in Unionville. Caleb had been under his care a couple of times before he had joined the Army. Torrey was now the assistant to the regimental surgeon, Dr.

Norman S. Hamlin, who Colonel Morgan had signed up in St. Catherine. Caleb wished one of those doctors could be here now instead of contemptible, ignorant Harold Masterson.

"Where's Doc Torrey?" Caleb moaned. "I want to see him. He'll understand …"

"Torrey's busy," Masterson fired back. "Everybody's busy. Now stop scratching, boy. You don't want to be all scarred up, and don't want infection to set in."

The pressure lessened on his hand, and he saw Sergeant Masterson moving toward Ewald.

"Keep those covers pulled up," Masterson said.

Caleb muttered an oath. That rotter had eyes in the back of his head.

*    *    *    *    *

Sometime during his sleep, someone—undoubtedly Sergeant Masterson, hard rock that he was—had tied his arms to the cot. Caleb groaned, twisted, pulled at the twine until it cut his skin. He itched all over. He yelled for Sergeant Masterson, screamed for Seb Woolard, but no one came. Later he prayed for his mother, his father, even his sister to come help him through this torment.

"Nobody's coming, Caleb," Ewald Ehrenreich whispered. His voice sounded ancient, coarse, terribly weak. "Let me die in peace, will you?"

Caleb felt tears streaming down his face.

"Just shut up, Caleb, and let me die in peace."

*    *    *    *    *

Sunlight bathed him when he opened his eyes. Beside him, Ewald Ehrenreich whined and groaned. He should be staring up at the dingy yellowing canvas of the tent, but instead looked over the mounds of Fort Morgan's dirt walls at the pale blue sky.

"Thanks, *friends!*" Seb Woolard spit out the words, and some saliva, with sarcasm.

"What?" was all Caleb could manage.

"They're gonna burn my tent." Seb gestured outside the fort, and Caleb saw black smoke billowing into the sky.

"That's enough, Woolard!" Sergeant Masterson said. "Fall in and march."

Caleb turned as far as he could and watched Masterson lead a handful of men, loaded down with clothes and bedrolls, Seb Woolard's tent, knapsacks, and bags. They marched across the sod, between rows and rows of sick men, toward the fort's gate and the fire somewhere beyond the earthen walls.

He turned back to look at Ewald, but, when he saw the rash covering the twin's face, he jerked back his head, and stared at the dirt wall before him.

*Does my face look like that?* he wondered.

* * * * *

The hand on his forehead felt cool, a calming closeness as if Jesus himself had touched him. He wanted to raise his arms, hold that hand on his head forever, but his arms were still tied.

"How do you feel, Master Cole?"

His tongue felt parched, swollen. The hand moved away, then cold, refreshing water dribbled onto his chapped, cracked lips. It felt as wonderful as his mother's buttermilk.

Opening his eyes, Caleb saw, above him, Dr. Torrey's hand squeezing a wet cloth, releasing cool water into his mouth. Caleb swallowed, wet his lips, watched the doctor dip the rag in an oaken bucket beside the cot, and perform the procedure again.

"The last time I saw you, I was treating Bessy for a bowel

complaint," Torrey said. "How is your sister?"

Caleb let the water run down his throat. He sighed and found his voice. "I haven't seen her since August."

"And your folks?"

He tried to remember the last letter he had gotten from his mother, but couldn't recall what it had said, or how long it had been. For that matter, he didn't know how long he had been sick. Yet he answered: "They're as well as can be expected."

Doc Torrey nodded and smiled an ancient smile. His lips moved, but Caleb didn't catch what he had said, if he had said anything at all.

"Measles have struck down many of our brave lads," Doc Torrey finally said, "like a pestilence unleashed by our Lord Jehovah."

Caleb wished Doc Torrey would give him some more water, but instead he had dropped the rag in the bucket, and now was checking Caleb's pulse.

"I thought only children got measles," Caleb said.

For the first time, Doc Torrey smiled a true smile. He released his hold on Caleb's bound wrist, and patted his shoulder. Suddenly Caleb felt embarrassed. He was a soldier, not some farmer's kid any more. Doc Torrey should know that.

"I'm afraid this case of measles knows no age limit," Doc Torrey said, his good-humored countenance replaced by a haggard face with bloodshot eyes and four days' growth of beard covering his cheeks and chin. "Do you still itch?"

"No, sir." The answer surprised Caleb, who looked down at his arms.

"I don't think Sergeant Masterson needs to keep you shackled any more, my boy." That was almost as wonderful as the water. But urinating in a chamber pot like some wretched, ancient invalid made him ashamed. "However," Doc Torrey continued, "I'd like you to stay in bed, keep covered, at least another day or two."

Caleb's head bobbed.

"I'll write your father, son, and let him know you're all right."

More good news. Relief swept through Caleb's body. He wasn't going to die in Fort Morgan after all.

"Thank you," he said.

The doctor picked up the water bucket with his left hand and stood. "I'll see you tomorrow, Caleb."

He nodded a reply, but, as Doc Torrey turned to leave, Caleb called out: "How's Ewald?"

An old tongue ran across Doc Torrey's dried lips. "Tomorrow," he said. "You rest. And stay warm."

Wearily Doc Torrey made his way out of the tent.

* * * * *

"It's your fault!" Seb Woolard jammed a finger inches from Caleb's nose.

He was squatting by the fire, new blanket draped over his shoulder. They had burned his cot, and the old blanket, too. Caleb sank back, stunned.

"What are you talking about?"

"Thanks to you and Ewald, I've lost my tent, my knapsack, just about everything I come to this war with."

"It is no one's fault," Rémy Ehrenreich said without looking up.

"It sure is. That was a good tent. I never should have joined this man's army. It's brought me nothing but misery and a bunch of louts for messmates."

"You?" Rémy looked up. His eyes were bloodshot, but Caleb saw no signs of a rash on Ewald's twin brother.

"That's right." Seb rose. "I'm glad your brother's dead. Cost me my tent, him and this sick son-of-a—"

Seb was gesturing toward Caleb, but Rémy exploded from his crouch and sent a looping right that slammed into the Milan farm boy's jaw, not allowing him to finish the curse. Before Seb could rise, Rémy was on top of him, swinging, slashing, pounding. Caleb tried to rise, but his legs buckled, and he found himself sitting on the ground, watching Rémy Ehrenreich turn into a mad dog, mouth practically foaming, face red as the blood spurting from Seb's face.

Almost instantly a crowd surrounded the fight, cheering, shouting, betting. Caleb had managed to push himself to his knees, tried to call out for his two bunkies to stop, when two men stormed through the circle of soldiers, flinging men and boys right and left.

"Stop this!" Captain Clark ordered, but it took Sergeant Masterson's strong arms to pull Rémy Ehrenreich off the whimpering Seb Woolard.

"What's the meaning of this?" Captain Clark said. Without waiting for an answer, he whirled to face the circle of men. "Haven't we buried enough of our boys over the past two weeks? Do we need to bury more from a round of fisticuffs?" He turned back to Rémy Ehrenreich. "There's a war going on, lad. We should be fighting Yankees and Kansas trash, not each other."

Rémy just stood there, shaking with rage, Sergeant Masterson pinning his arms behind his back.

Captain Clark looked at Seb, who had curled into a ball. "Two of you men assist this soldier to Surgeon Hamlin."

Four volunteers immediately helped Seb Woolard to his feet.

"No, belay that order." The men backed away, and Captain Clark stepped closer. "Hamlin and Torrey haven't slept in … I don't know how long, and I dare say they are busy enough trying to save lives so they certainly don't need to waste their time on the likes of you." He looked up, his face tight, angry, and staring at Sergeant Masterson. "To the guardhouse with both of them, Sergeant."

"Yes, sir, Captain."

"They can heal there or die there."

"Yes, sir."

\* \* \* \* \*

"Ewald's dead?" Caleb shook his head.

"Pneumonia," Sergeant Masterson spoke softly. "Thought you might be called to Glory yourself."

Caleb drank the broth in his coffee cup.

"His parents came for his body." Masterson sipped something stronger than broth. "That was a terrible day. Mother and father crying up a storm, his mother pleading with Captain Clark and Colonel Morgan to let them take young Rémy home with them, that they'd lost one son and wasn't that enough. But Colonel Morgan would not allow that, said that Rémy had signed an oath. Sent them home, he did. Their father driving the buckboard, the poor old mother just kneeling over the coffin in the back, wailing her little head off."

Caleb couldn't finish the broth. He set the cup down and stared at the fire. "How many others have …?" He couldn't finish, but Sergeant Masterson did it for him.

"Died?" Masterson let out a mirthless chuckle. "I don't know. Lost count of the funerals Chaplain Garner has led. Many families have come to claim their young men."

With a sigh, Caleb shook his head. "This isn't the way war is."

"Oh, lad, it most certainly is. It was that way when we fought in Mexico. It was that way when my father took part in the campaigns against the Seminoles down in Florida. I've buried far more soldiers felled by disease than those that died from lance or ball."

Caleb had to inhale deeply, and summon up his courage as he exhaled. "Doc Torrey says you likely saved my life."

"Not me, lad."

"He said …"

"Doctor Torrey saved your life, son. He and Doctor Hamlin. Or God Almighty did. I did as I was told, as any soldier would do."

"Well …" Caleb smiled. "Thanks."

To his surprise, Harold Masterson grinned back, almost like he was human, a barber again, fingering scissors back in Pennville, and not that gruff, no-account sergeant with the foul mouth and horrible attitude.

"Well, what's the matter with Seb Woolard?" Caleb asked, and immediately regretted bringing up that subject.

The smile left Masterson's face. "He's a bad one, that boy. I wish he wasn't in Company E, that's certain sure."

Caleb felt his eyes well with tears, but he would not cry. "I thought he was my friend."

"He's no one's friend. And you shouldn't make friends, not these days. Friends are here one minute and gone the next."

"He blames me and …" He couldn't say Ewald's name. "*For a tent?*"

"He's trash. Dirt poor trash. All of those Woolards from Milan are trash. Likely his pa stole that tent. And those brogans he wears, I suspect they was procured by a quick hand, as well. Me thinks it's a mighty good thing he doesn't yet have a musket. He'd likely murder one of our own rather than some Yankee."

Caleb didn't want to think about that. "How is Rémy?"

Masterson snorted. "Rémy. That boy will be fine. Don't you ever fret over Rémy, Cole. If this regiment had a hundred Rémy Ehrenreichs, we'd lick the Yankees in sixty days." Masterson slipped the flask into the mule-ear pockets of his britches. Rising, he extended his right hand. "And with a hundred lads like you, Caleb Cole, we'd cut that time in half. Let's go."

"Where?"

"Into town. About thirty Kansas Yanks, captured at Lexington and paroled by General Sterling Price, are in town. Let's go see who we're really supposed to be fighting."

# CHAPTER EIGHT

"Right turn, march!"

Musket on his shoulder, Ryan followed the order in perfect time with Matt Bryson. He almost even smiled. Thousands of heels clicked on the paved streets.

No slackening or quickening the cadence—no shortening or lengthening the step.

Conforming, naturally, "with the principles prescribed in the School of the Soldier, Number 402" as written in *Hardee's Rifle and Light Infantry Tactics*.

If he ever met that W. J. Hardee, once a Union officer but now, he had heard, a Confederate commander, Ryan McCalla would like to shove that little book down Brigadier General William J. Hardee's throat. Heck, he didn't have any need for it any more. Nobody in the Second Texas Infantry did. They had those dad-blasted one-hundred-and-fifty-plus pages memorized.

The Houston band's blaring of "Dixie" wailed closer, and Ryan could see the gazebo, stands overflowing, and a throng of Texians lining the parade grounds of what was now called Camp Bee.

"Platoon, halt!" Sergeant Rutherford shouted, and Company C, once the Bayland Guards, stopped.

"Right, dress!"

They moved as if machines, never faltering, never stumbling. The second platoon followed the first, then he heard Captain Smith call for the company to form into two ranks, single file. Again they marched. Stopped. Formed into two ranks.

"Left, face!"

One fluid motion.

"Right, dress!"

The band, if Ryan could call it a band, reached a crescendo. A cymbal clashed, followed by the applause of the onlookers.

"Gentlemen," he heard Colonel Moore tell Captain Ashbel Smith and the other company officers, "that was an excellent display. You, your sergeants, and your men are to be congratulated."

"Hear, hear!" shouted Houston's mayor. "These soldiers are an excellent representation of Southern manliness and discipline. They will show those Yankee mongrels that they have gravely misjudged Texian mettle and Confederate fortitude." Ryan couldn't see the city official's face, only his tall gray silk hat bobbing as the mayor must have nodded. More applause. At least, the city band had stopped its butchering of "Dixie" and other patriotic tunes.

"That was glorious, Colonel Moore," a woman's voice rose above the din. "These men march beautifully."

"We should," Gibb Gideon muttered down the line, "we've been doing it since summer."

Ryan would have smiled, however, back to the men, eyes facing the officers and viewers, Sergeant Rutherford said: "Another word, and I cut out your tongue and feed it to the dogs."

\* \* \* \* \*

In October, the Second Texas had left Galveston Island for Houston, establishing Camp Bee on the flat grasslands just outside the city. A Union ship had sailed into the harbor under a flag of truce, and the

Yanks had basically said: "Surrender or be blown to Kingdom Come."

A few shells were traded, to no effect, before Confederate Colonel Joseph J. Cook had negotiated a truce with the Federals. The Yanks agreed to a four-day cease fire in which non-combatants could evacuate the island for the mainland. They did. So did the Second Texas, weapons and all, and so did every other Rebel soldier on the island. Cook and the other Texas commanders had a great laugh at that, imagining the Yanks' reaction to having no prisoners, no confiscated weapons, only a deserted town to their name, but now only seven miles of salt water separated the Yankees from the Texas mainland. Galveston lay less than fifty miles from Houston.

At some point, the Yankees would have to invade, Ryan figured, or Colonel Moore would try to take back the island and reopen the Texas port.

Instead of bunking in a Galveston warehouse, Ryan now shared a conical tent with his messmates. Called a Sibley tent, it resembled a Comanche teepee rather than any other type of tent Ryan had ever seen, with a smoke hole at the top and pegs along the bottom, except an Indian's lodge was made from buffalo hide, and the Sibley was canvas.

The tents, like the .69-caliber muskets many of the soldiers carried, had once been property of the US Army, recently conscripted into the Confederate Army.

Those tents had been designed and patented by an officer named Henry Hopkins Sibley, a West Point graduate who had risen to the rank of major in the First Dragoons. Now, according to Little Sam Houston, Sibley was a brigadier general leading an army of Texians to claim New Mexico Territory and the Colorado gold fields for the South.

That made Ryan wonder how the North could ever hope to win this war. A gifted inventor like Henry Sibley had resigned his commission to join the Confederate Army. A tactician and author like William J. Hardee—even if Ryan despised the manual Hardee had authored—had left the North for the South. Albert Sidney

Johnston, formerly a general in the Texas Army and in the US Army, now commanded the Confederacy's Army of the Mississippi. Even the Second's commander, Colonel John Creed Moore, had been graduated from West Point and had fought against the Seminole Indians. Ryan wondered who was left to command the Northern armies.

They stood at attention, then at ease, and listened to the mayor and Colonel Moore pontificate and praise, stump and speechify. A preacher prayed for deliverance from the Yankee blockade. A woman sang a hymn, a cappella, and the mayor talked for another fifteen minutes before the brass band launched into "Bonnie Blue Flag." More applause, and, finally, Colonel Moore told the captains to dismiss their troops, the captains passed down the word to the lieutenants, who, in turn, ordered the sergeants, and, at last, Sergeant Rutherford barked out: "Dis-missed!"

Yet even as the assembly ended, as Gibb Gideon and Harry Cravey led the way back to their Sibley tent, Ryan McCalla noticed that everyone still acted like soldiers. Harry Cravey, who had started drilling with an axe an eternity ago, carried his musket properly. Only a month ago, Sergeant Rutherford had screamed in Baby Cravey's face for a good twenty minutes for dragging the weapon behind him. Now, it remained on his shoulder, hand clasped firmly on its stock, bayonet glistening in the sun.

"You boys almost look like soldiers," a long-bearded man in duck trousers and a muslin shirt told them as they marched past.

*Almost.*

Well, the man did have a point. Sam Houston Jr. looked resplendent in his tailored uniform, but Gibb Gideon wore ragged britches that needed hemming, and the closest thing Ryan had that resembled an Army uniform was a woolen vest with brass buttons.

"Sergeant Rutherford," Ryan called out to the gruff, mustached non-commissioned officer walking alongside, "when are we getting uniforms?"

"You don't need uniforms to kill Yankees, McCalla!" Rutherford barked.

That was the same answer Rutherford had given last week when Matt Bryson had complained about the lack of uniforms.

A city of canvas appeared before them, stretching out across the dead winter grass. Rutherford veered off for his personal tent. Captain Williams' Company D, formerly the Confederate Grays, turned sharply down what had been dubbed Moore Lane, and disappeared into their Sibley tents. Gideon and Cravey kept marching down San Jacinto Boulevard for thirty rods before stopping. Lowering their weapons, removing the bayonets, the soldiers stacked the long guns in a circle in front of their tent.

Gideon stooped by the pit, piling a piece of fat lighter in the ash, and covering it with broken twigs. "Who wants coffee?" he said, and, although no one answered, he knew his messmates well enough to know that everyone wanted coffee.

"Need help?" Ryan asked.

"You know better'n that. Give me a few minutes."

Ryan disappeared inside the tent, unfolded his camp chair, and sat down by his bedroll, reaching down for the case holding his fiddle. Little Sam had peeled off his coat, slipped his arms through his suspenders, and was pulling off his shirt. Matt Bryson had dropped onto his bedroll, removed his brogans, and began massaging his feet. Outside, Harry Cravey announced that he'd fix a pot of beans if anybody else was hungry.

"Sounds good," Gibb Gideon said. "I'll do the coffee, you cook the beans."

Matt Bryson snorted. "This feels like Sunday."

It was, however, Wednesday.

"Maybe you'd rather be drilling the School of the Company again." Little Sam pulled on a freshly laundered ivory shirt, with an inset bib of rose-colored stripes, and began tucking it inside his blue trousers.

Ryan plucked a string on the Miremont, frowned, turned the knob to tighten it.

Outside, the fire crackled. Somewhere in the tent city, a jew's-harp began twanging out "Old Dan Tucker" accompanied by the sounds of laughter and a cacophony of voices. It certainly did feel like a Sunday.

Ryan moved to the next string, tuned it, then the next. By now, he could smell the aroma of Gibb Gideon's coffee, and heard Harry Cravey pouring beans into a pot. He hoped Baby cooked them through this time. Last time, it had been like eating pebbles.

"Are you going like that?"

He looked up from his violin at Little Sam, now busy tying a red silk cravat around the paper collar he had affixed to his shirt.

Ryan glanced at his shirt, vest, and trousers, then looked back up at Houston.

"It's only three-twenty," Matt Bryson said, checking his watch. "The ball doesn't begin for more than three hours."

Little Sam shrugged, adjusted his cravat, pulled up his suspenders, and began combing his hair.

"You going to eat Cravey's beans in that clean shirt?" Ryan asked.

He caught Little Sam's eyes from the reflection of the little mirror they had tacked to the center pole. Sam Houston Jr. winked.

"I'm not eating with y'all, boys." He slipped a comb into a pocket, and grabbed his coat and wide-brimmed gray hat. "I'll be seeing you gents tonight. Play 'Jeannie with the Light Brown Hair' for me, Ryan."

"I always do."

"And you boys don't spike the punch."

\* \* \* \* \*

Built by Captain E. S. and James H. Perkins, Perkins Hall stood in Houston at the corner of Franklin and Main Streets, the first opera house in the city. The last time Ryan had been here was back in November, playing with other amateur musicians in a benefit concert for the Hospital Fund.

There had been no alcohol at the concert hall that time, but, three songs into the ball, Ryan could smell the beer and ale flowing out of the kegs supplied by Peter Gabel's brewery.

Seeing Little Sam Houston lead a young redhead onto the dance floor, Ryan turned toward the guitar player on his right as soon as they had finished "Barbara Allen" and mouthed the title of Stephen Foster's song.

Applause sounded politely as Ryan began a violin introduction, and he had to smile as Little Sam gave him a wink while leading the young girl in a pink grenadine dress and fringed sash of pink ribbon around the floor.

Forty minutes later, the guitar player, a Company E lieutenant named Arnett from Robertson County, announced that the band would take a break for fifteen minutes, but that the choir from the city's First Baptist Church would come on stage and sing.

Ryan put his fiddle in the case, closed it, and headed off the stage, avoiding the onrushing girls and elderly women of the choir. He turned to his left, went down the steps, and exited onto the main floor, ignoring Gibb Gideon's calls for him to join him and several other infantrymen by the Gabel kegs. He found himself beside the tables of punch bowls, fruits, cakes, cookies, and pies.

He slaked his thirst with a glass of punch, and looked across the crowd for his mother and father.

"Do you ever get to dance?"

Turning quickly, Ryan almost splashed the remaining punch in his glass across his buttoned vest.

The best he could answer was: "*Ummmm.*"

She smiled, and bowed. Her blue dress was satin de Mai and thin silk, more fitting for the summer than winter, although Houston rarely felt winter's breath. Trimmed with blue and white ruches, with a blue belt and clasp, the dress featured sleeves made of white muslin, and she wore a hat of mixed chip and straw, accented with a blue rosette and ostrich plume.

It was only later, lying in his bedroll back in the Sibley tent, that he remembered her dress. At that moment, if he had been asked to describe what she was wearing, he would have been only able to say: "*Ummmm.*"

"I saw you play at the benefit for the hospital in November," she said.

"Yes." He set the glass on the table before he dropped it on the floor. "I was there."

*Idiot.*

Her hair was midnight, tucked up in a chignon somewhere behind the hat and plume, her face dark, her eyes a far-reaching brown. She extended her delicate white-gloved hand.

"I am Irene Vardakas." He would never be able to pronounce that last name.

His right hand shot forward. "Ryan McCalla."

He was about to formulate a complete sentence when a fat man wearing an ill-fitting plaid sack suit tapped a brass-headed walnut cane on the floor near Ryan's brogans, muttered something, and slapped Ryan hard across the back.

"Why don't you kids get into some boats, row your way out to sea, and take the fight to the Yanks?" He laughed. His breath stank of ale.

The Baptist choir finished its first song.

Reluctantly Ryan turned away from his Greek goddess, and looked at the triple-chinned man with bloodshot eyes.

"I'm sorry, sir?"

The drunk repeated his question, and Ryan suggested he take up his battle plan with Captain Smith. He jutted his head toward a figure two tables down, standing between a chocolate cake and a picked-over ham. Captain Ashbel Smith seemed busy fending off an assault by a man wearing a green jacket that had been in fashion back when Sam Houston was president of the Republic of Texas.

The drunk looked toward Captain Smith, then back at Ryan, then at the Greek goddess, finally let out a chortle, and used his cane to push back his silk hat, before waddling back toward Gibb

Gideon and the kegs of beer and ale.

"So …" Irene tried again. "Do you ever get to dance?"

"Sometimes," Ryan said. He couldn't remember ever dancing with anyone anywhere.

"My father says it's my duty to dance with a brave young soldier defending Southern womanhood and Texas honor."

The choir finished another song.

"Your father is an erudite and patriotic man."

Ryan couldn't believe what he had said, and found it even harder to believe that Irene V-something was laughing.

"So …?"

He couldn't believe it. This Helen of Troy was suggesting that they dance … to a Baptist hymn?

He moved closer to her, but Lieutenant Arnett stopped him by calling out his name. Ryan looked at Arnett, who was gesturing toward the stage, and Ryan cursed all officers of the Second Texas Infantry underneath his breath.

"Maybe later?" Irene offered hopefully.

"It would be my honor," he said, bowed graciously, and followed Lieutenant Arnett through the people, past the kegs, and back to the stage.

He spent the rest of the ball scanning the hall for the goddess, wondering if he had dreamed the entire thing since all he saw was his mother dancing with his father, Little Sam Houston dancing with every other woman—excepting Irene—and Gibb Gideon laughing at the jokes of the fat man with the walnut cane.

They closed with "Dixie," which caused a deafening applause. Ryan wiped his sweaty brow with his handkerchief, packed away his fiddle, and pretended that he didn't hear his mother's beckoning. When he looked up, however, he saw Irene Vardakas walking out the front door and into the midnight, her white-muslined arm intertwined with the black broadcloth of Matt Bryson's frock coat.

# CHAPTER NINE

The measles epidemic had long since passed. For a while, Caleb thought it would be the only battle he and the other soldiers in Missouri would ever see. A few weeks ago, however, Major General Henry W. Halleck, new commander of the even newer Department of the Missouri, had ordered Colonel Morgan and the Eighteenth to leave Fort Morgan and head west to Weston in Platte County, north of Kansas City.

"Our glorious mission," Morgan had told his troops before they boarded the train in Laclede, "is to suppress those Rebel bushwhackers, provide assistance to our brave settlers who still honor the Stars and Stripes, and enlist enough men who will fight to the death to preserve the Union and provide our Rangers with a final company to make us a true regiment."

It sounded like a noble expedition, but Caleb would soon learn that Morgan apparently had forgotten to mention another part of the mission.

To plunder.

Oh, that cut both ways. Rebel bushwhackers murdered, burned, pillaged. On December 1, two Union cavalrymen had been ambushed while crossing the bridge over Bee Creek, their horses stolen, along with their greatcoats, high boots, sabers, and carbines. One of the dead trooper's gold teeth had been pried out of his mouth, and both men had been scalped. Caleb could expect such atrocities from Rebels, but from the men he called comrades?

Within two days of the Eighteenth's arrival in Weston, Seb Woolard brought a silver candleholder and nickel-plated cigar case into the new tent he shared with Rémy, Caleb, and two new recruits for the company, a farmer from Milan named Folker, and Sergeant Masterson's first cousin, Boone Masterson.

"Where did you get those?" Boone asked.

"Confiscated from Rebel trash." Seb pushed the plunder into his haversack.

When Caleb complained to Sergeant Masterson, the former barber snapped: "It's his business, Cole, not yours."

For a few days afterward, Caleb considered Harold Masterson as big a thief as Seb Woolard, but Boone later told him that when his cousin had complained to Lieutenant Roberts, going through proper military channels, the one-time mercantile clerk from Unionville had proudly displayed a tray of silver utensils, asking: "And what did you confiscate, Sergeant?"

Since then Seb Woolard had filled his haversack and now had an additional two pillowcases stuffed with valuables liberated from Rebel sympathizers.

They had arrived in Weston on the blustery evening of December 9. As the American flag was raised once again, Colonel Morgan proclaimed that he would bring peace to Platte County if he had to kill every bushwhacker in sight.

Missouri irregulars, however, proved really good at staying out of sight.

They had burned the railroad bridge at Iatan, had shot down those two cavalrymen at Bee Creek. One had even sneaked into Platte City, lowered the Union flag Caleb had helped raise himself that morning, dropped the flag into a watering trough, and raised instead a filthy pair of men's red flannel underwear.

When Morgan himself raised the relatively dry Federal flag the next afternoon, he declared that if any American flag was ever lowered in any city or town in Platte County, that town would be sacked.

Thus, the Eighteenth Missouri became night raiders.

Caleb found himself storming into farm houses, watching as Sergeant Masterson or Lieutenant Roberts or even Seb Woolard pulled a man out of his house, wearing nothing but his undergarments, while his wife and/or mother and/or children cried, begged, prayed.

Sometimes the man was flogged, then forced to take the oath of allegiance to the Union. Sometimes he took the oath willingly, then was flogged as a reminder not to forget his loyalty to the Union. Once, the man of the house was not home that night, so Colonel Morgan had the home, barn, privy, and lean-to burned. The milch cow, pigs, and chickens were, Morgan proudly bragged, "conscripted into the Union Army."

The next time Colonel Morgan gave orders to burn a citizen's home and farm, Captain Clark wheeled his horse, drew his LaMatt revolver, and faced the men of Company E. Then he announced: "If any one of you falls out of line to help perpetrate this crime, so help me God, I will shoot you myself."

From where he stood, Caleb could hear Seb Woolard's curse, but the boy did not move.

Slowly Colonel Morgan, his orderly, and his adjutant eased their horse toward Captain Clark and Company E.

"Is there a problem here, Mister Clark?" Morgan asked hesitantly.

Keeping the massive revolver aimed skyward, without looking back at his commanding officer, Captain Clark answered: "Yes, Morgan, there most definitely is."

The absence of rank, and a respectful *sir*, did not go unnoticed by anyone.

"You have your orders, *Captain*."

"I answer to a higher authority." This time Clark turned savagely toward Morgan, but kept the pistol, now shaking in his right hand, up and away. Had he moved it, Caleb just knew that Jacob Clark would have blown Colonel Morgan out of his saddle. "*Sir!*"

If he lived to be a hundred, Caleb would never forget this incident.

* * * * *

Things had gotten worse. Oh, Colonel Morgan hadn't pressed charges, or hadn't ordered Captain Clark's arrest for insubordination. Instead, he had meekly turned his horse again, and watched the inferno begin. During future raids, Captain Clark and Company E remained behind in Weston, which limited Seb Woolard's thefts to the city proper. The farm kid resented Captain Clark and the rest of his messmates. Caleb could have cared less.

Then, on December 14, Morgan had ordered Clark to procure mounts for six men, and send them toward Centerville, a stronghold of slave owners and Southern extremists. Morgan had received information that bushwhackers might be congregating there. Captain Clark detailed Sergeant Masterson to lead a patrol to Centerville, to pick and choose his own men. Once Morgan left, the captain fished out a few silver coins, and put them in Sergeant Masterson's hand. "Rent the horses, Sergeant," he had said softly, and Masterson had answered with a proud, understanding nod.

"I'll return the mounts with the captain's compliments."

Rémy, Caleb, Boone, and Folker joined Sergeant Masterson, who said he could not find Seb Woolard, so they would have to keep the patrol to five men.

"You give Seb privy duty, Sergeant?" Folker said.

"What's that, Folker?" Masterson kicked the horse he had rented from a farmer along the Missouri River into a trot. "I didn't hear you."

Folker was slow, but not stupid. His smile almost matched Caleb's as he kicked his roan into a trot, and they rode out of Weston toward Centerville.

They caught two Rebels coming out of the New Zion Baptist Church, surrounded them, disarmed them, and lashed their wrists to their saddle horns and their legs underneath the bellies of their weary mounts.

"Caleb!" one of the prisoners called.

He blinked, staring, not comprehending. Actually it was the other prisoner Caleb thought he had recognized, not this shaking kid with cornbread crumbs covering his face. Finally it hit him.

"Parker?"

Parker Pruitt, recent recruit of the Keytesville Methodist Rangers, couldn't hide the tears welling in his eyes. His smile seemed genuine, however, as if he thought Caleb Cole could get him out of his current predicament.

"You know this boy, Cole?" Sergeant Masterson asked.

"He's from Unionville, Sergeant. His daddy runs some flour mills in town."

"Land's sakes," said the other prisoner, spitting out a mouthful of tobacco juice, "it's the pig farmer."

Now Caleb remembered him. The straw hat and gauntlets were gone, replaced by a wretched felt slouch hat, ragged clothes, not even a coat or gloves to fight off the winter chill. Captain Benedict Crane, leader of his Keytesville militia.

"And this one?" Masterson asked.

Caleb found no sympathy for either of them. "Last time I saw him, it was after midnight, and he was threatening my folks. They came calling for me." He tilted his head toward Pruitt, whose smile quickly vanished. "They *both* were there."

He left out the part that he had been hiding in a pigpen, and had dug his way to freedom, escaping assassination, by covering himself with dung and hay. His face flushed in anger, and he felt his fingers clenching into fists that shook.

"What are you doing here?" Masterson asked the two Rebel militiamen.

The captain turned silent, but Parker Pruitt sniffled and said: "Furloughed. On our way home."

"I see you furloughed some cornbread and fatback from the preacher here," Boone said.

"The parson here"—Captain Crane had found his voice—"he is a good Southern man, not scum like you darky-loving scoundrels."

Which prompted Folker to launch into a verse of "John Brown's Body," until Sergeant Masterson told him to shut up.

"Any more of you boys been furloughed?" Masterson asked.

No answer, and with Centerville residents beginning to congregate outside the church, Sergeant Masterson decided that two prisoners would satisfy Colonel Morgan, and that they'd best light a shuck back to Weston.

* * * * *

The colonel had been pleased, too. The two prisoners were locked in a root cellar, and Sergeant Masterson was rewarded with a bottle of wine, and a promise that his name would be mentioned in the colonel's next report to General Halleck.

On the way back to their camp, Masterson left the wine in the root cellar with Captain Crane and Parker Pruitt.

Captain Clark was gone, though, sent back to Laclede with a platoon to guard the railroad and look for Rebel irregulars. Lieutenant Roberts took command of Company E, and it was Roberts who led Caleb and the others into Platte City on December 14.

Colonel Morgan met seventy or more soldiers of the Eighteenth Missouri in front of the courthouse.

"The American flag has been removed," he said, and Caleb's eyes rose to the flagpole. "When God destroyed wickedness in the days of Noah, he did so with flood, but promised that the next time he would do so with fire. Well, I am the arm of the Lord, and these Secessionist sinners will kneel before me … in ash."

Silently the various companies went throughout the town, while Morgan, his adjutant, and his orderly crossed the square and entered a dram shop.

Lieutenant Roberts led Company E's detachment to the livery. "You know what to do, Sergeant." He spoke directly to Sergeant Masterson.

His head lowered, knowing he was powerless to defy an officer, Sergeant Masterson turned. "This fits you, Woolard," he said.

Woolard bolted out of line as soon as Masterson had spoken, and Caleb's head dropped, his eyes closed. If only Captain Clark were here.

He wasn't, of course. He was off on some fool's errand.

Before the lieutenant led Company E to its next assignment, Caleb could smell the smoke.

They set the opera house on fire, and the mayor's home. They marched by in silence as a white man stopped swatting, futilely, at flames inside a store with a wet rug, coughing, slowly retreating with other recruited firefighters, men of color. Freedmen or slaves, Caleb didn't know, and Company E didn't stop to ask, or help.

"Hey." Rémy Ehrenreich nudged Caleb's shoulder, and jutted his jaw toward the town square.

Smoke burned his eyes, but Caleb could spot the red-orange glow in the cupola of the courthouse.

By the time they reached the square, Colonel Morgan had stormed out of the dram shop, and was shouting furiously at a sergeant from Company E.

"My orders were explicit, you numskull!" Morgan raised a half-full whiskey bottle toward the courthouse. "I said the courthouse was not to be burned."

The sergeant stammered something, but Morgan whirled, flung the bottle into the street, pivoted to face the sergeant again. "Go put it out!" That's when Morgan noticed Lieutenant Roberts and Company A. "Help him. Save the courthouse!"

It was a lost cause already. Even Caleb knew that, but it felt better, trying to save a building from burning even if it didn't quite atone for the sin of burning down a livery—and the mayor's home—and an opera house.

By morning, when the Eighteenth Missouri Infantry marched out of Platte City, the town lay in smoldering ruin.

* * * * *

"We now tighten all cinches," Colonel Morgan said to an assembly the next day.

"National flags will fly over every house. Every man in this county will take the oath of allegiance. Anyone in Weston leaving town must have a pass. Any person visiting Weston must have a pass. Those who do not will be arrested and fined ten dollars."

What went unsaid, Caleb soon learned, was that passes would cost 5¢. Morgan also did not announce that fines and fees collected would fill his pockets.

"And we shall make an example of the two bushwhackers who have refused to take the oath. This will bring peace to this wretched county. And it will avenge the foul murders of two Union cavalry troopers."

Caleb Cole had serious doubts about this man's army.

Instead of acting like well-disciplined soldiers, most of the Eighteenth Missouri had become no better than brigands.

On this snowy morning, it struck him that Ewald Ehrenreich, dead and buried for some two months now, had been lucky. At least Ewald wasn't part of this. Freezing, teeth chattering, fingers numb from the cold, and sick to his stomach from the orders he had been given, Caleb gladly would have traded places with Rémy's dearly departed twin brother.

"Unlock the door, Private," Sergeant Harold Masterson told a farm boy from Company D on guard duty, "and let out the prisoners."

Benedict Crane stumbled out first, blinking, shielding his eyes from the light, even though the sun dared not show itself on such a miserable morning. Parker Pruitt followed, shaking, face masked in confusion.

"Captain …?" he began.

"Buck up, Pruitt. Be a man. For once in your life."

The boy's eyes widened. "Caleb?" he called out.

Caleb stared at the snow falling on his brogans.

"Prisoners," Sergeant Masterson called out, "march!"

The three-mile trek southeast out of Weston felt like thirty. No one spoke, except Rémy, and all he did was whisper a prayer, repeating his Hail Marys over and over.

At last, the bridge over Bee Creek came into view.

The snow had stopped, but the wind still howled.

Caleb tried to tell himself that for all he knew, the Keytesville Methodist Rangers had ambushed those two Federal troopers, that Captain Crane and Parker Pruitt were murderers. That they deserved to die.

He couldn't convince himself, though. Instead, a new thought popped into his mind: *I should desert. Go back home. Slopping pigs is better than this. This isn't my fight. Let the South leave the Union, and why should I care about freeing any slaves?*

In the center of the bridge waited Colonel Morgan, his orderly, his adjutant, and the captains of the other companies.

"Prisoners, halt!"

Masterson nodded for his squad to line up on the opposite side of the bridge. Reluctantly Caleb followed, and fell in place, at the end of the line closest to Colonel Morgan and the others.

Masterson moved Captain Crane and Parker Pruitt across the bridge. Pruitt's knees buckled, and he began sobbing as Masterson jerked him to his feet, shoved him almost too hard. The sergeant had to grab the boy's shirt front and jerk him forward to keep him from toppling over the railing and into the icy waters of Bee Creek.

"Proceed, Sergeant." Colonel Morgan was the only soldier mounted, looking like Death riding a towering black stallion.

By now, Parker Pruitt was screaming over the wind's roars, begging for his life.

Masterson headed back and fell into line beside Caleb.

"Ready!" Colonel Morgan said.

Nobody moved. Not even Seb Woolard.

"By thunder, I said ready!" the colonel roared, and this time the firing squad raised muskets, rifles, one fowling piece. Gently Sergeant Masterson helped push Caleb's weapon to his shoulder.

"Aim!"

Captain Crane spit tobacco juice at the firing squad.

Parker Pruitt turned, stepped around Captain Crane, and ran.

"Shoot the prisoners! Fire! I say, fire!"

Crane just stood there, defiant.

Caleb lowered his rifle, and watched Parker Pruitt run. Beside him, he heard Rémy whispering as he lowered his rifle: "Hurry, boy. Run. Run like the wind."

Hoofs echoed on the bridge. Caleb watched Colonel Morgan race by, heard a blast. Only then did he realize that Morgan had fired his revolver.

Captain Crane crumpled, folded over.

At the edge of the bridge, Parker Pruitt screamed.

Another shot. A third.

The horse raced past the prone body of Parker Pruitt. Morgan jerked the black to a stop, wheeled the horse around, galloped back toward the assembly. He lowered his pistol and sent another ball into Parker Pruitt's body without stopping, and reined up in front of Captain Crane's lifeless body, cocked the revolver, aimed, fired again.

When Morgan dismounted, the orderly raced forward to take the reins to the black, and the colonel handed him his smoking revolver, too. He stormed toward the firing squad: "That was a disgrace, Sergeant."

"Yes, sir."

"You almost let that prisoner get away."

"Yes, sir."

"Discipline wins battles, Sergeant. Discipline wins war. You and your men showed no discipline whatsoever."

"Yes, sir."

"The next time I give an order, I expect you to obey it. And your men. If not, the next time it will be you and these boys who face a firing squad."

"Yes, sir."

Morgan spun on his heels, drawing his saber. Caleb watched in horror as the colonel dipped the point of the saber in the lake of blood pooling underneath the dead bushwhacker's body, then raised the tip to the bridge's railing and wrote, in blood, the letters US on the wood.

"What have I gotten myself into?"

A moment passed before Caleb realized he had spoken those words, loudly, so that everyone on the bridge had heard.

He did not care.

# CHAPTER TEN

Even her friends called her String Bean.

Grace Dehner had learned to accept that nickname, much as she had realized she could not do a thing about her height. In her bare feet, she stood just an inch under six feet tall and had towered over even her mother back when she had turned thirteen years old. Now, four years later, she could look her father in his eyes, and easily look down upon practically every boy her age that she knew in Corinth. She could outrun them all, too.

Which was what she was doing.

Laughing hysterically, holding up the hems of her green hoop skirt, she ran down the sidewalk, then, without even slowing down, crossed the warped plank that a slave had laid across the muddy street. Behind her, a boy swore, which was followed by the dull sound of a body falling into thick mud. She knew that it was Jimmy Evans who had fallen, and even though she couldn't hear the ragged breathing of the other boys chasing her, she picked up a little speed just to be safe.

Turning onto Waldron Street, Grace Dehner slammed to a stop, just barely missing knocking Miss Prudence Caxton onto her hindquarters.

Nick O'Brien and Johnny James rounded the corner, turned sharply, and raced away from the Waldron Street Christian Church. Johnny James shouted a warning as he tore through the mud on Taylor Street. Everyone else retreated, leaving Grace alone to face Miss Prudence Caxton.

"Grace Dehner, you should be ashamed of yourself!" Miss Prudence stuck up her nose, brushed herself off indignantly as if she had been knocked onto the sidewalk. "Why, just look at you! Running around like a termagant. What has become of you, child?"

Grace lowered her skirt, tried to look properly ashamed of herself.

"Look at your hair, goodness gracious. Fringe! Fringe hanging down into your eyes."

Grace tried to brush the bangs off her forehead.

"And you are perspiring in these frigid conditions!"

It was sunny, maybe fifty degrees. Of course, after running for a half mile, she couldn't argue the fact that she was sweating.

"You are too old to wear your hair down in curls, young lady." She pointed to her own silver hair, neatly tucked up in a bun and covered with a lace net. "Where is your snood? For that matter, where are your gloves?"

Grace would have sworn her mother had pinned up her hair before she left the house that afternoon, but Miss Prudence was right. The lace net was gone. Must have fallen off when she had tripped crossing Bunch Street. As far as the gloves, however, she detested wearing gloves. They cut off the circulation to her long fingers.

Standing at the entrance to the Waldron Street Christian Church, the other fine ladies nodded in approval of Miss Prudence's observations. Grace felt her face begin to redden, and she wished Miss Prudence and every other lady in Corinth would mind their own business. She had never been one to bite her tongue, and was about, instead, to bite off Miss Prudence's head when Dr. Kenton Landon arrived, stepping between Miss Prudence and Grace, and extending his right hand.

"Grace, my dear Grace, thank you for racing to see me. I feel if we hurry, we might just manage to save Darius McGillicudy from being called to Glory." Smoothly he turned Grace around, tucked his hand underneath her arm, and led her back to Taylor Street and crossed that plank.

"Aren't you coming to hear the Wednesday sermon?"

The question, from Mrs. Hildegarde Beaumont and directed at Dr. Landon, was sarcastic. Everyone in Tishomingo County knew Kenton Landon to be a freethinker, although Dr. Landon liked watching the horrified faces when he proclaimed himself to be an atheist.

Dr. Landon released his hold on Grace's arm, and turned, tipping his bell crown hat without slowing down, calling back: "I'm sure someone will tell me all about Parson Mark's preaching. But please pray for Grace and me. Better yet, please pray for relief for poor Darius McGillicudy. Cholelithiasis is a terrible way to die."

When they were safe from view behind the walls of Weatherby's Mercantile, Grace asked: "What is cho— what is chole—" She gave up, and began again: "And who is Darius McGillicudy?"

Kenton Landon had pulled a tobacco twist from the pocket of his green frock coat. "Darius was a childhood friend an eternity ago on the Thames River, though his surname has long since faded from my fleeting memory. McGillicudy was the scoundrel who told me Cross City would be a great place to hang my shingle."

Back in 1853, Cross City had been the original name of Corinth, until a newspaper editor suggested that they name the city after a place in Greece that had been a crossroads of some sort. Two railroads, the Mobile & Ohio and the Memphis & Charleston, crossed here at this swampy settlement in northern Mississippi.

Grace and Dr. Landon were heading toward those railroad tracks now.

Nobody had sounded really enthusiastic about the name change, so the editor had made a compromise. Try Corinth out for size. If nobody liked it after a year, they could always go back to

Cross City. They hadn't gone back to Cross City, and that had been four or five years ago.

"And that disease?" Grace asked.

"Cholelithiasis?" Dr. Landon had bit off a substantial chaw from the twist, and had shoved the tobacco back into his pocket. "I have yet to hear of anyone dying from that indisposition, although many have sworn they felt like they were about to. Most people call it gallstones."

They crossed the tracks, moved between bales of cotton, and among slaves, who quickly dropped their gaze lest anyone accuse them of improper glances at a white woman.

Dr. Landon stopped, started to say something to Grace, then bit his lower lip. "Come on," he said, and continued his long gait, which Grace easily matched. Standing six feet, three, Kenton Landon was one person Grace could look up to, literally and figuratively.

"And what did you do to incur Prudence Caxton's wrath?" he asked after a while.

She shrugged. "I was racing Johnny, Jimmy, Nick, George, some others."

"Winning, I presume."

Of course. Grace didn't have to answer that question. And it wasn't even fair. All the boys had on were their pants, shirts, coats, and shoes. Grace was laden down with a chemise and other unmention-ables—stockings, whalebone corset, crinoline, camisole, bodice, skirt, belt, jacket, and shawl. And those velvet slippers on her feet slowed her down. She would have been even faster had she raced barefoot.

"Where were you supposed to be going?"

"I was there," she said with indignation. "Church. Papa and Mother will be madder than hornets when they hear that I missed the Wednesday Bible meeting and sermon."

The doctor spit into the mud.

"I can tell you exactly what Parson Mark will say." They had started winding down Tate Street.

"Preston Childs has two sons at Fort Donelson. He'll pray for their deliverance from Yankee tyrants. He will pray for President Davis' wisdom and for the hand of God to strike down that Abolitionist rascal, Abe Lincoln. He will ask God to see our great city and wonderful congregation through these dark days, and will pray that the Almighty infect the Northern troops in Tennessee with dysentery. He will lead the entire congregation in a long, spirited prayer that God will spare Corinth, this blessed city, from the savages of war. He will find a passage in the Bible and use it as justification for what he seeks, thus making it right, holy, and just."

"What passage would that be, Doctor Landon."

"You may call me Kenton, Grace, as I've told you a hundred times."

"Mama says I shouldn't be that familiar with a man old enough to be my grandfather."

A smile cracked granite face. "*Grandfather?*" He spit again.

"Well ...?" She asked again about the Bible.

"String Bean," he said, "I've never cracked a Bible's spine."

Silently she made a vow to pray for Kenton—Doctor Landon's—soul.

They turned down a tree-lined dirt path. It was colder here, much colder, and Grace shuddered as a chill raced up her spine.

"Doctor Landon," she called out, her voice suddenly timid, "where are we going?"

He answered with a tilt of his head, and she saw the picket shack, saw a bearded white man, shoeless and shirtless, smoking a corncob pipe, rise from a wooden keg he was sitting on and use his right foot to slide a clay jug behind the keg and out of view of his guests.

"How is your quest for higher learning coming at the college?" Landon asked, and then stopped to use thumb and forefinger to hook out the tobacco from his mouth.

He meant the Corona Female College up on the knoll now called College Hill. The Reverend L. B. Gaston had established the college four and a half years ago, getting city officials to donate ten acres and then having a domed, three-story brick building erected. Grace had spent two semesters there.

"I won't begin my third session till next month." Grace looked at the wretched man living in squalor. She'd never seen a white man living in such a miserable home.

"Learning anything?"

She snorted. "Arithmetic that I already know. Geography that I don't give a whit about. History's all right, I guess. But I'd rather be reading Lord Byron or William Gilmore Simms than going over all that English grammar stuff."

"All right." Landon took a step forward. "You're about to get a real education, Grace Dehner." He rarely called her by her full name. He stopped, turned, his face sober, serious. "You don't have to do this, Grace. I had planned on leaving you at the depot, but … Well, never mind. You're here. But you can run back to church, or home, or bury your nose in Lord Byron's poetry."

She shook her head, though at that moment she really wanted to be standing on Waldon Street, being yelled at and embarrassed by Miss Prudence Caxton.

"All right," the doctor said. "Come with me. If you get sick, don't be ashamed. If you cry, cry long and hard. If you want to run away, run away. This isn't Byron or Dickens, Simms or Cooper, or Jesus of Nazareth. This is life, String Bean. And you shall learn why I say there is no God. And, why, sometimes there should never be any doctors."

\* \* \* \* \*

She stepped out of the stinking hovel and into the night, looking for stars but finding only tall pine trees and clouds. She felt herself trembling, but managed to block any tears. She wanted to breathe, deeply, hold it in forever, wanted to go home and take a scalding hot bath. Wanted to bundle her clothes, give them to her father, and plead with him to drop them in Dismal Swamp.

The stink of death would never leave her.

Behind her, she could hear the husband, now widower, and Dr. Landon step outside, talking in whispers. What to do next? Should there be a funeral for his wife? His two daughters? His infant son? Would the citizens of Corinth burn down his home, not that it was much of a home, to keep the sickness from spreading?

The man, now alone, wandered to the keg, reached down, found the jug. It was the best, the only thing Kenton Landon could prescribe.

She heard him come near her, felt his arm on her shoulder.

"They would have died no matter what. The baby was dead when we got here. They ...."

"I know." But she didn't.

"Medicine can be fragile. There is no known treatment for diphtheria."

So that's what had killed that poor man's family. Diphtheria. She had heard of it, but had never seen it.

"What a great way to bring in this new year," she said. Her bitterness surprised her. It also eased the rage boiling inside her.

The oldest daughter had been maybe Grace's age, although Grace had never seen her, not at the subscription school, not at church, certainly not at the Corona Female College, not even along the railroad tracks or anywhere. Her eyes had seemed paralyzed, along with her throat. She had just lay there, unable to move, unable to breathe, until her heart had finally stopped beating. Her eyes had never closed, until Dr. Landon came over and shut them with his own shaking fingers.

"No treatment," she began, hating how her voice quavered. "That tube ...?"

He shrugged, released his hold. "I just thought ..." He turned away. "An experiment. Had it worked, they would have written me up in all the medical journals."

They had tried pushing a thin tube down the mother's throat, Grace holding the woman's face, trying to keep her mouth open, feeling the woman's desperate fight, but she had no strength. And Dr. Landon hadn't been able to get the tube through the obstructions. So she had died, gagging, choking, with Grace still holding her face.

Church bells rang out, signaling the new year, celebrating something. Not mourning the dead.

Grace wondered what time it was.

"I shouldn't have brought you here," Dr. Landon said, "but I needed you."

She looked at him, saw tears in his eyes. That surprised her. "No," she said, her voice urgent. "No, I'm glad I came. I just had hoped …" She turned away.

"You've been coming to my office for two years now," Dr. Landon said. "I told everyone … your father included … that you wanted to become my nurse, but I always said that in a joking manner. Yet deep down, String Bean, I knew. You can help people. You can be a nurse. You can become a doctor."

She laughed. "A woman doctor!"

"Believe me …" He started to say something else, but excused himself, telling her not to leave, that he would walk her home, explain everything to her parents, assure them that she was never in harm's way, that there was no cause for alarm, that diphtheria … that diphtheria … Shaking his head sadly, he joined the man on the porch, and waited for him to pass the jug.

* * * * *

Back on Tate Street, they could see the depot, illuminated by street lamps, and could make out a puffing black locomotive preparing to head northwest toward Memphis.

"Why did you bring me along?" It had struck her back at the shanty, while Dr. Kenton Landon helped kill a jug of corn liquor with a grieving man who had just lost his entire family. "You knew there was nothing you could do for any of them."

"I had to try."

"That was not my question." She stopped, turned, faced him.

"I will need your help, Grace."

She blinked. "Help with what?"

His smile held no humor. "Remember when I told you that the parson at your brick church will pray that God spare Corinth from war?" She didn't answer, didn't blink, didn't move, just waited. "It will be an unanswered prayer, and not because I say there is no God, and not because God, in His infinite wisdom, does not always answer those prayers of hopeful believers. War will come here, String Bean, and soon. Because of that."

He pointed, and Grace turned.

Ahead of her, a powerful black American locomotive—a 4-4-0, she knew the type, had seen them often enough—began coughing and sputtering as it came to life, pulling its tender, several boxcars, and a caboose away from the depot.

# CHAPTER ELEVEN

MARCH 15–18, 1862
HOUSTON, TEXAS

There was no drill duty, no fatigue duty that blustery morning of the fifteenth, no mock battle to be executed under Sergeant Rutherford's and Captain Smith's critical eyes, and no ball or party honoring the Second Texas Infantry scheduled that evening.

As they assembled, Colonel John Creed Moore looked grim, and it couldn't have been that the men had performed horribly in Friday's "sham" campaign the previous day. If anything, the Second Texas Infantry drilled better than any troop in the Confederate Army—at least those troops still in Texas. Moore had commended the captains that evening, and his praise had been passed down to the lieutenants and to the sergeants and finally to the *real* soldiers themselves. Even Sergeant Rutherford had not found anything to criticize.

"Men"—Colonel Moore stopped to clear his throat—"we have our orders."

All whispering, all clanging of metal, and the restless footsteps of soldiers stopped. Every eye trained on Colonel Moore, who wet his lips and said: "On Tuesday, we will depart for Arkansas and report to General Van Dorn."

No sergeant tried to squash the excited whispers ripping down the lines.

"It will be my honor, men, to lead you into battle."

Already most of the soldiers had started cheering.

"For honor!"

Hats soared into the air.

"For Texas!" Even Ryan found himself screaming.

"For glory!"

* * * * *

"Arkansas?" Harry Cravey sat on his bedroll, long legs extended, shaking his head. "Arkansas?"

Gibb Gideon slapped Cravey's back. "I've been there. It's full of mosquitoes, just like Houston. Only difference is there're no shrimp and the trees are a lot bigger."

"More Yankees there, too, I reckon," Sam Houston Jr. said.

"Yankees are here." Cravey sniffed, and Ryan realized that Baby was crying. "Not more than fifty miles from here."

Ryan wet his lips, tried to think of something to say.

"Yeah, and all those Yankees in Galveston are doing is sitting and crabbing, I warrant," Matt Bryson said. "The Yankees have already taken Fort Donelson up in Tennessee, opened up the Cumberland River for those Northern despots. Van Dorn's marching to whip the Yanks and hold onto Arkansas, maybe recapture Missouri. That's where soldiers are needed."

"Besides," Gideon said, "I'm sick of all those shams we've been fighting. It would be nice to fight someone in a blue uniform, and shoot real lead balls at the real enemy."

"It would be nice," Little Sam added, "if we had uniforms."

"Look who's talking," Gideon fired back, his face lighted with amusement as he brushed imaginary lint off the sleeve of Little Sam's coat.

"You don't need uniforms to kill Yankees." Matt Bryson's exaggerated impression of Sergeant Rutherford's drawl made everyone in the tent laugh. Except Baby Cravey.

"Well, I didn't sign on to fight nobody in Arkansas." Cravey leaped from his seat, wiping his eyes. "I was told we'd just defend Texas." He slammed his hat against the center pole, and stormed outside.

Ryan started to go after him, but Little Sam stopped him. "Let him go, Ryan. He'll be back."

"He better be," Gideon said.

*  *  *  *  *

That evening, Harry Cravey returned. He said his mother made him come back, but he sure didn't see any reason he should march off to Arkansas when there were Yankees only fifty miles south.

"Let yellow fever kill them," Matt Bryson said. "I'd rather kill them with buck and ball." He patted the stock of his musket.

*  *  *  *  *

They drilled on the sixteenth, all day, and again on the seventeenth, but only that morning. Afterward, they retired to their quarters to prepare for one more glorious ball.

*  *  *  *  *

Although Captain Ashbel Smith himself ordered Ryan to leave the Miremont, saying that this social was to honor the fighting men of the Second and that a Houston band—and only a Houston band—would play that evening, Ryan brought the violin, secured in its case, anyway.

He stood back in Perkins Hall, searching for Irene Vardakas, but did not see that Greek goddess. He hadn't found the courage to ask Matt Bryson about her, and Matt was busy trying to match Gibb Gideon at the kegs of ale in the corner. Instead, Ryan smiled at his mother and father.

"I dare say you have grown some," Josiah McCalla said stiffly, nodding in approval. He wore a blue and white checked shirt to show his patriotism. His breath smelled of rye.

Thinking of nothing to say, Ryan merely nodded.

"Are you going to play?" his mother asked. Tears welled in her eyes, but Ryan tried not to look at them. She pointed a gloved finger at the case.

"No," he finally answered, swallowing, and bringing up the case and handing it to his father. "I was hoping … hoping you might … keep it safe … till I get back."

Reluctantly his father took the case, and Ryan prayed that his father would not remember that he had bought the violin in New York and that, even though its maker was a Frenchman, it might be considered Yankee, and thus unacceptable to find shelter in the McCalla home.

"I thought …" His mother paused to bow to Matt Bryson's father, exchange some pleasantries with Mrs. Bryson, and then returned to her conversation with her son. "I thought you were in the regimental band, that you needed the violin in place of a bugle."

"We have our own instruments," Ryan lied. "For the band. And the regiment is supposed to get bugles and drums …"

His father cut in: "You can't kill Yankees with a cello, Reine."

"It's a violin, Josiah."

"Doesn't matter." His father looked away, staring across the hats of straw and felt and dresses of lace and silk, toward the tables lined with kegs of Peter Gabel's brews. He tucked the case underneath his arm, then announced: "I will take this to Randall, have him keep it in the phaeton." Randall was his father's manservant. Josiah McCalla strode off.

"Have you been eating well?" Reine McCalla asked her son.

He choked back a laugh, and bobbed his head. "'Bab—um … Harry Cravey's turned into a pretty good cook."

"And are your bowel movements regular?"

"Mother!" He blushed, realizing anyone near him had heard his shout. Lowering his voice, he announced sternly: "I am almost eighteen years old."

Her reply came equally rigid. "You will turn seventeen in June."

"Well ..." He gave her a smile, and she returned one just as forced.

The band had started playing "Jeannie with the Light Brown Hair," and he was about to ask his mother to dance, when a towering figure came between then, and he heard the legendary Sam Houston's voice.

"Missus McCalla, I see your husband has left you defenseless against the masses. Would you honor me?"

He watched his mother's bow, then, mouth open, stood amazed while the leviathan swung his petite mother onto the floor.

When Ryan turned back, Irene Vardakas stood in front of him. He almost staggered backward.

Smiling, she stepped closer. "You are not playing tonight," she observed.

"I don't even have my violin," he said. At least he thought he said that. Whatever had sprung from his mouth, she seemed to understand, and tilted her head toward the crowded floor.

"We didn't get a chance to dance last time," she said.

"We must rectify that." How he managed to find those words, he didn't know.

She smelled of peach blossoms. Her blue silk skirt rustled as they waltzed—or tried to waltz. Ryan bumped into Lieutenant Simons of Company K, and that could have been disastrous because Simons' right leg had been amputated just below the hip after taking a musket ball during the Mexican War. Ryan stopped, horrified, but Simons stayed the course and never even slowed down. Irene squeezed his hand, laughing, and they resumed their dance. At least twice, Ryan was aware that his own brogans were atop Irene's feet, yet she never complained.

When the band finished Foster's song and went straight into "Buffalo Gals," Ryan stayed on the floor, and led Irene again around the room, until Matt Bryson tapped him on his shoulder.

"Mind if I cut in, Ryan?" he asked.

Ryan stepped away, started to retreat, then stopped. He stood in the center of the dance floor, waiting until Matt Bryson led Irene back toward him. When they started to pass, Ryan tapped his friend's shoulder.

"Do you mind?" he asked.

He had to give his friend credit. Matt almost doubled over laughing, then slapped Ryan, hard, across the back, and walked toward the kegs, leaving Ryan to finish the dance with his Greek goddess.

\* \* \* \*

"Second Texas, fall in!" The bellow echoed across Perkins Hall.

Ryan had just handed Irene a glass of punch. Now he turned, confused. Citizens hugged the walls, leaving a cavernous space in the center of the hall where its patrons had been dancing.

"You heard the colonel!" Sergeant Rutherford stood inches from Ryan's face. "Fall in! Move, you petticoats. Move!"

Ryan turned, hurried, still confused, maybe even a tad frightened. *Have the Yankees left the island, brought the war to the mainland?* He moved behind Little Sam, saw Gibb Gideon weaving, heard him complaining between burps. They moved together like a train, found Captain Ashbel Smith waiting, and then lined up in their proper places. Other non-commissioned officers echoed Sergeant Rutherford's shouts, until at last the full company had assembled.

"Ladies and gentlemen!" Colonel Moore shouted. He was smiling. That meant, Ryan hoped, that they were not about to engage the Yankees in battle tonight. "The ladies of this wonderful city have a gift for these fine young men I will soon have the honor of leading into splendid battle."

The hall fell silent. Four women walked onto the stage and slowly, ceremoniously unveiled a silk flag. In that instant, all the trepidation Ryan had felt vanished as he gazed upon the Texas flag. On this one only olive branches circled the single lone star with the word SECOND over its top and TEXAS below. He felt pride. His right arm raised, and he cheered. The yell bounced off the rafters and balconies, matched by hurrahs and huzzahs from the other enlisted men of the Second Texas Infantry.

When the din died down, Captain Ashbel Smith stepped forward. "If it pleases the colonel, might I ask an old friend to address our troops before we depart for glory?"

Moore nodded, but whispers raced through the crowd of soldiers and citizens as Sam Houston stepped in front of the battle flag.

"Well," Little Sam whispered, "here's where my father gets hanged."

Yet Sam Houston did not speak of the great mistake, of Yankee supremacy, of sinking into fire and rivers of blood. He did say that the North had an almost endless supply of resources, that the South, or at least Texas, already was feeling the bite of the blockade. He also warned that the South could be split easily—the Union victory at Fort Donelson was evidence of that—and that the Mississippi River was key to the entire war.

Always the statesman, ever the general, he said that the best way to win the war was to control the West, stretch the Union resources thin, hold out until the people in the North—the voters—grew sick of war, of death. Let England and France recognize the South. Let the Union negotiate a peace.

"Understand, brave lads," he said, "that I can never be against the Union. I am for peace. But I honor you as you honor me. You are, by luck and God's will, Texians. You will fight bravely. You will bring triumph to our state, to the Texas name." He was walking off the stage, through the door, but talking as he moved, his ancient body tired but towering, his voice strong. He stepped onto the floor, walked to the assembled troops, nodding as he passed the officers, heading straight for Ashbel Smith and Company C.

"I am not shamed by having my name, my namesake, attached to this regiment." He paused long enough to shake Ashbel Smith's hand. He turned, stood beside Rutherford—even the sergeant looked like a dwarf next to Sam Houston—and, eyes glistening, he continued.

"My own son, a boy I love dearly, is committed to your cause, and I am committed to my son."

Little Sam let out a sigh of relief.

"Be strong, you men of the Second Texas. Be valiant. Know that my eyes and, above all, my prayers will follow you."

More applause, and Sam Houston tucked his cane underneath his arm, and held out his hand. Gibb Gideon shook it, and then Houston reached into his pocket and withdrew a plug of tobacco. Gideon glanced at it, uncertain.

"It is not much," Houston said, "but a chaw of tobacco got me through many troubling and difficult times."

Harry Cravey stared comically at the plug Houston gave him. "You'll learn the habit, son. Just don't swallow the juice."

Matt Bryson thanked the general, and shoved the quid into his trousers pocket.

Like Cravey, Ryan could only stare at the brown plug Sam Houston placed in his hand. "Your mother will say it's a nasty rote, son, and she's right. But we men are known for having a myriad nasty consuetude."

"Thank you, sir." Ryan slid the tobacco into his pocket.

"No, Mister McCalla, thank you."

Now Sam Houston stood in front of Little Sam.

"I'm out of tobacco, Son," he said, but gold coins jingled in his hand as he fished them out of his pocket. Little Sam cupped his hand, and let the coins drop in. Ryan couldn't believe it, but tears rolled down Sam Jr.'s face. "Don't spend that money on corn liquor, Son. Nor on some lovely Arkansas belle." His voice lowered. "You might need it. Remember that in case ..." He cleared his throat, turned abruptly, and, using his cane again, made his way back to Captain Smith.

As he raised his hat, cheers roared, and Ryan would have sworn the roof of Perkins Hall lifted six or seven inches.

* * * * *

To the sound of "The Girl I Left behind Me," Ryan climbed into the car. He walked behind Little Sam to the back of the coach, leaning his musket against the wall beside young Houston's, and shrugging out of his haversack. He sat next to the window, pressed his head against the glass, and looked outside.

For a half hour he did not move. Not even when the train began pulling away from the station. Silently he watched the city pass slowly.

"Is she out there?" Little Sam asked.

"Who?" Ryan asked, not moving his head from the glass.

"That handsome woman you were dancing with last night."

"I don't know."

"Well, do you see her?"

"No."

"She's out there. Keep looking."

He bit his lip to keep it from trembling. He couldn't tell Sam Jr. that he wasn't looking for Irene Vardakas. He was just looking at Harris County, Texas, his home, the place where he had grown up, the only real place he had ever known, watching it roll away.

Feeling that he would never see it again.

# CHAPTER TWELVE

6 Febr., '62

Dear Maryanne:

I take pencil in hand hoping you and your family are well. I received the lemon cookies that you sent for Christmas, and suffice to say they have all been devoured by now. I think they were gone within hours after they arrived. Thank you.

Well, I don't know if the news gets to Unionville from Platte County, but ….

Maryanne, this is the fifth time I have tried to write this letter. The first time I was writing Mother, but I just can't tell her about all the horrors I have seen. So I have been trying to write you. I just have to tell somebody, somebody who does not wear the mark of the Eighteenth Missouri.

Our leader, Colonel Morgan, is a scoundrel. He should be hung. He has been collecting fees and tariffs from the citizens here that we are supposed to be protecting, and cares not one whit if they are for the North or favor the Southern cause. Two nights ago, while I was walking from church, a woman spit on me and called me "trash." At first, I thought that she was one of those slave-lovers with all of her brood riding around wearing bushwhacker shirts and armed with dozens of pistols, but she said that her son wore the blue with Col. Sigel, but that I was a disgrace.

The thing of it is, Maryanne, I could not argue with her.

Do you remember Parker Pruitt? Does his daddy know that he is dead? We killed him. Well, Col. Morgan killed him. Executed him without a trial or anything. He was supposed—I mean Parker Pruitt—to have been shot by firing squad. And I was part of that squad, but, praise God, we did not pull a trigger. But Col. Morgan did. Shot him and the captain of that bunch of Methodist ruffians from Keytesville. I cannot write of what our colonel did to the bodies. I wish I could forget that horrible scene.

There are good men in our regiment, Maryanne. Please know that. We are not all murderers and thieves and rapscallions. Sergeant Masterson, tough as he can be, is an honorable man. So is our captain, Jacob Clark. And many others hate what we are doing, but we are told that we are soldiers and that we must follow orders, even when they are issued by a fiend like W. James Morgan.

Our chaplain—you've heard him, that Methodist circuit rider— well, he preaches fire and brimstone like a Baptist and his sermons are more blood and thunder than just about anything I have ever heard.

We have chased some enemy. I do not count our capture of poor Parker Pruitt and his captain. Yet we have not fired a shot in battle yet, and the only casualty we can boast of is that two days back, Petrus Folker lost his hat. The wind took it off. The Rebel bushwhackers we were chasing, one of them lost his hat, too. So I guess that battle would have to be called a draw. Petrus picked up the Reb's lost hat as a replacement to the one the wind blew away. It does not fit, but he wears it, anyway.

Two regiments from Wisconsin arrived late last month, and they dress and march and act a lot more proper and military than we do. Yet I heard one of them say that he had heard of the Eighteenth Missouri all the way back home. I lack the courage to ask him what he had heard, however, fearing the worst.

I hear that the citizens of Weston and Platte City have written to Jefferson City and St. Louis and even Washington City demanding satisfaction. I ...

I did not write about Platte City, did I? Mayhap you heard that the city burned. We burned it. As far as I know, nobody was hurt badly during our action, but, can one not be hurt by watching his or her home go up in flames, flames set by their fellow Missourians? When I returned to Weston, reeking of smoke, I threw up.

Because of what I had done.

I was not alone. Boone Masterson—he is Sergeant Masterson's cousin—cried. Just bawled like a baby. I heard that the captain of Company D procured a keg of whiskey and gave it to his soldiers so that they might drown away any memories of that horrific scene. I do not imbibe, Maryanne, but I was tempted to drink John Barleycorn, if my comrades of Company D would let me, until ...

Yes, I have recovered completely from the measles. I am thinner now than I have ever been, but I think I am stronger. Thank you for your prayers. I am sure they helped pull me through that terrible time.

I wish that Ewald Ehrenreich had not died of that terrible disease. I wish it had been Seb Woolard, instead. Oh, I should not say that. It is wrong, and un-Christian. Forgive me. It's just that Seb is as rotten as Colonel Morgan. He steals from not only the Secesh families but good Union people. He is no better than Col. Morgan, who I heard owes the hotelkeeper, where he is staying, $50, and refuses to pay. I don't know why that hotelkeeper does not throw Col. Morgan out. Well, I guess I do. He has heard about Platte City, and about poor Parker Pruitt. He does not want to be executed, or have his home and place of business left in a mound of ashes.

Maryanne, please don't show this letter. I don't know why I

even write you about these horrors. I pray you won't think I am an evil man. It is just …

* * * * *

He crumpled the pages, swearing, and tossed the letter into the fire. How could he let Maryanne Corneilison know what he had done? Why torment her?

Watching the flames envelope the paper, he sat there, his eyes dead, his heart aching.

"Caleb. Caleb!"

Caleb blinked, looked up to find Boone Masterson pulling on his hat with his left hand, grabbing his rifle with his right. "Can't you hear?"

Only then did the notes of a bugle reach his ears. Confused, he rose to his feet. "Assembly?" he asked, and thought: *At three in the afternoon?*

Boone didn't answer. He was already running to fall in.

Fetching his rifle, Caleb trotted through the mud. Men scurried like ants, equally struck dumb by the blaring call for assembly. Once he located his company, he took his place in line, stood at attention, and waited.

No one spoke. In front of them strode Colonel Morgan, whose face seemed ashen. Near the commander stood a stout, thick-bearded man in a Union frock coat and wide-brimmed black hat that he had to hold down with his gauntleted left hand. At last Colonel Morgan stopped pacing, shot the stranger a glance, and took a step toward the regiment. He had to shout to be heard over the wind.

"Officers, chaplain, and men of the Eighteenth Missouri!" He swallowed. "It is …" His voice cracked, and he stared ahead blankly for several minutes. "My fight is not done! I leave for Palmyra immediately to seek redress, to defend my rights …"

Boone Masterson shook his head. "What the Sam Hill is he talking about?"

"Be quiet," Sergeant Masterson growled.

"There are traitors within these ranks!"

That caused Caleb to blink. His lips parted.

"Men envious of my command! Men who desire my position!"

Caleb tried to crane his neck, to look toward Captain Pratt, the big planter from Linn County, the one he had heard many men say should be running this outfit.

"Cole!" Sergeant Masterson snapped hoarsely, and Caleb's head shot back straight, eyes forward, barely breathing.

The wind carried away Morgan's words. He turned, saluted the newcomer, who merely nodded—too scared to lose his hat, Caleb figured—and stormed angrily away.

"He resigned," a whisper shot down the ranks.

"Relinquished his command."

"Bet General Halleck made him quit."

"Good riddance."

The barrel-chested man removed his hat and held it at his side. "Men of the Eighteenth." A big man, yet one who looked mild, downright timid, his firm voice rose above the howling wind. "I am Colonel Madison Miller, until recently captain of the First Missouri Light Artillery. Now, by orders of General Halleck, General Schofield, and Governor Gamble, I am colonel of the Eighteenth Missouri." He walked toward the assembly as he spoke. "Let me say this once. I am a black Republican from Saint Louis. The lot of you, it strikes me, are nothing more than a bunch of long-haired Democrats. A rough set of men, I'd dare say." He stopped in front of Caleb's company. "I do not see soldiers. I see swine."

*Swine.* Caleb's heart beat. *He knows I'm a pig farmer. He's talking right at me.* Colonel Madison Miller's powerful eyes sure looked as if they were trained on Caleb Cole. He almost wet his britches.

"All right, so you can burn down a town. So you can murder

two prisoners of war and write US in their martyred blood on the railing of a bridge. So you can ride or march after a bunch of cowardly bushwhackers but are unable to shoot down even a horse. The only prisoners you've been able to catch are two boys coming out of church. Hurrah!"

He jammed his hat on his head. "I do not command banditti. I command a volunteer regiment in the United States Army that is fighting to hold our precious Union together." At least now, Colonel Miller was heading down the line, away from a trembling Caleb Cole. Caleb could breathe again.

"You have enlisted in this regiment, and so you will become soldiers. Soldiers with honor. Soldiers who are devoted to duty. Soldiers. Disgrace me, disgrace our United States, disgrace the state of Missouri, disgrace this regiment, disgrace yourself, and I will see you condemned to Hades."

\* \* \* \* \*

Caleb couldn't believe it. If not exactly vindicated, at least he felt excited. He wrapped a handful of coffee beans in the neckerchief Folker had given him, then dropped it into the pot, which he set on the glowing coals. He wasn't alone.

"That Colonel Miller, he doesn't look like much, but he'll make the Eighteenth a regiment those Rebs will sure remember." With a little whoop, Boone Masterson smiled and shook his head.

"He's a soldier. A soldier's soldier," Rémy said, his head bobbing in agreement—as if he really knew what a soldier's soldier was.

"That's straight." Even Harold Masterson had forgotten about the sergeant's chevrons he had sewn onto his coat sleeves. He tossed a piece of salt pork into the skillet, and began gossiping more like a barber than a non-commissioned officer in this man's army. "He was a captain in a volunteer unit from Indiana or Illinois ... maybe it was Iowa ... during the war in Mexico. Got wounded at Buena Vista."

"Left behind a big job with the Saint Louis and Iron Mountain Railroad, I heard, to join that artillery regiment," Folker added, "and is big in politics. Governor. In the assembly, and …"

"Governor?" Sergeant Masterson laughed. "You mean mayor."

"Well, he holds some office."

Masterson added more salt pork to the skillet. "That's not all. He wasn't just a captain in that artillery regiment. When the Rebs started acting up, when we knew it would be war or disunion, Colonel Miller helped form the First Missouri Infantry. You boys might not know this, but there's a law that anyone who tries to recruit a militia without the governor's approval, he can be hanged by the neck until dead. But Colonel Miller did it, anyway."

Rémy's head bobbed. "Soldier's soldier," he said.

Sitting a few rods away, his back braced against an oak tree, Seb Woolard snorted, spat, and swore. "Ask me, he don't amount to much."

Caleb turned, angered, but refused to be goaded into a fight or argument with the likes of that bit of trash.

"What do you mean, Woolard?" Sergeant Masterson asked.

"Colonel Morgan put up his own money to get our regiment going. You talk about him like he's just some common thief."

*No*, Caleb wanted to say, *you're the common thief.*

"But …" Seb pulled himself to his feet. "But you forgot all about that. All that money he spent. It wasn't for glory or riches. It was to preserve the Union. Now, boys, you tell me what this Miller bloke has put up. Can you? 'Course, you can't. Because this Miller, he ain't put up one dime. He ain't nothing to me."

"He's your commanding officer, Woolard." Harold Masterson pushed the salt pork with a knife. "Best not forget that."

* * * * *

Colonel Madison Miller wouldn't let them forget it.

For the next week, they drilled. Miller pushed them harder

than Morgan had ever dared. Where Morgan didn't like target practice, saying it was a waste of powder and lead, Colonel Miller had them shoot until their faces were blackened and their muscles screamed in agony.

They marched. Double-stepped to the Missouri River and back. They carried full packs northwest to Iatan, east to New Market, south to Platte City, and back to Weston. Their socks became threadbare, their brogans ventilated from marching over stones. Their legs stiffened. They swore they would die.

Yet they went on.

Until their legs no longer hurt, until the muscles hardened in their arms, until they could load and fire their rifles, muskets, and shotguns four times a minute, and—those still not toting shotguns—hit a target eight hundred yards away.

* * * * *

"Rise and shine, you green peas of Company E."

Caleb's eyes fluttered opened. He shut them and rolled over. "The sun isn't even up."

The blanket ripped off him, and Sergeant Masterson's voice roared: "I said up, you lazy tramps! Up! Pack your gear and fall in!"

Somewhere in the darkness, Boone Masterson cursed his aunt for ever giving birth to his older cousin. Caleb fumbled for his britches. Seb Woolard complained that he couldn't find his hat.

"You'll find it when we come back to camp," Rémy told him.

"We're not coming back!" Sergeant Masterson thundered.

* * * * *

Silently they marched north, spending the night in a field outside St. Joseph. On Sunday, February 16, the Chaplain Garner led them in prayer. He delivered his sermon, which he called "This is the

Last Time," but it lacked the bombastic assaults, the clamor, the demands for salvation, the pleas for the destruction of the South. It was quiet, moving. Beside him, Rémy sobbed. Even Seb Woolard seemed moved.

They started the doxology, but couldn't finish. Tears flowed freely. Chaplain Garner started the benediction, but stopped. His voice cracked. He brushed aside his own tears, and muttered: "Please, lads. File out. Go to your homes."

*Home? Unionville was, what, a hundred, two hundred miles from here? North? Northeast?* Caleb didn't really know. He'd never been out of Putnam County until … His head shook. Numbly he walked out of the field where Chaplain Garner had held service. He went back to his camp, and sat there, quietly.

Two days later, they left their makeshift camp for the Hannibal & St. Joseph train. There was no singing, no chorus, no cheers. The men quietly loaded onto the cars, found their seats.

"Where are we going?" Rémy asked at last.

That had been the question everyone had been asking since they had marched out of Weston. Asked a hundred times. Hundreds of answers.

Caleb let out a mirthless chuckle. It was so unlike him. Or would have been unlike him six months ago.

"To war," he said flatly.

# CHAPTER THIRTEEN

APRIL 1–3, 1862
CORINTH, MISSISSIPPI

April 1, 18 and 62

Mother and Father:

This will be quick as we just arrived in Corinth. I am now one experienced traveler as we got here by rails (as you know), steamboat, and what we call the "ankle express."

I'm at the depot now, but we did not arrive by train, but on foot. Ladies are meeting us here and have been passing out coffee and cake. As I scribble this hurriedly, they are serenading us with "Dixie," although nary a one has as fetching a voice as yours, Mother. A young girl is waiting patiently for me and others to finish these notes so she can take them to be mailed out soon.

Colonel Moore has gotten us new uniforms, and I must get mine before they are all gone.

If you see Mrs. and Mr. Bryson, tell them that Matt is well, though his face is dotted with mosquito bites. We did not go to Arkansas. Like as not, you have heard that General Van Dorn was defeated at some place called Elkhorn Tavern and he retreated. General Ben McCullough was killed in that battle, or so we were told, although you can't believe everything you hear. Father, let me know if you have heard about McCullough. Van Dorn retreated, but now General Johnston and General Beauregard are saying that we march to meet the enemy—Grant, who caused the forts along the Cumberland to surrender.

Must run now. Love to you all. Tell Mrs. Cravey …

\* \* \* \* \*

He couldn't finish. The girl was waiting, so he signed his name, stuck the paper he quickly folded into the envelope he had already addressed, and thanked her as she took it with a smile. Somehow, she reminded him of the likeness of the girl on the cover of the sheet music for Stephen Foster's "Jeannie with the Light Brown Hair." Her eyes weren't as haunting, her face not as round, but this girl was real, not an artist's fantasy. Maybe, it struck him, she was even more real than Irene Vardakas, who he still imagined to have been only a raven-haired dream. This Mississippian certainly was much taller. He wanted to ask the girl her name, but that would have been too forward. She had been walking along the depot with other young girls, each one carrying a wicker basket, to collect letters to mail home to loved ones. Watching her walk away, Ryan couldn't believe how tall the girl was.

Matt Bryson whistled for him to hurry, so he grabbed his musket, and rejoined Company C.

The huge depot reminded him of the wharves along the Texas coast, although even at Galveston he couldn't remember ever seeing so much cotton. Bales were stacked higher than buildings. He crossed the tracks of the Memphis & Charleston in front of a smoke-belching, steam-hissing engine, and slogged through the thick mud. He had to stop, let mules pulling caissons and cannon pass. He started again, only to have to duck away as a Confederate officer galloped down the road, the horse's hoofs spraying Ryan's legs with thick gobs of mud. He didn't mind the mud. By now, he was used to mud, mosquitoes, and bowel complaint.

From Memphis, they had marched a hundred miles, slightly south but mostly east, through hilly forests that teemed with ticks and other bloodsucking parasites, trudging through swamps and quagmires in rain showers that never seemed to let up.

For two weeks they had been on the move, beginning with a locomotive from Houston to Beaumont, then by steamboat up the Neches River to Weiss' Bluff. From there they had marched—although it often felt as if they swam more than walked—to Alexandria, Louisiana. Back on another side-wheeler, they made their way up the Red River and then the Mississippi to Helena, Arkansas. That's where they learned that Van Dorn's army had been turned back at Elkhorn Tavern near the Missouri border earlier that month. That's where the Second Texas had been issued new orders: REPORT TO GENERAL JOHNSTON'S ARMY OF THE MISSISSIPPI AT CORINTH. So it was back onto another steamboat, this time a sternwheeler, and up the Mississippi to Memphis, Tennessee, and, from there, footing it on the "ankle express" to Corinth.

It was a city of fewer than three thousand, Ryan had been told, but he had never seen so many people—mostly soldiers, then slaves, and well-dressed women of all ages, ignoring the misting rain, running to men clad in gray, offering them Bibles, cups of coffee, slices of cake.

A long brick building stretched out before him, and he read a sign, TISHOMINGO HOTEL—he had no idea how to pronounce that—dripping rain water. Many men of the Second Texas had crowded under the long porch roof to escape the rain. Canvas-topped wagons lined the front of the hotel, and, from them, some Brazos County boys from Company E tossed down bundles of white cloth to various corporals and privates while sergeants and lieutenants barked out orders.

Sniffling, Ryan hurried across the street.

"General Johnston!"

Captain Ashbel Smith's shout caused Ryan to stop and turn.

He looked rougher than a cob, this Albert Sidney Johnston, certainly not as tall as Sam Houston, but a solidly built figure all the same. Ryan altered his course slightly just to get a better look at the general who would soon lead the Second Texas, and scores of other regiments from across the South, into battle.

Drops of rain glistened on the gray wool of Johnston's frock coat like diamonds, and he sported a thick mustache, flecked with gray. His face seemed too small for his body, but those blue-gray eyes, which shot a quick glance at Ryan before training on Ashbel Smith, could drill through a mountain of granite.

"Ashbel." Johnston's voice sounded like a mix of grits and gumption. "It is good to see an old friend's face. How is Texas?"

"Texas is Texas, Albert … I dare say, General."

"We must march soon. Get your men their rations, Captain Smith. I don't know how much we have left." Johnston's tone softened, and he smiled warmly at Captain Smith. "We will talk later, old friend. After we drive the enemy across the Tennessee River."

Ashbel Smith fired off a salute.

"Conquer or perish," Johnston said, his voice full of power again. After returning the salute, he mounted and kicked his towering black horse into a trot.

Captain Smith's eyes left the figure of General Johnston and landed on Ryan. "Better get your new uniform, McCalla," he said pleasantly enough, and strode through the mud toward the depot.

The Memphis & Charleston locomotive was pulling out as Ryan squeezed onto the hotel's porch. The whistle blew, and, as the train picked up speed, every eye of every soldier standing on the first-story porch of the Tishomingo Hotel looked up at the wooden second-story porch that served as their roof. The whole thing shook, and several soldiers, fearing the upper porch would collapse, jumped back into the boggy streets.

"Get back up here, you fools!" a sergeant yelled. "That's been shaking that way every time a train passes for five years."

*Five years?* Ryan shook his head. *The place looks like it's fifty years old.*

"Hey, Ryan! What do you think?"

He turned, blinked, and had to try not to laugh. Matt Bryson had shed the clothes he had been wearing and put on his new "uniform." He wasn't alone, either. A lot of soldiers had stripped down to their undergarments and were pulling on the uniforms. Ryan sure hoped the good ladies of Corinth weren't watching this wretched display.

Colonel Moore had requisitioned gray uniforms, but the trousers and coats being passed out weren't gray, but white. Matt Bryson looked not only like a ghost, but one of the funniest Ryan could have ever imagined. Maybe, just maybe, the pants would have been long enough for Sam Houston, but on Matt they stretched six inches past his feet, and he needed his belt to keep them from falling down. The coat, on the other hand, had sleeves three inches too short.

Matt laughed, found a spot to squat, pulled up his pant legs, and shoved on his old brogans. "Beats the rags I was wearing," he said.

Ryan somehow made his way to the end of the porch, where Sergeant Rutherford was barking orders at two privates who were handing out the bundles of white wool uniforms, wrapped in twine, from the back of a covered wagon.

"Here you go, McCalla!" Sergeant Rutherford tossed him a bundle.

Ryan caught it turned around, uncertain.

"What about shoes, Sarge?" someone asked.

"No shoes," Rutherford snapped. "Wear what brought you here."

"My feet brought me here. I ain't had shoes since Alexandria."

"Then your feet will take you to battle."

An unfamiliar voice drawled: "Sergeant, shouldn't we dye these duds gray?"

"No time for that, Warren."

Although men were peeling out of their filthy clothes all around him, Ryan wasn't about to undress in the middle of a bustling city. He saw the door to the hotel's lobby, and maneuvered his way there. The ground floor was full of dirty, stinking men changing out of their old clothes. Behind the counter, a bespectacled man in sleeve garters, book-ended by a bald Negro and a wide-eyed white boy, stared in amazement.

"Best hurry, Ryan," Little Sam Houston said.

Ryan set his new uniform on the back of a settee. "You, Sam?" He couldn't believe it. Sam Jr. had taken off the uniform his father had hired a tailor to make.

"We boys of the Second have to stick together," Little Sam said with a grin. "What do you think?"

Ryan managed to shake his head and smile. At least Sam Jr.'s uniform fit him better than had Matt Bryson's. Ryan stepped behind a curtain, and, leaning rifle and haversack against the colorful wallpaper, began unbuckling and unbuttoning.

\* \* \* \* \*

"You look like a horned toad stuffed to the brim," Little Sam said, looking at Gibb Gideon.

"Yeah," Gideon said stiffly.

Ryan didn't see how Gibb could breathe, tight as the coat was. Ryan felt lucky. His uniform fit, more or less. So did Little Sam's.

"Some of the boys say they'll gather up some pecan shells," Matt Bryson said, "crush them, and use that to dye these funeral suits a fitting color after we whip the Yanks."

"At least we got uniforms." Gideon took a stick and began rubbing one end against his mud-darkened sock. Like many others in the Second, Gideon no longer had shoes to wear.

No shoes. And little grub. They had exhausted their rations, which had been issued in Houston, somewhere between Memphis and the Mississippi border. Being the last regiment to arrive in Corinth, they had found most of the food the Army of the Mississippi had ordered already gone. Most soldiers had been issued four days' rations. The commissary had been able to give the men of the Second only two and a half.

Little Sam leaned over the pot that Matt Bryson stirred. "What is that you're making?"

"Something one of those Alabama boys from the Nineteenth showed me. They call it kush."

Ryan peered over Little Sam's shoulder, and frowned. "What is it, exactly?"

Matt didn't bother to look up. "Cornmeal, bacon, and water. Exactly."

Gibb Gideon spat out tobacco juice into the flames. "I wouldn't feed my hogs that."

"Hogs wouldn't eat it. *Soldiers* will."

Shaking his head, Ryan let out a long breath, and squatted by the fire. At least the coffee smelled good.

"Where's Baby?" Little Sam suddenly asked.

Matt stopped stirring. Ryan looked across the rows of Sibley tents and campfires, across the ghostlike figures moving about in the mud.

"He was writing a letter by the depot," Matt said, "last I saw him. Didn't you see him, Ryan?"

His head shook.

"He'll turn up." Gibb Gideon began unbuttoning his coat. "It's not like he can run off to his mama's house on Galveston Island."

* * * * *

Harry Cravey, however, wasn't there that night, or the next morning. Ryan even checked in at sick call, and was directed to a tent that served as the hospital. The stench of that place made him walk through in a hurry, but he didn't find Baby Cravey. He even walked along the depot, and went into the lobby of the Tishomingo Hotel.

Harry Cravey, it seemed, wasn't anywhere in Corinth.

He wasn't there before dawn on April 3, when the men of the Second Texas fell in, and began marching through ankle-deep mud, following the gray-, brown- and blue-uniformed soldiers of regiments from Mississippi, Arkansas, Alabama, Tennessee, Louisiana, Kentucky, and Texas, leading scores of other troops, some in uniforms, some without.

Sidewalks, porches, balconies, and platforms were lined two- to three-deep with the citizens of Corinth. A band played "The Bonnie Blue Flag." Women sang along. A preacher read from the Gospel of St. Matthew. Men removed their hats.

"Hey, mister, where does this road lead to?" Matt Bryson called out to a man in a brown sack suit.

"Monterey in Tennessee," he said. "Then all the way to Pittsburg Landin' on the Tennessee River."

# CHAPTER FOURTEEN

APRIL 6, 1862
PITTSBURG LANDING, TENNESSEE

At least the rain had stopped. Between the rivers, the steamboat, and what seemed like forty days and forty nights of a constant deluge, Caleb Cole felt so water-logged, he half expected to turn into a tadpole.

He woke that morning not to the sound of rainfall, but of horses' hoofs plopping through the mud, and the splashing of freshly brewed coffee into a cup just outside the canvas tent. Since he had slept in his socks, trousers, and boiled shirt, he pushed off the blanket, stepped into his brogans, grabbed his blouse and hat, and eased outside.

Smiling, Folker handed him the cup of coffee he had just poured for himself.

The tin cup burned his fingers, so Caleb set it on a stump to cool. He looked up at the dark sky, finding a few twinkling stars. Fewer clouds. Maybe today it would not rain.

"'Morning, General," Boone Madison said, and waved his hat at a small figure with a scraggly red beard and well-chewed cigar.

Turning quickly, Caleb blinked as he espied General William T. Sherman, who ignored Boone Madison's greeting, lead a small group of riders down a quagmire some might call a road.

"Morning?" grunted Seb Woolard, squatting by the fire to warm himself. "The sun ain't even up."

The sky was turning gray in the east, but the only real light came from lanterns and cook fires that cast an eerie glow on the endless expanse of canvas that stretched out over several acres. A drummer tapped out something over to the east, and the sounds of a military camp—a military *city*—could be heard: curses and laughter, prayers and complaints, matches striking, bacon sizzling. The aroma of breakfast, of coffee, blended with the moist scent of the water-soaked earth and rotting leaves, of spring in western Tennessee.

Now Boone squatted by a nearby fire, turning a rotisserie crank. Caleb's mouth watered. Chickens. A dozen chickens being roasted over hot coals. Well, it was Sunday. Nothing like chicken, coffee, and bacon for Sunday breakfast.

Picking up his cup of coffee, Caleb tested the hot liquid and shook his head in wonder. If he lived to be a hundred, he'd never be able to comprehend this army of thousands that had turned a rugged, wet country, full of thickets and fleas, into a city that would have dwarfed Unionville, probably all of Putnam County, and might have even rivaled St. Louis.

Over the past week Caleb had met soldiers from all over— Illinois and Michigan and Wisconsin. He felt so far from northern Missouri, and couldn't wait to write to Maryanne Corneilison, or his parents, about all he had seen, all he had done. Those nightmares of Platte County, of Parker Pruitt and Colonel Morgan, lay in his past, he hoped never to return. He had just seen William T. Sherman ride so close that he could have swiped the general's cigar. He had listened to General Ulysses S. Grant, the hero of Fort Henry and Fort Donelson, give a speech or two. Neither Grant nor Sherman looked like heroes. Gee willikins, they didn't even look like soldiers, at least not officers, with mud-splattered boots, rumpled coats, and savage countenances.

By grab, he might even write his sister, let Bessy know everything he had seen since leaving Missouri. She'd likely have a conniption over his brags. Only they wouldn't be brags, just facts.

He was in Tennessee, the Confederacy, enemy territory. So close to actual war. That proved hard to accept, too. The Rebels, real Rebs, not the slippery bushwhackers he had chased in western Missouri, were massing only twenty miles south.

A muffled crack in that direction caused Caleb to stiffen and Seb Woolard to jump to his feet. "What's that?"

"Some dumb sentry." Folker filled a fresh cup of coffee. "That's probably where old Cump's heading this early in the morning." Cump was what a lot of the soldiers called Sherman, though Caleb didn't know why. "To arrest some fool for shooting off his musket, and have him hanged by his thumbs."

"He'll have to arrest more than one," Seb Woolard said. "Been hearing a lot of shots this morn."

"I wish it was the Rebs." Boone shook his head. "Tired of all this prancing around for Colonel Miller."

"Hold your horses." Sergeant Masterson had finally stepped out of his tent. "We'll have our fight soon enough. We're here, aren't we?"

\* \* \* \* \*

Getting here had been a long, roundabout journey. The train they had boarded in St. Joseph had taken them to St. Charles, with a long delay—and quite a bit of excitement in Breckenridge after several cars had derailed. No one was injured, however, and Caleb had wished he had been in one of the cars that had slipped off the tracks. It would have been a good story to tell his folks.

From the Missouri River, they had marched to Benton Barracks, a miserable place in St. Louis that made the dirt redoubt of Fort Morgan in Laclede look like a grand hotel.

While in St. Louis, Colonel Miller had dismissed several other officers of the Eighteenth—those who had been close to Colonel Morgan—but Captain Clark remained in command of Company E. For that, Caleb felt grateful. The colonel's actions, however, had riled many of the regiment's enlisted men to threaten desertion, but no one, not even Seb Woolard, had made good on the threat. Maybe because as soon as Colonel Miller had replaced the officers he had kicked out of the service, the Eighteenth was on the move again.

Ordered to join General Grant's army at the District of West Tennessee, more than eight hundred men had crammed aboard a ship called the *Nebraska* and steamed to Cairo, Illinois. The *Nebraska* was as pathetic as Benton Barracks, a wooden vessel that creaked, moaned, and often leaked water. Between the hundred horses and mules in the ship's hold, the filth on the deck where the men camped out, and the stink of the river, most of the soldiers suffered on the journey. Half the men of the Eighteenth came down with diarrhea, which got so bad that the *Nebraska*'s crew cut holes in the wheel covers to accommodate the persistent purgings of hundreds of sick, miserable soldiers.

Caleb felt blessed. He had no loose bowels, and he loved the scenery.

Back in Missouri he had traveled by train, and now he was on a steamboat, heading to war with his friends. While more than a few boys hung their heads over the sides of the ship to vomit, Caleb just sat or stood, watching the river, the tree-lined banks, the other ships, boats, barges. There was just so much to see. The world, he decided, was a wonder. When this war was finally over, he wondered how he would be able to return to slopping hogs.

He had marveled over Kansas City and St. Louis. Cairo, Illinois had been equally something to behold. For Caleb, anyway. Chaplain Garner had another view.

"What do you think, Parson?" Caleb had asked when they had stepped onto the levee.

Head shaking, the preacher had replied: "Why, Private Cole, this is a splendid site for a town … if only they had land to build on."

From Cairo, they had moved down the river, still aboard the *Nebraska*, on to Columbus, Kentucky, and then down to Island No. 10, where they had gotten their first taste of war.

"An appetizer," Sergeant Masterson had called it.

Actually all Caleb and the others had done was sit on the *Nebraska*'s decks, and watch shells from Confederate batteries on the island and Union ironclads in the river light up the night sky. Caleb had often heard about fireworks, had seen an illustration or two in some magazine his father had brought home, but he had never seen even a firecracker. Not on Independence Day. Not on New Year's Eve. The cannons had sounded like thunder, and the *Nebraska* had shuddered with the explosion of every shell. It had been something to see—beautiful, awe-inspiring, but hard to believe how deadly it must have been closer to where those shells kept exploding.

"What would happen if one of those bombs hit us, Sergeant?" Seb Woolard had asked.

"You'd never know," Masterson had answered.

The next morning, the Eighteenth Missouri had learned what war was all about.

They swung axes, picks, shovels. They worked cross-cut saws. They joined engineers and "contraband"—runaway slaves, or slaves who just happened to find themselves surrounded by Federal soldiers. The Eighteenth worked alongside these black men and Union engineers, removing timber and limbs, leaves and mud, driftwood and sandbars. Some fool general had gotten it into his head that trying to run steamboats like the *Nebraska* past Rebel cannon was too risky. Instead, they would clear these flooded woods northeast of New Madrid, Missouri, and create a fifty-foot channel.

Those soldiers who weren't still feeling the effects of dysentery had taken to the forest, working even after blisters formed atop blisters, even after their muscles screamed in agony and kept them awake at night. Caleb soon wished he had gotten sick. He often wished he had died. Until he had helped bury two Missouri farm boys who had died.

Then came new orders. Once the *Nebraska* turned around, the Eighteenth Missouri had climbed back onto those putrid decks, and returned to Cairo, leaving behind the graves of privates John A. Blake and William Pate, and one unfinished canal. "Much work as we did on that," Rémy had complained, "seems that we could at least stick around and sail down it when it opens!"

That, of course, was not the way this man's army operated.

Back to Cairo, then up the Ohio River to Paducah, Kentucky, and down the Tennessee River where, finally, they had pulled ashore at Pittsburg Landing.

As soon as they had gotten off the *Nebraska*—by then, even Caleb had grown sick of river life—they had marched a mile and a half southwest, and set up camp in a grove of hickories and oaks near some pike the locals called the Eastern Corinth Road.

Colonel Miller had wasted no time. South of the woods lay a farm, and in the clearing the new commander of the Eighteenth had decided it was time to drill.

And drill. And drill.

The problem, of course, was that most of the soldiers—Sergeant Masterson and Rémy Ehrenreich, among them—had not fully recovered from their bouts with diarrhea while on the *Nebraska*, or from all the back-breaking work on that stupid canal. Others, like Folker, had merely complained that they hadn't gotten their land legs back.

Colonel Miller had not really cared. He had drilled them anyway, until, at last, on Friday, April 4, he had ordered the regiment for a general review. The colonel had closed the review with one long, flowery, patriotic speech.

Yesterday, they had drilled again.

And today? It was Sunday, so maybe, the good Lord willing, they wouldn't have to parade or march.

So here he stood on a crisp morning, a private in the Eighteenth Missouri Infantry, part of the Sixth Infantry Division, Army of the Tennessee, Brigadier General Benjamin Prentiss commanding.

\* \* \* \* \*

Caleb set his cup down long enough to pull up his suspenders, and slip on his blue blouse. Slowly the sun began creeping over the trees. Matt dropped bacon into a skillet, and the sizzle and scent reminded Caleb that he was starving. Another smell caused his stomach to growl, and he looked around until he saw the Dutch oven, its lid covered with coals and ash.

"Folker, are you making biscuits?" He couldn't remember the last time he had tasted biscuits. *Back home on the farm, a lifetime ago?* He shook his head.

"Amen, brother. It'll be a Sunday feast, boys. Even got us butter for the biscuits."

"When are we going to march to Corinth?" Folker changed the subject. "I'm like Boone, here. Tired of waiting."

"We march when General Grant says we march," Masterson said, helping himself to coffee.

There was a pop. Followed by another. This one closer.

"Stupid fools," Boone Masterson said.

"Wish they'd stop that infernal racket," Seb Woolard said. "It's making me all jumpy."

As the sun climbed higher, Caleb looked at the sky again. The clouds had moved away. "Hey," he said, "I think it's going to be a beautiful day."

Rémy snorted. "At least my clothes might dry some."

A raw-boned graybeard from the nearby camp, one of those boys from the Sixty-First Illinois, wandered into camp. At first, Caleb thought he was coming to borrow grub, but the old man hooked his thumb southward and said: "That's gunfire, ain't it?"

Sergeant Masterson nodded. He was about to say something when a volley sounded.

Suddenly the morning stood still. The stoppage of time ended almost immediately. A bugle blared. A horse galloped past.

Folker rose slowly, ignoring the bacon and biscuits.

"You don't reckon ..." somebody said, and Caleb didn't recognize the voice.

"Hey, Chaplain." That was Rémy talking.

Caleb turned to see Chaplain Garner walking by.

"You expect to give us a sermon?" Boone said lightly, and jerked a thumb toward the Methodist meeting house in the distance.

"No." Garner didn't even stop. He was making a beeline toward Colonel Miller's tent. "I expect to fight today."

Gunfire, closer now, became steady. Caleb thought he could see wisps of gray smoke rising above the tents in the early light. He took a step to get a closer look, only to be jerked back by Rémy. A horse galloped past him, leaping over the chickens on the rotisseries, and almost trampling Garner.

"Colonel Miller!" the horseman roared. His tunic wasn't even buttoned, and he appeared to have his boots on the wrong feet.

Rémy whispered: "That's General Prentiss."

"Get out your brigade! They are fighting on the right!" Prentiss did not wait for a response. Slapping the roan with the side of his saber, the general galloped down the muddy, tent-lined path toward the Sixteenth Wisconsin.

Caleb felt his bladder release. He didn't care. Feeling the blood leave his face, he turned and found Sergeant Masterson. "It's Sunday," he said, his voice quaking. Surely, he thought, even a bunch of Secesh wouldn't attack on a Sunday.

"It sure won't be like any Sabbath you've ever seen, boy," Sergeant Masterson said as he reached the stack of weapons. He began tossing rifles, muskets, shotguns. "It'll be wormwood and gall."

Caleb dropped his rifle in the wet grass.

# CHAPTER FIFTEEN

APRIL 6, 1862
NEAR SHILOH MEETING HOUSE, TENNESSEE

Ryan McCalla's stomach growled, prompting Matt Bryson to stifle a laugh, and whisper: "Careful, Ryan." He hooked a thumb in the direction of the cornfield. "They might hear you."

*Not a chance*, Ryan thought. Apparently all Yankees were deaf. The Second Texas Infantry and who knew how many other Southern outfits were here, less than four hundred yards from the Federal Army, so close, in fact, that last night Ryan had heard the Yankees' roll call, and yet the enemy hadn't heard a thing. Certainly the Confederate Army had made enough racket during that miserable, arduous, muddy march from Corinth.

Thanks to rain and muck, they had made only two miles that first day. When the downpour finally had stopped, several soldiers had fired their muskets, shotguns, and rifles.

"What the Sam Hill are you boys doing?" Captain Ashbel Smith had shouted.

"Just making sure our powder ain't ruint!" somebody had replied, and Captain Smith had let loose with a cannonade of curses. The Yanks hadn't heard that, either, and the captain's voice must have carried all the way to Kentucky.

A short while later, Albert Sidney Johnston had ridden over—

undoubtedly to see what idiot was firing his weapon—and the entire Second Texas had let loose with a cheer. The general had waved his hand urgently, begging the soldiers to be quiet. Last night, as the regiments began assembling into battle lines, someone had even shot a deer.

Ryan lay in the remnants of a muddy cornfield, thinking how good venison would taste right about now. He hadn't eaten since the first night out of Corinth. Those two-and-a-half days' rations had been consumed immediately.

"When you get food," Sergeant Rutherford had told them, "eat it. Food lasts in your bellies, boys. It won't last in haversacks. And you never know when you'll get a chance to eat again."

Lying here, clothes still soaked, he wished he had picked up one of the knapsacks, coats, belts, hats, canteens—you name it—that the soldiers had shucked on the march. He remembered Gibb Gideon's comment—"All that trash … those boys are just marking our way back to Corinth in case we have to retreat!"—and Little Sam's serious reply: "Don't you dare mention a retreat, Gibb Gideon. No, sir, don't you even think it!"

Ryan had left his bedroll a few miles back, along with his rotting brogans. Now he wished he had the blanket, though not the shoes. He wished they hadn't left those cozy Sibley tents back in Corinth. Most of the boys in Company C had spread oil cloths over the ground, paired up with a friend, and shared a blanket. Ryan just lay on the ground. Even before the sun had risen, the sound of musketry woke those who had managed to sleep.

Ryan's heart pounded against his ribs as horses and mule-drawn wagons raced behind him. He rolled over in the thick goo, and looked across the cornfield—weathered crops from last year, just stubble, standing in the field or toppled over, covered with what resembled a lake. The farmers hadn't gotten a chance, Ryan guessed, to plow the fields and plant crops this spring. Beyond those bent or fallen brown stalks, men in blue had begun assembling.

Cannon cut loose, and Ryan flinched. His ears rang. Loud primeval screams chilled him as a wave of gray-clad soldiers charged.

The battle was on.

Ryan and the Second Texas began rising, moving back however, instead of forward, falling into place along the road, far from the raging fight somewhere ahead. They stood there, waiting.

"Sergeant, why don't we join this here fight?" a Texian drawled angrily.

"Shut up, Fletcher!" Rutherford snapped. "We'll get our share of Yanks soon enough."

Minié balls whistled overhead. A cannon ball exploded in the center of the cornfield. Bullets and grapeshot thudded against hickory trees, and still the Second remained silent. The sun was well up, Ryan guessed. He couldn't see the sky because of thick, gray-white smoke.

"Forward, men! Forward!" Captain Smith shouted.

Sergeant Rutherford sprang to his feet. "You heard the captain. Fall in, Company C. Fall in!"

Beside Ryan, Matt Bryson grinned.

Surprisingly Ryan felt relaxed as he marched. Lying on the ground, listening to the sounds of war, then forming into a battle line and just standing around and listening to the screams of horses and men had pricked every nerve in his body. Now, as he was about to join the onslaught, relief swept over him.

"I'll see you boys at the banks of the Tennessee River!" Captain Smith roared, and the cheer of Texians drowned out the din of musketry and artillery.

"Fill that gap on Lick Creek!" someone shouted, and Ryan's feet moved.

He didn't know where Lick Creek was, wasn't even sure Captain Smith or Colonel Moore knew. They just marched, listening to Sergeant Rutherford's cadence. Ryan stepped over a dead body. He didn't even care.

"Company forward. Quick time!"

That soon became double-quick, staying in close-order formation, and Ryan was running, gripping his musket, face grim, grinding his teeth. After all of those drills, those sham battles back in Texas, he moved as if by rote. Double-quick time, one hundred and forty steps, covering one hundred and nine yards.

He saw the line of gray, the San Jacinto Guards and companies from other regiments deployed as skirmishers some four hundred yards ahead. Another regiment angled off to the right, to protect the flank. The skirmishers had stopped. Men were ramming loads down the barrels of their weapons.

"Second Texas!" Colonel Moore shouted. "Fill that line. Fill that gap!"

Ryan was turning, moving, finding a wall of dead men. Stopping, he capped the nipple on his .69-caliber. Ahead of him, the first line fired, stepped back.

"Captain Brooks is killed!"

The words meant nothing to Ryan.

"Ready!" Sergeant Rutherford yelled.

Bullets whistled. From right and left came the sickening thud of bullets striking flesh. Some men groaned. Others merely fell.

"Aim!"

He could see log cabins behind a mound of bluecoats, tents beyond that, smoke not from long guns and cannon, but fires. The Federals marched forward, deliberately. He saw the Stars and Stripes fluttering in the breeze, spotted a bluecoat tapping out a beat on a drum. Saw another flag, but all he could make out were red bars and gold stars. The blue line in front of him disappeared in a cloud of gray smoke. A ball whistled past his ear, and then he heard more of those thuds, more groans, more men falling.

"Fire!"

The rifle's stock slammed against Ryan's shoulder. He stepped back, letting the first line move back into place. He butted the rifle in the mud, felt his hands moving, pulling out a cartridge.

His teeth bit into the paper, tore. He poured powder down the barrel, then buck and ball, three buckshot, and a one-ounce ball. Moving, not thinking. In front of him came a deafening roar, echoed by the musketry from the Federal lines. Thuds. Groans. Somebody wailing like a baby.

Ryan shoved the ramrod down the barrel. He blinked. The soldier in front of him, Billy Wells from Houston, was on the ground, eyes staring up, but where his nose should have been, was an ugly, gaping hole.

Ryan stepped over the body into his place, and listened for Sergeant Rutherford's command.

"Fire!"

His rifle kicked again. The Yankee carrying the other flag—not the American—staggered and fell. Ryan wasn't sure if his shot had struck him. Another soldier dropped his rifle, lifted the flag, began waving it. Shots down the line boomed, and that flag bearer also fell.

Ryan stepped back, but no one had filled Billy Wells' place. He wondered if he should, but was too busy reloading with buck and ball. Rebel muskets roared, and the Yankees were turning back, running.

"Where is that Texas regiment!"

Somehow, despite the thunder of muskets, Ryan recognized the voice. He fired, stepped back, began reloading, heard Colonel Moore's answer.

"Here we are, General!"

Albert Sidney Johnston loped forward on a big bay horse, his face hardened as he pointed toward the Union lines. "Drive those men out of that camp!"

"You heard the general, boys!" Colonel Moore pulled off his hat, stuck it on his saber, which he raised over his head.

A blast deafened Ryan. He couldn't hear a thing, not Colonel Moore's order, but he could see Matt Bryson drawing his bayonet, putting it on his Mississippi rifle. Others did the same, so Ryan drew his from the scabbard. He stared ahead, across a field. The

Union line looked to be three thousand, maybe more. The Second Texas numbered just more than seven hundred.

"Charge bayonets!" He could hear again, but only briefly. A horrifying yell followed, a mix of coyote and banshee, of every lost soul in hell. Ryan shrieked himself, savagely, and, holding his rifle, he charged across the field.

Ever since Houston, he had this premonition of death. That's why he had given his parents his violin. He knew he wouldn't survive the war, and this morning, April 6, he figured it was his time to die. Still, he felt no fear of death, but, rather, acceptance. Last night, he had watched officers and men write out their last wills and testaments. He had seen Sergeant Rutherford scratch his name on a sheet of paper, which he then pinned to the inside of his blouse—so his body could be identified. He had heard of a lad from Company A writing in his diary: APRIL 6, 1862: TODAY I WAS KILLED.

Ryan hadn't felt the need to do any of that. If he died today, so be it.

A soldier running near him toppled. Ryan leaped over a dead Yankee. Another. The blue line in front of him turned, fleeing. Smoke burned his eyes. He tripped over a dead man's foot, almost fell into the mud, somehow recovered.

"They're running, boys!" He did not recognize the voice. "Pour it to them, lads. Give them ..."

Ahead, Lieutenant Hawthorne turned, waving his kepi over his head. Then the back of his head seemed to explode. Something splashed into Ryan's face. It felt like a mixture of mud and pebbles. He kept running, wiping his eyes and forehead with his free hand, carrying his .69 with the other. He didn't see the lieutenant any more.

An instant later, the Second stopped. It had run into an invisible wall. Five men fell. A bullet tugged at Ryan's side. Smoke poured from the cracks in one of the log buildings. A muzzle flashed. That terrible thud.

"They're in that cabin, boys!"

He had dropped to his knee. Aimed. Fired. Dozens of muskets

echoed his shot, splintering the log walls. A bluecoat charged out of the doorway, clutched his blouse, pitched to his side. Another ran out. He, too, died.

Ryan rammed another charge down the barrel.

"Come on, Ryan!" Matt Bryson shouted.

He was up, chasing thousands of Federals. The Yanks dropped their weapons. Some shed their coats, bummer caps, cartridge boxes.

Ryan cut loose with another Rebel yell. That premonition of death disappeared. Never had he felt so alive.

"Chase them to Kentucky, lads!" Captain Smith's voice.

*Kentucky? Those Yanks won't stop until they're in Canada.*

The log cabins lay behind him now. He wove through a township of tents, past camp desks and camp chairs, kettles left on coals. Coffee pots set on tripods. Mess chests, many of them still open. A candle burned atop one table, and Sergeant Jardine sat down in a rocking chair, tucked a napkin inside his blouse, speared a piece of ham with a silver fork.

Someone else had stopped, pulled a chunk of beef out of a kettle, dropped the meat, began shaking his burning hand.

Ryan blinked again as the face registered. He stopped running. "Little Sam?" he asked.

Sam Houston Jr. grinned. "I'm hungry!" He picked up the beef he had dropped. "Beats corn, salt, and apples, don't it?"

Just like that, Ryan remembered his stomach. He leaned his rifle in a stack of arms—Federal arms, he realized. Some of the Yanks hadn't even gotten to their guns, or had ducked out at the first sound of battle. He knelt beside Little Sam, found a loaf of fresh bread. His mouth tore off a hunk. He was in heaven.

Sam filled a Union cup full of coffee, passed it to Ryan, then wrapped a bandanna around his scalded hand.

Washing down the bread, Ryan looked around. Gibb Gideon was lugging a dressing case out of a tent. What he planned on doing with it, Ryan couldn't guess. A bearded corporal from

Company D yelled, "Huzzah!" jerked the cork out of a bottle of claret, and started guzzling. Someone held a tin box, and was pulling Yankee script from it, tossing it into the air. Most, however, only stopped for food.

"Criminy," someone said, "I might join the Yanks if they always eat this good."

Another one cried: "Fellas, we're in clover now!"

Matt Bryson exited a nearby tent. Rifle cradled underneath one arm, he held out a blue sheet of paper in his other hand, showing it off for Ryan and Little Sam.

"Boys," he said, "you're now looking at a stockholder of the Mound City Manufacturing and Real Estate Company." He shoved the paper inside a trousers pocket.

"Where's that?" Little Sam's mouth was so full of meat, Ryan could barely understand him.

"Mound City. Where else?" Matt's eyes widened, and his mouth dropped as he stared at Ryan. "Ryan?" he said at last. "Are you all right?"

Ryan eyed his friend curiously. He could only nod as he lowered his cup of coffee and reached again for the sourdough bread.

"Your face, man."

Even Little Sam, noticing Ryan for the first time, studied him with measured concern.

After wiping his face, Ryan looked down at his hands. They were blacked by gunpowder, but wet with blood and bits of something else. His stomach knotted, and he wiped the gore on his pants.

"It's not me," he said.

"Likely a bluebelly you killed!" Matt cackled, and wandered to another fire pit to wolf down burned bacon. "I bet I've killed a dozen already, and it's not even noon yet."

The coffee and bread had lost their appeal, and taste, but Ryan went right on eating and drinking. *Let Matt think that.* Ryan put the image of Lieutenant Hawthorne behind him.

Shots and cannon roared in the woods and fields. A horse

whinnied. Captain Smith screamed a litany of curses. "Don't stop! We've got them running."

Colonel Moore echoed Captain Smith's rallies. "Come on, Second Texas, come on! For glory! Kill them all!"

A few soldiers picked up their long guns, and stumbled after the Federals, stuffing their pockets with boiled potatoes and roasting chickens as they ran.

The bulk of the men kept filling their bellies.

"Up, McCalla! Up, Houston! This battle isn't over."

Ryan looked up to find Sergeant Rutherford standing over him, brandishing a nickel-plated pistol in his right hand. A gold chain—no three gold chains—hung from one of his pockets. Even Rutherford had taken a few moments to plunder some Yank's tent.

"Let's go!"

Ryan gulped down more coffee, tossed the cup aside, found his weapon.

"You, too, Bryson!" Rutherford began trotting. "We can all feast after the enemy is whipped."

"They're already whipped, Sarge!" Little Sam spit out chewed beef and saliva, but he, too, began to follow Sergeant Rutherford.

They crossed a road to another camp, moved through the grove of oaks with caution. Something fluttered through the smoky haze, and Ryan stopped, turned.

"Ready!" Sergeant Rutherford yelled.

"Hold your fire!" came a panicked cry from the trees, and Ryan saw the white flag. A hatless bluecoat stepped forward. The handkerchief was tied to the barrel of another Yank's rifle. "Hold your fire!" the Union sergeant repeated. He led about a dozen men through the trees.

Rutherford repeated the Yank's request. Ryan took a deep breath, and slowly exhaled.

"All right!" Lowering his rifle barrel, Matt Bryson raced over toward the surrendering Yanks. "I'm five hundred dollars richer, have killed two dozen Yankees ..."—the number had risen, and Matt Bryson hadn't fired a shot since stopping at the Federal camp—"and now I'm about to capture a passel of birdies."

The Yankees halted.

"Ready!" the hatless sergeant yelled.

Ryan rose. His heart pounded. To his left, he heard Sergeant Rutherford say: "What the ...?"

"Aim!" The Yanks raised their weapons. Even the one with the white flag tied to its barrel.

Matt Bryson slid to a stop, lowered his gun, and turned around to find Sergeant Rutherford. His face puzzled, Matt opened his mouth as if to ask a question. Two other Second Texas boys who were running to take the prisoners also halted. One began to aim his shotgun.

"Fire!"

# CHAPTER SIXTEEN

## APRIL 6, 1862
## PITTSBURG LANDING, TENNESSEE

"Fill your canteens, boys! Some of you will be in hell before night, and you'll need water!"

Caleb almost stopped. He didn't know who had shouted those words, but it reminded him that his canteen remained inside the tent.

"Forget it!" Boone Masterson said, reading Caleb's mind. He tossed Caleb one of the roasting chickens, while shoving two into his pockets. "In case you get hungry."

The juicy chicken hit Caleb's coat, fell into the leaves. He started to pick it up, but Sergeant Masterson kept screaming, so Caleb, his rifle feeling as if it weighed a ton, followed Boone Masterson and the rest of Company C.

"We just finished eating," complained a private from the Sixty-First Illinois.

"Don't gripe to me," Seb Woolard shot back. "We ain't even et yet!"

They formed a haphazard line behind stumps, felled rotting logs, and thick brush just north of the cleared field of a farmer named Spain. Where the Eighteenth had paraded, drilled, and lined up for Colonel Miller's inspections, where they had listened to General Grant speak flapdoodle about winning the war, and General Sherman tell them how the Rebels dared to "trample our glorious flag," and General Prentiss say it would be his honor to lead "you stalwart Missourians against those louts of the South."

Finding a thick oak stump, Seb Woolard squatted behind it, using the jagged top to steady his Harpers Ferry musket. He had pilfered the musket back in Platte County, replacing that $11 monstrosity he had bought off that peddler in Laclede.

Everyone else remained standing.

Behind them, cannon roared, sounding as if the artillery had moved down the Eastern Corinth Road near where Caleb had slept just last night. Where he had been about to eat a filling Sunday breakfast. Captain Clark came jogging over, hurriedly scribbling something in a small booklet. Finished, he stuck the booklet in his vest pocket, and put the pencil over his left ear.

"Colonel Miller!" It was Prentiss galloping back. The general jerked savagely on the reins, and his horse almost stumbled in the thick mud. "Your deployment is unacceptable to me, sir." He pointed. "Take your regiment there. The enemy shall be attacking from that direction."

"Yes, sir!" The colonel snapped a salute, although Caleb knew from Madison Miller's face that he did not care much for the general's decision.

Without returning the salute, General Prentiss galloped off, and the Eighteenth was moving again.

"By thunder," Seb Woolard said, "this ain't no way to fight a war. We had good cover with all those stumps and things."

"That's the way a bandit would fight," Folker said.

"Or bushwhackers," someone agreed.

Said Folker: "We're soldiers."

"Yeah." Woolard shouldered his musket. "And a bunch of us is about to become dead soldiers."

Captain Clark directed the company, and Caleb and others fell into line as the regiment formed an L facing south and west. Over toward Spain's field, a bunch of Cincinnati artillery boys were unlimbering their cannon. The Sixteenth Wisconsin began forming on the other side of the road.

Caleb saw a bunch of Federals from Michigan scurrying around like ants. The commander stopped tucking in his shirt and said: "Colonel Miller! I am Colonel John M. Oliver, sir, of Monroe County. We have been directed to form to your left."

"Well, hop to it, Colonel. Rebs will be upon us at any minute."

"But, Colonel. We have not been issued ammunition."

Miller's mouth dropped. Cannon boomed.

"Just form your line, Colonel Oliver. Stand at order arms." He shrugged. "I guess."

What else could those Wolverines do?

Caleb heard the Michigan soldiers running behind him, and could picture their faces, ashen, eyes wide—much like his own.

"Company A ready!"

"Company B ready!"

Captain Clark: "Company E ready!"

Other company commanders' calls ran up and down the line.

The Ohio artillery blasted again.

The Eighteenth Missouri stood, waiting. A minute. Two. Three. Although it felt like hours.

"There," someone whispered. No, not someone. Dully Caleb realized he had spoken. Out of the trees and brush on both sides of the road, Confederate guns glistened in the sunlight. Behind the woods, visible above the tree line, a sea of gray and light brown covered the hilly slopes.

"Heavenly Father," Boone Masterson said, "there can't be that many … not in the whole South."

"Stand ready!" Captain Clark said, but his voice cracked. "Remember you are the Eighteenth Missouri!"

Skirmishers had stepped onto the road, into the fields. Gray smoke lifted from their barrels, and a moment later Caleb heard the sounds of musket fire. Something buzzed over his head. Someone groaned.

"I told you we never should have left those stumps!" Seb Woolard's high-pitched wail.

"Shut up, Woolard!" Sergeant Masterson raised his hand.

A musket boomed.

"Hold your fire, Boone! All of you, on my command!"

Something struck Caleb's chest. His knees buckled. His right hand released his rifle, clasped his ribs at the third brass button of his tunic. Sinking to his knees, he jammed the butt of the rifle on the ground to keep from pitching forward. No pain. He turned his hand over, pushed himself up, looked at the dark lead ball lying on his lifeline.

"It's spent," Folker said, laughing. "Boy, you're one lucky bas—"

*Thud!*

Folker let out a gasp as if sucking in all the air around him. Blood pulsed from his chest like water from an artesian well. His musket dropped into the mud, and he fell backward.

"Fire!" Weapons thundered, but Caleb hadn't heard Masterson's orders. He had just pushed himself back to his feet, just escaped from death. He fell back, let the line behind him step ahead. Blinking, he looked down, his eyes meeting Folker's, only Folker's did not blink, did not see.

"Fire!"

The pungent smell of gunpowder stung his nostrils, his eyes. He moved back into position, started to prime his rifle, only to realize that he still hadn't pulled a trigger.

"Ready-aim-fire!" Sergeant Masterson's orders ran together as one word.

Caleb felt the rifle slam against his shoulder. The mass of gray-clad men in front of him disappeared in a haze of steaming gray smoke. He fell back.

The Rebs answered with their own volley. Men pitched forward, fell backward. One turned, dropping his rifle, and ran.

Caleb had stepped back. He poured powder down the barrel, seated a ball with his ramrod, heard the second line's cannonade, filled the flash pan, was stepping back into place. He fired. Again. Slowly he realized the Missourians had moved to the southern side of Spain's field. He didn't know how much time had passed since he had fired his first shot, didn't know where Folker's body was. His tongue tasted like gunpowder. His eyes teared from smoke.

Reaching for another ball, he stopped and stared. In horror, he sought out Harold Masterson. "Hey, Sergeant!" Masterson's head was bleeding around his left temple. "I'm out of ammunition!"

"Look around you, Caleb! The dead can't shoot!"

He knelt, found a cartridge box on a soldier's body. Dropping his rifle, the long rifle his father had given him when he went off to join Jacob Clark's militia, he had to pry the musket from the dead soldier's grip. This was better. He could fire this musket faster than his flintlock. Caleb made a mistake. He looked at the dead man's face.

"Boone?" he called out, but Boone Masterson could not answer. Briefly Caleb's eyes found one of the roasted chickens sticking out of a pocket, and a wild thought raced through his mind. *Poor Boone ... never got to eat his breakfast.*

Bile rose in his throat, but he jerked the weapon free from Boone's viselike grip, picked up the cartridge belt, and then heard the screams from hell.

Shrieking Rebels in gray and butternut charged from the brush on the right, bayonets flashing in the sunlight, bayonets slashing.

Sergeant Masterson swore. "They've flanked us!"

A ball tore off Caleb's hat. Kneeling, he fired, thought he saw a Secesh pitch forward. More cries from behind him, and Caleb whirled, half expecting to see a horde of demons in gray come killing, but it wasn't the Rebs. It was those Wolverines, charging out to meet the enemy, armed with empty muskets but bayonets.

Caleb was up, too, reversing the grip on Boone Masterson's musket, grabbing the barrel still hot from a murderous rate of fire, swinging. The stock crushed a bearded graycoat's skull, and the momentum carried Caleb into the mud. He pushed himself up, spitting out gobs of muck, saw a revolver sticking in the waistband of the man he had just killed.

*I've killed a man.*

He blocked out that thought. His right hand gripped the revolver's butt, jerked. Backing up, pushing himself to his feet, he thumbed back the hammer, aimed, pulled the trigger. The pistol bucked in his hand. He stepped back. Fired again. The revolver roared.

"Fall back! Fall back! We will reassemble at camp!"

Someone raced past Caleb, almost knocking him down. Caleb pulled the trigger, felt no kick, heard no shot, realized the percussion cap had misfired.

"Come on, Caleb!" Sergeant Masterson stopped, turned Caleb around, shoved him.

Caleb ran. He thought he could run all the way to the Tennessee River, swim across it, then keep running. In fact, some soldiers kept running, with no intention of stopping, but Caleb recognized the knocked-over rotisseries, a few chickens burning in the flames, the skillet, the Dutch oven. Smoke sizzled from the ashes of one fire pit. A bullet had pierced the coffee pot, and the fire was out. He was back at his camp.

"Take cover!" Captain Clark shouted. "Fire at will!"

"Now you're talking." That had to be Seb Woolard.

Caleb dropped near a hickory stump. A wave of gray and brown swept across the field. The Ohio battery blasted. Bodies, blood, and mud flew skyward. He still held the pistol, cocked it, fired. This time, it worked, but he knew the Rebs were out of range for a handgun. That, however, did not stop him from shooting again.

Cannon roared once more. He kept pulling the trigger, realizing that the pistol was empty, and had been for a long time. He flung the gun in the direction of the Rebs, turned, ran seven or eight yards, and pulled the Springfield off a dead Illinoisan's body. Grabbed the cartridge box, too, hurried back to the stump.

The Springfield was still loaded, even capped. Caleb pulled

back the hammer, aimed, fired. As he reloaded, he realized that the gray line had stopped. Another cannon ball blasted in the mud. For a moment he heard nothing, just concentrated on securing the ramrod, capping the nipple. Finally words reached his ears.

"They've stopped. We've stopped those vermin!"

Shouts. Cheers.

"Where's Sergeant Downey?"

"Come back. Don't run. Boys, you're the Sixty-First Illinois!"

"Caleb, have you seen Boone?"

Turning, Caleb saw Sergeant Masterson, his head still bleeding. "Boone?" he repeated. "Have you seen my cousin?"

Caleb's head shook feebly. "No," he lied.

He thought he might wretch. Sergeant Masterson wandered down the row of tents, his voice echoing hauntingly: "Boone! Boone! Boone Masterson, where are you?"

Caleb filled his lungs with hot, putrid air, and looked across the open field now littered with the dead and dying, Rebels and Federals alike.

"No! Them Rebs aren't retreating. Here they come!"

"This is our home, boys!" Captain Clark strode among the tents, mess chests, oaks, and hickories. "We shall not let the enemy force us from our camp, our home. Be ready, boys. We'll drive them out of Dixie."

Cannon roared again, but this time from Spain's field, and grapeshot tore through the trees, the tents. Men screamed in agony. Caleb hugged closer to the stump, looked at the campfires. A coffee pot had been blown into shreds.

Men staggered past, some from the Eighteenth, others from Illinois, Wisconsin, Ohio. Few bothered to stop. They kept walking, ignoring shouts and rebukes from officers and sergeants, just made a beeline for the landing at the river.

"This is crazy!" Seb Woolard dropped his musket, turned, took off toward the river.

Caleb looked down the line, across the road, turned, studied the broken line of men in blue in front of the line of tents. There was no way, not a chance, that the Union could hold this position. Caleb wasn't a master of war, yet even he knew that.

So did General Prentiss. He rode over, on another horse this time, reining in. "Get your men out of here, Colonel."

"Sir?"

"Get them out of here. *Now!*" The horse wheeled. "There is a sunken road." He pointed north. "Re-form there."

Sergeant Masterson was back, kneeling beside Caleb. "Have you seen Boone?"

Caleb's head shook. "He'll turn up, Sergeant."

Colonel Miller, Captain Clark, Lieutenant Ault, other officers, and sergeants were directing their men to fall back.

"To the *Nebraska?*" someone questioned hopefully.

Rising, Caleb tugged Sergeant Masterson's coat sleeve. The barber stared blankly, as if he had a bad case of chicken heart disease. "We're moving back, Sergeant," Caleb said quietly. "I imagine Boone's down that way, too."

Slowly he led Sergeant Masterson away from the tents, the dead, the dying, the charging Rebels. Hurriedly they moved northeast, away from the Eastern Corinth Road.

A Missouri battle flag lay in the mud.

He did not stop to pick it up.

# CHAPTER SEVENTEEN

APRIL 6, 1862
NEAR SHILOH MEETING HOUSE, TENNESSEE

Matt Bryson's dirty white chest exploded in a spray of garnet. The Mississippi rifle slipped out of his hands, and his eyes rolled back in his head as he slammed forward into the ground. The two other Confederates standing near him staggered, and dropped. To Ryan's right, someone screamed.

Hurriedly those Yankee assassins began reloading.

"No!" Ryan shouted, firing his musket as he ran, missing, not caring. Behind him, Sergeant Rutherford cut loose with a savage oath. Ryan knew Matt was dead, and he knew that squad of Union vermin would soon join him for such cowardly treachery. He planned on killing the hatless sergeant himself.

Sergeant Rutherford, however, robbed him of that revenge. Reaching the sergeant first, Rutherford rammed a bayonet into the Yank's chest so hard, the blade poked through the back of the man's blue tunic. So hard that Rutherford lost his grip on his musket, and that Union piece of filth was driven back ten feet, falling on his back, the musket sticking upright like a grave marker. Rutherford grabbed his weapon, pulled the trigger, the blast igniting the dead sergeant's clothes. He did not bother to put out the flames.

Curses and cries rose over the reverberation of Confederate

gunfire. A shotgun blast dropped a Yank. A musket ball tore into another as he turned to flee. One sobbing boy dropped to his knees, clasped his hands, begged for mercy. A bullet in his head dispatched him quickly, which might have been merciful enough.

All of that Ryan saw through peripheral vision. His focus remained on a white-faced old man in front of him, old, bony fingers futilely trying to finger a copper percussion cap onto the nipple of an Enfield rifle. The white handkerchief hung loosely from the barrel. Ryan drove his bayonet into the old man's gut.

His mother's voice raced through his mind: *Always respect your elders, Son.*

He pulled out the bayonet, dripping crimson. The old man sank to his knees, dropping Enfield and capper, blood spilling from both corners of his mouth. Ryan kneed the man's chest, watched him fall onto his back, his lips parting in a blood-frothed prayer. A glimpse of the perfidious flag of truce tied to the Enfield fueled his rage. He smashed the man's face with the stock of his musket. Again. And again. And again. He could have kept crushing the man's face for the rest of his life.

"Come on!" Little Sam pointed, began jogging away, following a line of white-uniformed soldiers.

The Yankees lay dead.

Ryan sucked in air, spit, turned, hurried to Matt Bryson.

He lay on his back, three bloody holes in the mud-splattered white coat, head turned to the right, mouth open, a small pool of blood mixing with the mud and grass. At least his eyes were closed. His white trousers, always too long for him, looked even more comical, the bottoms of the wretched legs covering his brogans, blackened with thick mud. Ryan started to kneel, but Sergeant Rutherford's harsh voice stopped him.

"He's done for, lad. Come on. Let's kill some more of Lincoln's hirelings."

＊ ＊ ＊ ＊ ＊

They moved through the woods, at first stepping around or over the dead, but soon unable to avoid it, and no longer caring.

"Hey, whereabouts you from?"

Ryan turned toward the molasses-soaked voice, spotted a toothless man puffing on a corncob pipe. He'd never seen the soldier before.

"Texas." He wasn't certain how he should answer. "Place called Cedar Bayou. It's near Houston. Second Texas Infantry."

The man, his face masked in gunpowder and dirt, removed the pipe. "You fellers fit like the devil. Was y'all at Manassas?"

Ryan's head shook.

"We was." The soldier, dressed in patched gray trousers, moth-eaten muslin shirt, and battered straw hat, tapped the cob against the handle of a massive knife sheathed at his side, and tucked the pipe in a pocket.

"This is our first engagement." Ryan's voice sounded hollow.

"Well, we didn't fit none at Virginy. Spent the winter there, then a-come home with fifty dollars on furlough. After we spends all that money, Capt'n a-sends us to Memphis, and here we is. Yep, this be our first battle, too, and it's been a hot one. So I reckon you and me has both seen the elephant now." He stuck out a filthy hand. "Name's Dick Hinton. Hail from Drew County. We's with the First Arkansas." He hooked a thumb to a blood-spattered man with a beard that looked like metal bristles.

"Ryan McCalla." Briefly they shook hands.

"I'm with the Sixth Tennessee!" someone else called.

"Fourth Louisiana." At least that's what Ryan thought the voice had yelled.

"Well, you're in the Second Texas now!" Captain Ashbel Smith snapped, and everyone cheered.

They moved past some Wheelock Prairie boys from Company

E, a corporal mounted on a cannon like a horse, slapping the barrel with a black slouch hat. Yankee prisoners sat on the ground, hands clasped behind their heads, guarded with bayonets at their throats.

"Hey, fellas!" one of the Rebels bragged. "We captured ourselves a cannon!"

A corporal spit out tobacco juice, nodding. "Didn't even fire a shot."

Another cheer, and they marched past the captured artillery piece.

Weapons blasted to the right, and Colonel Moore hurried over: "Captain Smith!"

"Yes, sir!"

"Assist Captains McGinnis and Christian. General Chalmers' Second Brigade needs some Texas-size help."

"You heard the colonel!"

With the others, Ryan pivoted. He expected the two guys from Arkansas to join them, but the pipe-smoker sniggered and said, "I ain't helpin' no Mississippi sidewinders," and they kept marching north.

They moved at a double-quick pace, through a section of woods that had been shattered by musket blasts, grapeshot, canister. It was like walking through a cotton field that had been cropped. Minié balls whistled overhead. Other shots kicked up soil and débris. Men moaned for water. Beside a stump, a dying Yankee mumbled a psalm. They marched on. Muskets blasted ahead. Bark flew off those trees that had not yet been stripped by grapeshot and bullets. A Texian dropped to his knees, crying out: "Fare thee well, boys, I am killed."

Out of the destroyed woods, they moved toward the Mississippi brigade, feet stepping on dead Union soldiers instead of earth. Wheeling westward, Ryan realized they were marching through another Federal camp. This time, however, no one stopped to plunder the tents or steal any food. They climbed out of the ravine, onto a hill.

Deafening and deadly musketry greeted them, killing many, wounding scores.

"On the ground, boys! On the ground!"

Ryan was already dropping to a prone position. A ball spit mud into his cheek. He aimed at a cloud of smoke, pulled the trigger, rolled onto his back, tried to reload. Balls whistled over his head.

*Thud!*

He looked to his left, saw a stranger—maybe the guy from the Sixth Tennessee—the top of his head blown away.

*Thud!*

*Thud!*

*Thud!*

Forgetting about reloading, he pushed his way back down into the ravine, rose, staggered ten yards, twenty, not stopping until he was fifty yards away. Other men scrambled into the ravine, breathing heavily. Quickly Ryan finished reloading the musket.

"Re-form the ranks!" Captain Smith ran down the line, waving that wrist-breaking saber of his. "We'll charge with bayonets."

He was moving, climbing back up the ravine, out of the woods. A row of Union cannon greeted them. He saw Yanks pull the lanyards, watched the muzzles belch flame and smoke. Shells roared overhead. Others exploded in the field. Men screamed as if their bodies were engulfed in burning oil.

They moved past the cannon. Some of the boys stopped, tried to turn around those artillery pieces, to fire at the fleeing Yanks. Infantry approached, another line of blue forming another barrier, a deadly wall.

"Charge bayonets!" someone ordered.

The Federal line fired. A ball tore off Ryan's hat. Dropping to their knees, the Texians returned fire. A man wearing a blue frock coat galloped into the open field, screaming, waving his hat furiously.

"For God's sake, boys. Stop firing! You are killing your friends!"

Rising, the Texians continued on, most of them not bothering to reload.

From the Union line came a cry: "Colonel! Those are Rebs!"

Too late, the man on horseback realized his mistake. In a panic, he pulled on the reins, spinning his horse, raking its flanks with spurs. Muskets roared, dropping horse and man in a heap.

Rebel yells rose above the din. Ryan ran harder, screaming, watching the bluecoats turn, skedaddle.

One Yankee officer jumped into a phaeton, began lashing out savagely with a whip, too crazed to realize the horse lay dead in its harness. When he finally realized that, he stood, only to be shot off the buggy.

Not every Yank ran. An officer walked back, waving a battle flag in his right hand, screaming, trying to rally his men. Soldiers stopped, turned. Canister ripped the earth, dropped several men on Ryan's left. He would concede one fact about Grant's soldiers. They were as brave, as resolute, as Colonel Moore's Second Texas.

He pulled the trigger, realized he had left the ramrod in the barrel.

Minié balls filled the air. He could hear them pass so close. One buzzed his ear. He pitched aside his rifle, stopped to pick up one in front of a dead Confederate.

They cleared another field, went through more ravaged woods.

Onward they moved, reloading now. Union bodies littered the ground. In their white uniforms, now soiled, the Second Texas marched through the slaughter like ghosts.

"Where's Captain Smith?" someone asked.

"Took a ball in his arm."

"How is he?"

"Looked mortal to me."

Ryan almost stopped, but Sergeant Rutherford barked: "Forward. Keep driving those yellow Yanks."

Spotting Little Sam Houston, Ryan hurried and caught up with him, tried to think of something to say. Even had he been able to come up with pointless conversation, he couldn't talk. His tongue was swollen, blackened with gunpowder, grit, mud.

Cannon roared behind them. Murderous shells ripped the blue lines. At last, the Second Texas and stragglers from other regiments stopped. Finally Ryan remembered his canteen. He pulled it over, uncorked it, lifted it, dropped it. Two balls had shattered it. It was bone dry. He pulled it over his head and shoulder, let it fall on a dead Yank.

"Here."

Sam Houston Jr. passed him his canteen, and, greedily, Ryan drank.

"Colonel! Over there!"

Ryan turned to the voice, saw a Federal officer step out of the woods waving a white flag.

"Oh, no, you don't." Ryan knelt, brought the rifle to his shoulder, drew a bead on the Yank's chest. Behind him, he heard Little Sam cock his musket.

"Corporal McCalla. Houston. Hold your fire," warned Sergeant Rutherford, who brazenly stepped forward, positioning his back in front of Ryan's musket barrel.

Muttering a curse, Ryan eased down the hammer of his musket, and pushed himself to his feet. He and Little Sam flanked Sergeant Rutherford, watching Captain Hood of Company G ride out to meet the flag-waving Federal. He couldn't hear the words because of the continuous blasts from Confederate artillery, but, after a moment, Captain Hood returned, dropping an armload of swords at Colonel Moore's feet.

"They're surrendering, Colonel." Ryan read Hood's lips.

The colonel asked something. Sergeant Rutherford said: "Look!"

Confederate cavalry had surrounded the Yanks, and began leading them away.

"That's just like a horse soldier!" Rutherford snapped. "We win the battle. They take the prisoners and glory."

"Hey!" Sergeant Jardine shouted. "These cornfields and woods are littered with dead infantrymen. I've yet to see one dead cavalry trooper, Southern or Yank!"

Ryan joined the laugher. He tried to remember the last time he had laughed. Shaking his head, he returned the canteen to Little Sam.

Other bluecoats staggered out of the woods, from behind the tents, hands raised. Many of them bawled like newborns. Others begged not to be shot. One promised that, if they'd let him go, they'd never see hide nor hair of him in Dixie again.

A blond-headed Yank stopped in front of Ryan, speaking in some harsh language Ryan didn't understand. He and Sam Houston Jr. just walked past him, Sam mumbling: "Surrender to somebody else. We're still fighting."

"Where are we, Colonel?" a lieutenant asked frantically.

"Lord knows," Moore replied with a short chuckle, "but we're marching that way. To the sound of guns. Press on, men. Press on!" Moore stepped over the surrendered swords, moving north again, toward the Tennessee River. Ryan joined the procession, entering another forest.

When they exited those woods, more Yanks stood waiting.

"How many Yankees can there be in this here world?" someone asked.

These men stood across a road, standing behind a split-rail fence, a few other buildings.

"Hey, Ryan?" He glanced over at Little Sam.

"How much ammunition have you?"

Quickly he opened his cartridge box. Blinking, he let out a sigh. "None."

"Same here."

Sergeant Rutherford had overheard the conversation. "You've got bayonets, don't you? Give them the steel, boys! Charge!"

He was running again, yelling like a banshee, feeling lead fly around him, over him, under him. A cannon ball blasted a portion of the fence, sending chunks of wood rails and Yankees in every direction. Little Sam leaped the fence. Ryan ran through a newly made hole. He found a bluecoat crawling, looking up, mouth agape, eyes wide. Ryan prepared to thrust the bayonet into the boy's gut.

"Please!" the Yankee cried.

Ryan breathed. Blinked. Shifting his musket, he stepped over the petrified Yank, and tried to catch up with the rest of the Second.

He ran across dead men, rounded a burning caisson, letting his yell echo those coming from the mouths of the charging soldiers in front of him. He wondered what time it was, how long he had been fighting.

Then, a bullet tore through his thigh.

# CHAPTER EIGHTEEN

APRIL 6, 1862
PITTSBURG LANDING, TENNESSEE

Caleb pushed through the woods, trying to fight down the panic rising in him. Bullets thudded into the trees all around him. Men fell. Several dropped their weapons, crying, and ran. Officers tried to rally their men. One got knocked over for his troubles.

Voices, orders, shouts, prayers mingled together.

"Where's Captain Clark?" ... "Mother! Mother!" ... "Almighty and everlasting God, who hatest nothing that Thou hast made ..." ... "Back there. Shot in the head." ... "Has anyone seen Lieutenant Hudson?" ... "Captain, where is your company?" ... "Was he wounded?" ... "Boone! Boone Masterson, where are you?" ... "... and dost forgive the sins of all those who are penitent ..." ... "Ma, what am I doing here?" ... "Major, this is all that's left of my company, sir!" ... "My arm's shattered. Benji, don't let 'em cut off my arm!" ... "Boone! Do you hear me, Boone?" ... "The devil with this, I ain't waiting around to get killed." ... "The lieutenant was trying to help Captain Cooper but, last I seen, he and the captain both was surrounded by a bunch of graycoats." ... "... we, worthily lamenting our sins and acknowledging our wretchedness ..." ... "Form a line here!" ... "Company G, here, lads, right here!" ... "... may obtain of Thee, the God of all mercy, perfect remission and forgiveness ..." "Why are we stopping?" ... "Oh, Doris, I never shall feel your lips on my cheek again." ... "... through Jesus Christ our Lord. Amen."

A mile or so later, they came out of the woods, dipping into a road, then moving up a ridge on the other side of the sunken pike. Captain Stults directed the remnants of his company to find a position in the forest, ordered them to reload.

"Which company are you with?" the captain screamed in Sergeant Masterson's face.

When the sergeant only blinked, Caleb answered: "Captain Clark's Company E."

"Clark took a ball through the head back at camp, is likely dead." Stults' eyes narrowed. "I know you, don't I?"

Caleb nodded. "You know my father, I think. We farm in Putnam County."

Smiling grimly, Henry P. Stults put an arm on Caleb's shoulder. "I wish we were back in Putnam County now, son, don't you?" The softness left him immediately, and he turned, pointing. "Welcome to Company B. There. Find a spot there. Stand ready." His voice softened once more: "God willing, maybe some of us will live to see Missouri again."

To his right, he saw Lieutenant McEfee, once a quartermaster sergeant before being promoted to second lieutenant, directing ten or so of Company E's boys into the thicket. Caleb thought about joining them, but Sergeant Masterson sat down underneath an oak tree, pulled out a knife, opened the blade, began cleaning his fingernails. Caleb decided he'd stay with Company B for a while.

General Prentiss loped down the road, shouting orders, jerking the lathered horse to a stop. "Where is the Sixty-First Illinois?" No one answered. Prentiss swore. Someone asked him something. He pointed down the road, barking: "Join the Twelfth Michigan. Hurry!" Prentiss kicked the horse into a gallop.

"Lie down." Captain Stults crept behind the men. "Prone position. Hold your fire until they are on this side of the road. Then we'll allow them to make Satan's acquaintance."

Caleb loaded and capped his weapon, snuggling into the bed of damp, rotting leaves and twigs. Beside him, Sergeant Masterson kept cleaning his nails, once stopping to turn and shout out: "Boone! Boone Masterson, where are you?"

"Shut up!" Caleb bellowed. He tried to slow his heartbeat, tried to steady his breathing. Looking across the road, he waited.

Faces flashed through his mind. Folker and Boone, now dead. Captain Clark, with a bullet in his head. The last he had seen of Seb Woolard, the lout was running for the river. Rémy Ehrenreich? He couldn't recollect seeing him since this morning.

Morning? He rolled over, tried to find the sun through the thick trees and brush. Failing, he let out another breath, and got back into a prone firing position.

All around him came the sounds of cannon and musket, that piercing, horrifying yell of the Secesh. In front of him, however, there was nothing but an empty road, and woods.

"Why don't they come?" someone whispered.

"They're likely eating our breakfast!"

"Maybe they're trying to flank us."

He looked left, right. Nothing.

"Maybe they've gone back home."

"Quiet! Quiet, men!"

All whispers ceased.

Pounding hoofs in the mud, the plowing of wheels digging through mud. Caleb looked, held his breath. Before he noticed they were bluecoats, other Federals down the line cheered, and Caleb watched cannon and caissons race down the road, disappearing around the bend. Somewhere down there, Prentiss barked orders at the artillery commander.

"Now, we'll show those Rebs!"

"Be quiet!" an officer yelled.

Silence.

Then ... the sucking sound of boots in mud, the cracking of limbs and branches ... a curse ... laughter ... the jingling of canteens. Butternut-clad men stepped out of the woods and onto the sunken road. Soldiers in gray joined them. They cautiously looked down the road, kept coming.

"Fire!" Stults shouted, and Caleb's musket barked. He rolled on his back, trying to block out the sounds of men crying. A bullet clipped bark off the oak. Something whistled over his head. He drew the ramrod, found a paper cartridge, tried to reload while on his back.

"Boone!" Sergeant Masterson said. "Boone, that you, cuz?"

"Fire at will!"

The Rebels sang out that ruinous shriek. Caleb rolled over, capping the nipple. A branch fell across the front sight, clipped by a Southern ball. He shook the barrel, watched the slender branch disappear, stared, found a brass breastplate against a butternut coat in his sights, pulled the trigger.

"They're falling back!" came a cry that was answered by a rousing cheer up and down the Union line.

Jubilance did not last long.

"Here come the dirty little ..."

Out of the woods, back on the sunken road, the Rebels charged again, screaming, firing, dying. Caleb's musket felt so hot it would melt. He checked the cartridge box he had picked up, withdrew the last load. When he had the musket loaded, he rolled over. A few Rebs had made it across the road. One stood only three rods in front of Caleb, his face a black horrifying mask with wide, red eyes. The musket roared. Face and man disappeared. Caleb rolled back over, looked at Sergeant Masterson, nonchalantly cleaning his nails.

"Sergeant!" He had to yell twice. At last, Harold Masterson studied Caleb. "Your cartridge box." Caleb jutted his chin toward Masterson's waist. "Do you have any ammunition?"

Masterson blinked. "I haven't seen Boone. Have you?"

Swearing vilely, Caleb inched down, turned, crawled away from Sergeant Masterson. A ball blasted dirt and débris into his eyes. He cried out, almost released his viselike grip on the musket, almost ran through the brambles, fled for home. General Prentiss' words stopped him.

"Boys, Grant says we must hold 'em. We must hold 'em here."

Someone called back: "Where the devil's Grant?"

A cannon blast silenced an officer's condemnation. Caleb pressed his face deep into the leaves. At first, he thought the Confederates were shelling these woods. Cries, moans, shrieks, coughs, curses told him otherwise. Union artillery had opened up.

"Take that, you butchers!" That sounded like Lieutenant McEfee.

Caleb reached a dead man, pried open the cartridge box, pulled out the cartridges, and stuffed them into his own box. He looked up, saw a crucifix drenched in blood around the corpse's neck. He almost reached for it, even though he was not Catholic, thinking that it couldn't hurt. Still, he couldn't do it. *I'm no grave robber,* he thought, but he took the dead man's capper, and eased his way back toward Sergeant Masterson. Balls slammed into the woods. Another artillery shell exploded. His ears rang.

The sound of the charge he could not hear, but he still saw. More Secesh pouring out of the woods, crossing the road without touching the mud, a carpet of dead at their feet.

Once more, the Rebs retreated back across the road, into the woods.

A new sound reached him. Something screamed across the sky, clipping the treetops above him, exploding somewhere deep into the woods across the road.

"What's that, Major?"

"Ironclads, boys. Gun ships back on the river."

Another cheer, silenced by another shell. A section of an oak crashed next to Caleb, limbs tearing into his left arm and leg. He let out a groan, pulled his arm free, rolled over, kicking at the timber until his leg was no longer trapped. He started to keep on, make it to Sergeant Masterson, only to realize this bit of wood, dropped by a Union shell, would make better cover than the mound of dirt he hugged ten yards west.

"Hurlbut's pulled out!" someone shouted. "Sherman's turned tail. We've got to get out of here or we'll all be massacred!"

"Stand your ground!" A cacophony of curses. "Stand your ground! We must hold!"

Caleb loaded the musket, heard that chilling scream, rose to a knee to see above the smoking treetop, aimed, fired.

"Save your powder and lead. Let them get closer. Fire. Fire, men, fire!"

"The Union forever!"

The ringing had left his ears, but he could not hear. Nothing. Smoke and sweat almost blinded him. Again he rammed powder and lead down the barrel. His fingers were thick with black dirt, powder, and blood that wasn't his, as far as he could tell. He saw a flag, recognized it as the banner of Company E, the one he had last seen in the mud back in camp. It was being waved by someone— George Preston, he realized—being carted off on a litter, away from the battlefield, toward the Tennessee River.

A bullet clipped sweaty hair hanging over his ear. He faced the never-ending sea of gray and brown. Horse soldiers burst out of the forest, firing, spurring, turning down the road. A steady waterfall of horses and cavalry. One horse went down, spilling its rider. Caleb aimed, fired, missed. By the time he had reloaded, the Rebels had vanished, but he could hear those horses crashing down an animal path somewhere in the thicket. His hearing had returned.

"They'll flank us!" a sergeant from Company G yelled.

"They've already got us flanked!" answered someone to the east.

Out of the woods, the Rebels moved again, screaming, firing, the rug of dead men even higher now. Caleb fired, knew he was out of cartridges again. He scrambled from the felled treetop, crawled and dragged himself to Sergeant Masterson. This time, he didn't bother to ask for ammunition. Frantically he opened the cartridge box, only to find it empty, too.

Lifting his head, Masterson roared in anguish: "I can't find Boone …!"

"He's dead! Boone's dead. And so are we!" Caleb wanted to run, but he crawled over Masterson's legs, clawing, digging, finding at last another dead soldier. As he was ramming down a load, he heard Prentiss' shouting.

"We must stop this slaughter! Company commanders, stack your arms! Stack your arms!"

Caleb capped the musket, rolled over, fired.

"Stack your arms!"

He looked to the east, the west. A bullet tore into the ground beside him. This shot came from behind him. They were surrounded. Spinning, he looked into the woods, saw nothing but trees torn apart by Rebel lead, as if God had swung a scythe four to five feet off the ground.

"Surrender! We surrender!"

"Will they shoot us, Lieutenant?"

"No!"

A white flag fluttered. Another.

Caleb swore again. All of this. All those dead. Boone Masterson. Folker. "*For nothing!*" He spit out the words, heard footsteps coming from that sunken road, and bitterly pitched his rifle to the north. It took a moment before he could make his arms work after that. Reaching out, he used the trunk of a tree to pull himself to his feet, although he wasn't sure his legs would be able to support his weight.

He was right. He slipped, felt himself falling, but long arms reached around his chest, stopped his plummet. He felt himself being turned around, expected to find himself staring into the treacherous face of a Southern demon.

"You all right, Caleb?" Sergeant Masterson asked. He seemed to have regained his faculties, and offered a reassuring smile.

Caleb started to answer, but a gunshot stopped him. Harold Masterson, one-time barber from Pennville, Missouri, staggered against Caleb, a soft moan escaping through his lips, and they crashed onto scattered limbs and leaves. Masterson's head slammed into Caleb's forehead, and the world turned black.

# CHAPTER NINETEEN

APRIL 6, 1862
PITTSBURG LANDING, TENNESSEE

He woke, clutching his mother, burying his head against her breasts while trying not to cry. Shuddering, he squeezed her tightly, but she did not return the hug. She didn't even stroke his hair or soothe him with her sweet Kentucky drawl, and when a cannon cut loose in the gloaming, rifling the woods with grapeshot, Caleb Cole knew why.

Releasing his bear grip, he pulled his arms underneath the body atop him and, grunting, pushed it off. That took some doing, even for the biggest farm-bred boy in Company E. Caleb sat up, lungs working feverishly, and touched his tunic, sticky, soaked with blood. Shaking, he reached inside, feeling for some hole in his chest made by ball or bayonet. Nothing. Then he remembered, and looked down at the dead man who had fallen atop him.

"Oh, Sergeant Masterson," he said softly, and quickly turned away. Tears welled in his eyes, but none rolled down his cheeks. He blinked, shaking his head, and leaned against an oak tree. Or, rather, what once had been an oak tree.

Rebel and Federal lead had served as an axe, toppling the tree about four feet above its roots. A canteen draped over the fallen timber next to Caleb's left shoulder, and Caleb realized just how thirsty he was. His mouth was coated with a mixture of powder and Tennessee mud and grass. Desperately he reached up and grabbed the gray-wool-wrapped tin container by its canvas strap. Only then did he realize that a hand gripped the canteen. The hand of a dead Confederate soldier.

He fell, pulling the canteen with him, backing away, but stopping quickly when he realized that that direction would bring him next to Sergeant Masterson.

"It's Sunday," he remembered telling the sergeant that morning, and recalled Sergeant Masterson's reply: "It sure won't be like any Sabbath you've ever seen, boy."

Like always, the sergeant had been right.

Caleb squeezed his eyelids tightly, shaking his head, trying to block out the image of the sergeant's lifeless green eyes staring up at him.

"Water," someone moaned, and his plea echoed all across the battlefield from other wounded soldiers, Northern and Southern.

"Water …"

"Water …"

"Water …"

In an eerie, out-of-tune harmony came sporadic musketry, but mostly other calls. For mothers. For wives. For mercy. For death.

"Oh, please, God, Mama, just give me one drop of water."

Caleb's eyes shot open. He still held the canteen, and savagely brought it to his mouth, feeling the tin slice through his palm. The canteen dropped into his lap, and he stared at his bleeding hand, then at the canteen. A Minié ball had punctured the bottom, emptying its contents hours earlier. He looked away from the canteen, his bleeding hand, and, blinking back sweat and surprise, watched what appeared to be a ghost, crawling through the brambles. Again, Caleb blinked, but the ghost kept coming, and, after one horrifying moment, Caleb understood. It wasn't some apparition, but a Rebel soldier in a white uniform, once brand-new but now covered with soot, powder, and blood.

The Reb moved around a broken gun carriage, and over Master-son's body. He crawled right past Caleb, never noticing him, just moving with intense purpose, underneath the shattered oak.

"That's right, Matt, there might be some frogs in that pond," the Reb said. "Maybe even some big ones, and I pity them fool frogs. I do indeed, my friend. Because we will drink that pond dry."

As the Secesh disappeared underneath the oak, Caleb stared at the soiled white trousers, the left leg soaked with blood.

"Water!" another voice cried from afar.

Caleb rolled over, hearing the canteen spin away, and crawled after those fast-moving legs.

He moved over guns, some broken apart, some dropped, others probably never even fired. Crawled over knapsacks, brogans, kepis, and bedrolls. Crawled over a wagon wheel, underneath a caisson. Crawled through mud. Crawled over dead men. Followed the blackened, shoeless feet of the man in front of him.

"Don't be a dunderpate, Matt," the Reb said. "We saw that pond. I know where I'm going, bunkie. It's this way. I know it. My nose smells that water. My tongue tastes it."

Twice, Caleb turned, glancing behind him, looking for Matt. Behind him, he saw nothing but a battlefield littered with the dead, the wounded, the dying. "The wormwood and gall," Sergeant Masterson had said.

He stopped, images of the battle hitting him in a rush, and trembled.

"There! Just a few rods more, Matt, and we'll slake our thirsts!"

Caleb turned, moving with a fury, did not want that Secesh to get out of his sight. Soon he felt others crawling or staggering near him. Wobbly legs carried one soldier who could still not only walk, but run. Only then did Caleb stop, thinking: *I can walk, too. Can't I?*

He reached out, found the broken wheel and axle from a wagon, and pulled himself up. Caught his breath. Took a tentative step. A man rushed past him, almost knocked him to the ground. Caleb started to say something, but his mouth felt too dry. He stumbled on, still following the wounded Reb. His shoes sloshed through damp grass. The Secesh crawled over the dead. Caleb walked over them, until he could no longer avoid stepping on them.

"Here we go, Matt," the shoeless Reb said as he pulled himself to the edge of a pond. He cupped his hands, drank, and fell head-first into the water.

Caleb knelt beside him, started to drink, but saw the bubbles rising from the Reb's submerged head.

"Gee willikins, Reb." He reached over, gripped the soldier's blouse, and pulled him out of the pond. The Secesh gagged, snorted, rolled over on the bank, and vomited.

Ignoring him, Caleb returned to the water. He knelt, bathed his wounded hand in the water, then with his good hand, cupped a handful of the cold water, and drank. He drank again. Then he removed his hat, soaking it in the water, and put it on his head to cool off.

Behind him, the Rebel moaned.

"Gee willikins," he said again, and dipped the hat in the pond, letting it fill like a gourd this time, crawled a few rods, and lifted the hat toward the Reb's face. To his surprise, he found most of the water leaking from holes in the crown. Holes that hadn't been in his black hat that morning.

"Here," he said, and tilted the hat to the young soldier's mouth.

*Soldier*, Caleb thought with a snort. Caleb was sixteen. The Secesh couldn't be much older.

Much water rolled down the boy's cheeks, splattering the grass and rotting leaves, but some must have made its way into the Reb's gullet. He smacked his lips and said: "Thanks, Matt."

"My name isn't Matt," Caleb said, surprised at the fury in his voice. "It's Caleb. Caleb Cole. Eighteenth Missouri."

The Reb's piercing blue eyes came into focus. He suddenly remembered his leg, and, grimacing, sat up, and bent over to tighten the filthy, rolled-up bandanna around his thigh.

Cursing underneath his breath, Caleb returned to the pond, but this time had to wait until another soldier, this one from some

Union artillery regiment, had his fill. When that man stumbled away, Caleb plunged the hat into the water, and hurried back to the Reb before the water spilled from his sieve of a hat, dumping the water onto the bloody thigh.

"Thanks."

Their eyes met, but only briefly, because Caleb returned to the pond. This time he drank until he noticed that the water smelled funny. He straightened, cupped another handful, and brought it closer to his face.

Caleb looked again at the red-tinted water dripping between his fingers. Then he looked into the pond. Bodies floated in the middle. One hung on a caisson's wheel. Corpses lined the banks. Caleb's gut roiled. He shuddered as the skies darkened.

Grass rustled around him, and he saw the Secesh crawling to the edge. When the Rebel splashed water over his face, and drank greedily, Caleb wretched. Water came out, and he vomited again, but he had nothing in his stomach. There had been no breakfast that morning. He gagged and spat until he thought he'd throw up his own innards, then desperately fell to the bank and made himself drink the bloody water again.

When he lifted his head, he saw the Reb beside him bathing the bandanna in the pond, then retying it over his thigh.

Again, their eyes met.

"You seen Matt?" the Reb asked.

Caleb couldn't talk. His head barely shook.

The young face turned ashen, and stiffened. "Oh." The Secesh's voice sounded a thousand miles away. "No … I guess you haven't."

Caleb felt a sudden panic. He was here with the enemy, but didn't have his rifle. Not even a knife. Then again, neither did the Reb.

"You hit bad?"

Caleb looked at the Reb. "I wasn't even hit at all." A mirthless chuckle escaped, and he held out his right hand. "Got this from a shot-up canteen."

"Lucky." The Reb drank again.

"Don't feel lucky."

"You're alive."

Caleb shrugged.

"I thought we'd drive them Yanks all the way across the river. Didn't you?"

Another humorless laugh. Odd, Caleb thought, earlier that day he had thought he would never laugh again for as long as he lived. Shaking his head, he turned to the young Secesh. "I thought you Rebs were going to make us swim across the river."

The boy tensed, straightened. "You're a Yank?"

Caleb nodded.

"But I thought you said you hailed from Missouri?"

"I did. I do." The Secesh, Caleb knew, didn't understand. "Missouri's been sending troops to the Confederate cause and to the Union. And some ..." His head shook.

"Seems like we ought to be fighting one another. Or me taking you prisoner or the other way around." The Secesh made no move, though. Instead, he drank again, then, noticing the color of the liquid, spit it out.

"I'm all fought out," Caleb said. "Most of the Eighteenth ..." His head dropped.

"Yeah." The Reb rubbed his leg. "What's Missouri like?"

Caleb smiled. "It's home."

"Yeah. Know what you mean. Home for me's Cedar Bayou, Texas."

"Can't say I've heard of that," Caleb said.

"It's on Galveston Bay."

"I think I've heard of Galveston."

"Yeah. Where you from? In Missouri, I mean."

"Just a farm. Outside Unionville. In Putnam County."

The Reb laughed, harder this time. "Well, I never heard of any of those places."

"You're not alone. Even some boys in the Eighteenth had never heard of Unionville. It's near nothing."

They sniggered again, this time full of mirth.

"Water …" someone groaned from the woods. A horse screamed to the west. And from behind them: "George. Kill me, George. My guts is on fire. I can't take this no more."

Silence. Except for the moans, groans, death rattles, the splashing of water, the gurgles of drinking men, and the wind in the trees.

"Reckon we'll go at it again tomorrow?" Caleb asked.

"Oh, we'll fight. The Second Texas … that's my outfit … we're far from whipped. We're …" His voice trailed off.

A pistol popped somewhere deep in the woods.

The Secesh's head shook. "Never got off the bay much till I joined up. Thought this soldiering would be …" His head fell. "Well, I've seen enough of Tennessee, thank you kindly."

Caleb tried to wash off Sergeant Masterson's blood from his tunic. "I'd never seen anything other than Putnam County before …" A scream stopped him in mid-sentence.

"Curse you Yankee dogs!" a voice shot from the woods to the south. "You've kilt Gen'ral Johnston! I'll kill ever' last one of you black Republicans tomorrow!"

"Come ahead, Rebel trash!" answered someone from the opposite bank. "You can join your treasonous general in Hades!"

No one spoke for a minute or more, unless they were calling for their mothers or for water.

The Secesh shook his head. "Lord, I hope that's not true. About General Johnston. He …" Grimacing, the boy gripped his wounded leg.

Caleb looked at the blood-soaked trousers. "How bad you hurt?"

"Didn't get the bone. I don't think."

"You ought to find your hospital."

The Reb stiffened. "No, sir." He backed up to a dead man, and began unlacing the soldier's brogans.

"What are you doing?" Caleb demanded in dismay.

"He's got no use for these," the Reb shot back. "And I have."

That was enough. Caleb pulled his bullet-riddled hat onto his wet hair, stood, began staggering away.

"Hey, Yank."

Caleb stopped, turned. The Reb reached inside his blouse, and withdrew a plug of tobacco. "I would have drowned if you hadn't pulled me out of that pond." His hand, blackened with blood, powder, and grit, stretched toward him.

"Take it. Tobacco's one thing the Confederacy isn't short on. That and corn, salt, and apples. That's the joke down in Corinth. 'What does the CSA stand for?'" He winked. "'Why, corn, salt, and apples, of course.'"

Caleb shook his head.

"Take it," the Reb demanded.

Caleb couldn't control his hand. He watched his fingers grip the tobacco, and shove the plug into the inside pocket of his tunic.

"It's apple-cured," the Reb said.

Caleb just stared.

"My name's, McCalla," the Reb said. "Ryan McCalla."

"Caleb Cole."

"Good luck, tomorrow, Cole."

Caleb nodded. "You, too, McCalla."

He walked away, trying to avoid the legs of men, living and dead, that lined the bloody pond, then walked across the dead as fast as he could.

# CHAPTER TWENTY

APRIL 7, 1862
NEAR SHILOH MEETING HOUSE, TENNESSEE

It was midnight before Ryan McCalla made his way back to the Second Texas. After packing the wound in his thigh with moss and mud, he used a sturdy branch as a cane and left the bloody pond. The branch broke after a half mile, but he replaced it with an Enfield rifle he found near a dead man. The woods and fields still smelled like smoke, like death. Most of the men he found were dead, and those still living couldn't help him locate his regiment. One said: "Mister, I don't even know where I am." Another joined him and they wandered through the woods together until Ryan's travel partner happened to run into someone from the Nineteenth Alabama. The Alabamans moved west. Ryan continued north.

Finally Ryan found Sergeant Rutherford, a blanket over his shoulder, chewing on a pig's foot in front of a fire. Rutherford rose, filled a cup with hot coffee, and passed it to Ryan.

Staring at Ryan's leg, Rutherford said: "You should go to a hospital, Corporal McCalla."

His head shook violently. "No. I won't do that."

He had passed too many of those makeshift tents on his way from the bloody pond. Beside one, he had stumbled and thrown up, the screams from inside pricking every nerve. When a doctor knelt beside him, his hands covered in blood, and said, "Son, we need to get you inside," Ryan had found more strength that he could imagine, pulled himself away, scrambled into the nearest thicket. Nor could he forget walking through that hospital in Corinth looking for Harry Cravey.

"Harry Cravey," he said, remembering.

"Back in Corinth, I warrant," Sergeant Rutherford said. "Maybe on his way to Galveston Island." He tossed the pig's feet into the fire. "By jacks, I wish I was with him."

"Captain Smith?" Ryan asked hopefully.

"Took a ball in the arm," Rutherford answered, "but he'll live."

Desperately he wanted to ask about Matt Bryson, to be told that Matt was fine, that Ryan had imagined him being shot down by filthy Northern swine. That, however, had been no dream.

"Gibb Gideon? Sam Jr.?"

"Sam's all right. Haven't seen Gideon since late afternoon." Rutherford answered listlessly.

Ryan wanted to sit, but wasn't sure he'd ever be able to stand again if he did. Leaning on the Enfield, sipping coffee, he watched Texas soldiers move from the fires to the tents that, earlier Sunday morning, had been part of Grant's army. Now, the Second Texas Infantry had made the Union camp their home for the night.

"Colonel Moore's been trying to find Jackson." Rutherford shook his head. "No luck. He came back about fifteen minutes ago. Guess we'll find a new brigade to fight with tomorrow. The colonel did send Lieutenant Gallaher to fetch any powder and lead. Gallaher hasn't come back yet." Rutherford pointed at the Enfield. "I see you got a new weapon. Any ammunition for it?"

Ryan shook his head. "You don't think the Yankees will retreat."

In reply, artillery crashed overhead and far into the woods.

"Yanks don't plan on letting us sleep," Rutherford said.

Ryan emptied the dregs of the coffee onto the ground. "Don't reckon I'd sleep, anyway."

Pulling the blanket back over his shoulder, Sergeant Rutherford pointed toward a tent illuminated from the inside by a candle. "You'll find Little Sam in that one. Try to get some rest, Ryan. You'll need it tomorrow." That had to be the first time Sergeant Rutherford had ever called him by his first name.

Another shell exploded, lighting up the night sky with brilliant orange and red flames. A Texian shouted toward the Tennessee River: "Can't you Yanks do better'n that?"

Ryan moved away from the fire, his leg throbbing, calling out Little Sam's name before stepping inside the canvas.

Houston rose, setting a Bible on a folding table, and helped ease Ryan down into a rocking chair.

*A rocking chair.* Yankees sure knew how to fight a war. Ryan leaned the Enfield against a mess chest.

"I thought you were dead," Little Sam said. Another shell exploded nearby, causing both to flinch.

With a weary smile, Ryan shook his head. "Almost drowned." He let out a small laugh. "A bluecoat pulled me out of that pond over yonder."

"I've thought about going to that pond," Houston said. "Filling my canteen."

"Don't. You'll want no water from that place."

Houston pointed at Ryan's leg. "You all right?"

He shrugged. "It didn't hit bone, I don't think. Went plumb through. No way I'm going to let some sawbones see it, though."

Instead of pushing the subject, Little Sam Houston sat back on the bedroll, picked up the Bible he had been reading, handed it to Ryan.

Ryan's forefinger pressed inside the hole in the back cover. He opened the little book until he found where the ball had finally stopped.

"'Make haste, O God, to deliver me; make haste to help me, O Lord,'" he read, and then closed the Bible, which he returned to his friend. "You suppose that means anything?"

"That I'm lucky," Houston answered.

"That God's looking after you?" Ryan tried again.

Houston grinned. "Ask me that tomorrow evening."

Another shell exploded, but this one knocked Ryan off the chair, left his ears humming, rocked the ground. Little Sam, blasted off the bedroll, scrambled to his feet, helped Ryan up, led him outside. Seven tents down they found a smoking crater. A few of the Texana Guards from Company K were screaming out names. A sergeant rushed into the hole. A lieutenant fired a string of curses at the gunboats on the river. The sergeant crawled out of the crater, shaking his head.

A soldier sobbed: "They were playing monte. That's all they were doing. Playing monte."

At that moment, the skies opened again, a cold, biting rain, as if Yankee mortars had punctured another hole in the clouds.

"Come on," Little Sam Houston said, and helped Ryan back inside the tent. "There's nothing we can do for those poor …" He choked out the last words. Inside, they stopped, staring. Water poured through bullet holes in the tent's roof, drenching the bedrolls, putting out the candle. Ryan collapsed in the rocking chair, and pulled down his hat. Rain water dripped off the brim.

\* \* \* \* \*

Somehow, Ryan did sleep, long, hard, dreamless. When Little Sam tugged his shoulder, however, he woke instantly. Outside the tent came sounds of soldiers, the beat of a drum, whispers, curses.

They stepped outside into the predawn blackness, gulping down coffee with the remnants of Company C.

"Colonel Moore's been promoted," Rutherford told his men. "He's commanding a brigade that includes us and a couple regiments from Alabama. Lieutenant Colonel Rogers is now Colonel Rogers, commanding the Second Texas. We're to re-form at Lick Creek." He spit. "Corporal McCalla, you need to march yourself to a hospital."

"I don't think so, Sergeant."

That prompted a cheer from his comrades, and they turned and moved through the woods, Ryan using the Enfield as a crutch, determined not to fall behind. They stopped only to strip the dead of ammunition. Even before the sun broke, sounds of musket and artillery swept all around them.

* * * * *

Ryan couldn't figure it out. As big a hurt as the Confederate Army had put on those Yankees yesterday, they still kept coming. Through a wheat field, into the woods, across a cotton field. The Confederates kept driving the Federals back, only to be forced to fall back themselves.

His knee no longer would bend. A ball had carved a furrow above his right ear, and blood matted his hair.

"Charge!" Colonel Rogers ordered.

"McCalla!"

Ryan turned painfully. Sergeant Rutherford handed him another rifle, this one sporting a long brass telescope. "You stay here. Cover us with this here gun. Kill as many Yankees as you can."

He took the weapon awkwardly, wanting to protest but knowing Sergeant Rutherford was right. He couldn't keep up with the charging men. Instead, he leaned against a tree, bracing the barrel of the rifle against another hickory, watching Sergeant Rutherford run to catch up with his men.

Looking through the telescope, he tried to find a bluecoat in the distance, but saw nothing but smoke and timber. In the center of the cotton field, the soldiers stopped. Gunfire erupted. He fired into the belching smoke. The kick of the rifle knocked him on his butt, and his leg throbbed painfully.

By the time he could push himself up, fumbling to reload the Sharps, he heard the panic in the voices of the men, his regiment, as they stormed off the field, through the brush. Officers yelled at them, but the Texians kept retreating.

"Colonel!" A general in a gray coat galloped over. "You command a pack of cowards, Colonel. Those men bring disfavor to the Southern cause." Without waiting to hear Colonel Rogers' defense, the general spurred his mount in front of the cotton field.

A bullet spit bark into Ryan's eyes, and he heard the Federals screaming as they charged across the field.

"Come on!" It was Sergeant Rutherford again. "We're falling back. We'll regroup. Come on!" He felt Rutherford's powerful hands under his arms, felt himself being half carried, half dragged through the timbers.

"Where's Little Sam?" Ryan asked.

Rutherford did not answer.

A quarter mile later, they stumbled. Cursing, Rutherford pushed himself to his knees. Ryan looked up at him, briefly, then closed his eyes.

* * * * *

He woke to the sounds of cries, prayers, pitiful moans, and realized he was lying on his back. A tree limb passed over his head, blocking out the stars. He was moving. He turned his head to find himself staring into the eyes of a dead man. Ryan tried to sit up, couldn't, although he managed to push himself up on an elbow.

The wagon he was in hit a hole, and the jarring bolt sent Ryan crashing down, crying out, but others crammed into the wagon like cordwood hurt even more. Again he looked around, and now saw a man leaning on the other side of the wagon, staring at a bloody, empty coat sleeve.

In a panic, Ryan rolled onto his back, made himself look down his body, and let out a prayer when he saw he still had both of his legs, though one was massively swollen, drenched in blood and mud. Fighting down the bile rising in his throat, he looked the other way, and spotted a corporal clutching his stomach, his pallid face drenched in sweat.

It appeared to be dusk.

"Hey," Ryan said to the wounded soldier. "Where are we? Where are they taking us?"

The man blinked, and did not answer.

He didn't have to. The truth struck Ryan, and he slumped down, using the dead man's stomach as a pillow, and not caring. He was in a wagon, moving south, back toward Corinth.

General Albert Sidney Johnson's Army of the Mississippi—or whoever commanded it now that the general was dead—was leaving Shiloh, abandoning the bodies of Matt Bryson and countless others on that hallowed battlefield.

Retreating.

# CHAPTER TWENTY-ONE

APRIL 7, 1862
PITTSBURG LANDING, TENNESSEE

"Your name's Cole, isn't that right?"

Caleb opened his eyes to find a somewhat familiar face only inches from him. When the head moved back, icy rain blasted Caleb, and he sat up quickly.

"I'm Joseph von Arx," the face said. "You get shot?"

Slowly Caleb Cole remembered where he was. The moans, the begging, the shouts of the dying and wounded reminded him. He had been walking away from that filthy, bloody pond when suddenly he had merely collapsed. His legs just would not function, so he had crawled to a bullet-riddled tree, leaned against the trunk, and shut his eyes.

"No." Caleb slowly shook his head. "I don't think so." His hand throbbed. He remembered cutting it on that canteen.

"I did." Joseph von Arx smiled, and showed off a bloody left arm. "Reckon they'll give me a medal?"

"Who?" he asked tiredly.

"The Eighteenth Missouri, of course."

That hadn't been Caleb's meaning. *Who was left in the Eighteenth?*

"You sure you're all right?"

Caleb nodded, and pulled himself up. His legs had found

their muscles.

"We best find Colonel Miller. You sure you ain't shot?"

"I'm all right." Caleb glanced at his hand, but it didn't look too bad. "Just tired."

"I took a ball." Joseph von Arx showed off his bloody arm again. "It's just a scratch, but it bled like the dickens."

Through chilling rain, they walked north, Caleb hoped, toward Pittsburg Landing, past makeshift hospitals, and stacks of bloody arms and legs, the screams of men hurrying along Caleb and his new partner. Shells burst overhead every few minutes, lighting their path.

Finally they heard laughter, so out of place after all they had been through, and walked down toward the landing. In the dim light from the ships, dark-clad soldiers filed onto the ships as a band triumphantly played "Hail, Columbia."

*It doesn't seem right*, Caleb thought. *Retreating. Men laughing. A band playing.*

He stopped so abruptly, Joseph von Arx continued a few rods before he halted and turned around.

"What's up?" von Arx asked.

Caleb tilted his head toward the ships. "They're not getting on those ships. They're getting off!" A loud cheer shot from his mouth, and he pumped his fist in the air. More Union soldiers, fresh troops.

He caught up with von Arx, and they veered out of the path of a marching group of men in blue uniforms, heard their sergeants barking out commands.

Caleb led his friend toward a tree, where a man sat underneath, lantern at his side, puffing a cigar. Another officer slogged over toward the seated, weary figure.

"Where we going?" von Arx asked.

"Ask one of those officers if they know where we can find our regiment. Or where we should go …" Left unsaid was: *if the Eighteenth has been wiped out.*

Caleb stopped, shivered, realizing who he had intended on

asking for directions.

"Well, Grant," said the slim man with the red beard, "we've had the devil's own day, haven't we?"

Caleb turned, grabbed von Arx's arm, led him back toward the river.

"Yes," he heard General Ulysses S. Grant answer General Cump Sherman. "Lick 'em tomorrow, though."

\* \* \* \* \*

They waited for another company of infantry to pass, then moved toward some fires along the riverbank.

A gruff major stopped them, spitting tobacco juice between their legs, waving a lantern in their faces. "Where are you heading?" the major asked. Rain water poured off his bummer cap, and the lantern hissed as drops splattered down its chimney and along the sides of the glass.

"Trying to find the Eighteenth Missouri Infantry," Joseph von Arx answered.

"The Eighteenth? Those who aren't dead are prisoners," he said. "C'mon. You've just been conscripted into the Fifty-Third Ohio." He started to turn, stopped, and held the lantern closer to von Arx. Slowly the major removed his cigar. "Not you, boy. You take that arm onto that ship." The cigar pointed. "Let a doctor look at it."

Joseph von Arx smiled brightly. "I'll see you around, Cole."

"Take care," Caleb mumbled, and followed the major.

\* \* \* \* \*

Sleeping proved impossible. Torrents of water and mud, mingled with blood, buttons, bits of uniform, locks of hair, unmailed, unopened letters flowed through the trees and brush toward the river. Rain pelted him. He sat all night with a water-logged blanket over his shoulders, hearing men beg for water in the woods behind him, others scream for mercy on the hospital ships on the river. As another regiment disembarked from a ship, a soldier cried out to the new faces, "You're gonna catch regular hell today, boys!" and laughed.

Armed with a Springfield rifle, Caleb rose with the other Buckeyes to a sergeant's command. It remained dark. Caleb didn't care. They filed past a man in an apron, who let each man take a swig of coffee and shove hardtack into his mouth before marching into the woods.

They headed away from the river, marching alongside the new recruits from some other regiment. It was easy to tell the veterans from the reserves, Caleb thought with a mirthless grin. Those who had fought yesterday did not bother to look at the corpses they stepped across. Those who hadn't, gagged, and prayed.

"Keep moving!" a captain growled. "If any of you turn and run, I'll shoot you myself."

Cannon opened the second day of battle. The Fifty-Third Ohio and a reserve regiment exited the woods into a cleared field. Yesterday, a blue line like this would have stretched a thousand yards. Today, it barely reached four hundred.

From the south charged a horde of screaming Rebels, and Caleb realized another change. Yesterday, those ear-piercing shrieks would have caused him to tremble. This morning, he barely even heard the yells.

"Fire!"

The Springfield misfired, its powder likely wet and ruined from last night's deluge. Cursing, Caleb stepped back. An Ohio private dropped beside him, a bullet hole in his chest, and Caleb tossed away his rifle, and grabbed the dead man's, began reloading.

"They're running! The Secesh are running. We've licked them!"

The dark-haired Ohioan standing next to Caleb turned to shout at the reserves: "They'll be back, buck-o. Don't you go counting your chickens quite yet."

Within minutes, the Rebels came charging again. Cannon erupted up and down both lines. The ground seemed to shake, but Caleb steadied his rifle, aimed, fired. He breathed a sigh of relief as the rifle's stock slammed against his bruised shoulder. Stepping back, he withdrew the ramrod, and went to work again.

Again the Rebels retreated. Again they came back across the field. To die.

Slowly the Union line moved, wheeling at an angle, out of the field, into the woods, crossing a road, following a branch that flowed like a raging river.

He stepped over the newly dead, heard Rebs moaning for water, begging for mercy. Bullets clipped the branches. A few thudded into bodies. New recruits wept. Veterans cursed the new recruits.

They stopped, took to their knees, as a lieutenant crawled behind them. "The Secesh are holed up in that camp yonder," he whispered. "That's our camp, boys. A camp that yesterday belonged to a regiment in Grant's army. We're taking it back. We're not going to let a bunch of treason-addled Southern swine keep one of our camps."

The lieutenant crawled on past, repeating his whisper.

The man beside Caleb spit out tobacco juice, and shook his head. He glanced at Caleb, nodded, and said: "Nice knowing you, kid."

Caleb could only nod a farewell back.

Those Rebs weren't stupid. They had piled logs upon logs, forming a fort in front of those tents that had now been ripped apart by Minié balls and grapeshot. Some Union soldiers affixed bayonets on their muskets and rifles, but Caleb had no bayonet. The dark-haired man on Caleb's right drew a long-bladed knife with a D-ring brass handle. Caleb had no knife, either.

"Charge!" the lieutenant yelled, and the Fifty-Third Ohio did its best to imitate that Rebel yell.

A cannon roared from behind the Confederate breastworks, cutting down several charging Federals. Rebel yells drowned out the Union cries. Muskets thundered. A bullet splintered the stock of Caleb's Springfield. He kept running.

Two soldiers on his left pitched forward.

He could make out the Rebel flag fluttering in the breeze.

The cannon spit out grapeshot again.

Caleb lifted his rifle, fired as he ran, only to realize that he was alone. He stopped, turned. A bullet spit mud over his brogans. Another grazed his neck. Behind him, Rebels laughed.

"Keep a-comin', sonny!" one called out. "You're almost here."

A bullet splintered the other side of his rifle's stock.

The Fifty-Third Ohio was running, dropping their weapons, ducking behind trees. With a curse, Caleb hurried after them.

"You disgusting bunch of poltroons!" a captain screamed as Caleb reached the Union line. "Cowards! The lot of you. Exactly as shameful as were your actions yesterday!" He kicked at one sobbing private with peach fuzz on his chin.

Caleb looked around for the dark-haired fellow with the knife, but couldn't find him. A bullet sang over his head, and he turned, saw the Rebels charging.

He reloaded his rifle, aimed, fired. Most of the Buckeyes were running, however, and Caleb methodically reloaded. He and a handful of men, including the captain, fell back in an orderly fashion, stopping, firing, probably keeping the Rebs from overrunning the fleeing cowards of the Fifty-Third, likely saving the regiment—if he could call it a regiment—from annihilation.

When they reached another cleared field, they were met by another Union regiment. Caleb let the new recruits pass, let them whip the Rebs. A few rods ahead, he saw the banner of the Fifty-Third Ohio, some officers and men gathered around it, trying to regroup, reorganize.

Caleb walked in the opposite direction. He was finished with the Fifty-Third. They disgusted him.

* * * * *

He wandered through forests and fields, dead and dying, across destroyed fields and decimated woods. Occasionally he would stop to let a wounded man, Union or Confederate, it mattered not, drink from his canteen. Once he stopped, and held a Reb's hand and told him all about Putnam County, Missouri, until the Reb was dead.

It started raining, but not for long.

Along a rutted road, he fought alongside the Seventy-Seventh Pennsylvania. Just to get the taste of the Fifty-Third Ohio out of his mouth. He also began to notice that he was moving with the Union lines again, and, this time, they were heading south.

During a hard though brief shower, he helped some artillery boys push cannon and caisson through knee-deep mud. The sounds of battle soon faded, and the sun began sinking behind the trees. Smoke and mist hugged the ground like fog.

He was alone now, lost, but he kept walking south.

Caleb stopped, staring at a log building, a wooden cross at the top of the roof. The skies had opened again, and rain fell in spates. Blue-clad soldiers stood in the clearing around the ramshackle old church. One played a jew's-harp. Another sang "John Brown's Body." A few of the men were dancing a jig.

"What's going on?" Caleb asked. His voice surprised him. He hadn't really spoken since talking to that dying Reb about the difference between Poland Chinas and Durocs, Unionville, his parents, and Maryanne Corneilison.

A boy even younger than Caleb grinned. "The Rebs are retreating. We've licked 'em!"

"Caleb!"

He turned, stepped toward the log church. Seb Woolard bolted out of the door, splashing through puddles of water. Caleb dropped his Springfield, embracing Seb Woolard in a hug.

Seb Woolard, who Caleb had despised. Seb Woolard, who had despised Caleb. Seb Woolard, who had turned and run from battle. Tears flowed down both boys' cheeks. They hugged each other tightly, now sobbing, falling onto their knees.

"It's ... so good ... see ..." Seb couldn't finish.

He would never be able to explain it, but Caleb cried, too. It did feel good, Caleb thought, to see Seb Woolard alive ... to see anyone alive ... after those two horrific days.

# CHAPTER TWENTY-TWO

MAY 28–29, 1862
CORINTH, MISSISSIPPI

Sitting on the edge of the cot, Grace Dehner slumped when she saw her reflection in a mirror. Her red-rimmed eyes were sunken, corners marked by crow's feet, her face pale, brow knotted, hair matted with sweat. She looked forty years old, not seventeen. Behind her reflection, she spied the lines of cots, beds, bedrolls filled with men, the slaves scurrying about collecting chamber pots, a handful of doctors kneeling over some patients, and women, including Miss Prudence Caxton—like her, far removed from the comfort of their parlors—tending to the wounded, the dying, the dead.

"Hey, String Bean."

Grace looked away from the mirror and to her right. Seventeen-year-old Johnny James stood in front of her, his face turning sheepish as he stuttered, shifted his feet, and corrected himself. "I ... I ... mean ... uh ... Grace."

He held a gray kepi in his left hand, and wore gray woolen britches, a matching shell jacket, and a wide black belt across his middle with an oval brass buckle stamped CSA. An oblong wooden box was tucked underneath his arm.

"You joined up." Her voice sounded ancient.

"With Bedford Forrest. Cavalry. Get to ride a horse."

Men, her father included, kept bragging about Nathan Bedford Forrest's gallantry, courage, leadership, and horsemanship, but, to Grace, Bedford Forrest would always be a foul, slave-trading scoundrel a thousand times removed from Southern chivalry.

Johnny's smile lost its youthful exuberance. "Well, I figured the South needed … well … I mean … you know …"

All too well she knew. This empty cot said it all.

Awkwardly Johnny James took the box, and offered it to Grace as if he were presenting her a bouquet of roses. "You mama said this come for you. Asked if I'd bring it over." He stared at the label. "Come all the way from Texas."

She found energy, and rose quickly, towering over Johnny James, and accepted the box. It was heavier than she expected.

"Come with me, Johnny," she said, and led Johnny James through the maze of wounded men. She needed to free up that cot, anyway.

Behind her, Johnny James sniggered. "Never thought I'd get to be inside the Corona Female College."

Grace shook her head. Johnny wouldn't find any young ladies learning college arithmetic, reciting Latin, or debating Plutarch's essays. No classes were being held, although Grace certainly was getting an education. Since the slaughter at Shiloh, the Corona Female College had been turned into a hospital ward. So had churches, businesses, and even homes in the city and across northern Mississippi. Once news of the battle spread, doctors had barged into Corinth from New Orleans, Jackson, Natchez, and all the way from Mobile. To lessen Corinth's burden, wounded men had been sent by rail to hospitals in Canton and Columbus, Holly Springs and Memphis, and countless other cities. Instead of shipping cotton, the trains these days carried the horribly maimed, or coffins to be shipped to loved ones back home. Corinth, however, still reeked of the dead and dying.

She and Johnny had to pause to let two slaves carry a corpse down the stairs.

In the room where she had once loathed geography, she found Dr. Kenton Landon bending his long frame over a young Confederate soldier. She hurried to his bedroll.

"How's he doing?" Grace asked.

Dr. Landon straightened. "After a month in bed, I'll dare say that he'll walk. He certainly has been getting excellent medical care. Hello, Master James. You look patriotic, young man."

Grace glanced at Johnny, who didn't look patriotic at all. He looked as if he were about to throw up. Maybe he should have visited the Corona Female College before he joined up with Forrest.

The soldier from Texas sat up, resting his back against the wall. "When do I get out of this pigsty?"

Shaking his head, Dr. Landon muttered, "Ask your doctor," and, winking at Grace, left the room.

"Well?" Ryan McCalla asked.

"Shut up," she snapped. "It's nothing short of a miracle that you still have both your legs. Any other doctor would have sawed that one off, and you'd be getting fitted for a wooden leg right about now."

"Well, I've been walking around," he protested. "You said I had to walk before I could leave. I'm doing that. So when can I leave?"

"Shut up."

His head shook. "That scratch on my head's all cured, now. Only a little scar left, and my leg doesn't ache any more … not much. What I'm saying, Miss Grace, is that I'm no good to the Second Texas stuck up in this …" He shuddered.

She couldn't blame him for wanting to get out of here. She threw up every morning in the privy just thinking about what waited for her up on College Hill. Her mother and father insisted that she stay away from that place, but if Miss Prudence Caxton could handle it, then, criminy, so could Grace Prudence. Besides, Dr. Landon needed her.

"Are all Texians as stubborn as you are?" she asked.

That did it. Ryan McCalla smiled. "I reckon," he said.

She hooked a thumb behind her. "This is Johnny James. He's a friend of mine since we were kids. He just joined Forrest's night riders."

"We're not night riders, String Bean. We're cavalry."

"Johnny, this is Ryan McCalla. He's from Cedar Bayou, Texas."

Johnny James started forward, but Ryan McCalla stopped him. He pulled himself to his feet, grimacing, and took four steps before shaking Johnny's hand. He kept standing, too, defying Grace to order him back to his place.

Instead, she handed him the package. "This came for you."

He held it awkwardly, before a wicked grin stretched across his face. "Thanks," he said, "*String Bean.*"

She made a promise that if Yankees didn't kill Johnny James, she would.

Johnny James must have felt her wrath. "Well, I best be going." He pulled on his kepi, and shook Ryan's hand again. "I'll call on you before we ride out, Grace," he said, "if you don't object."

She didn't answer.

Ryan pushed away the straw and sawdust, knowing what it was before he even pulled out the duck wrapping. He set it aside on his pillow, and fumbled with the letter. Grace had to open it for him, and she handed him the paper that smelled of perfume. She fought down jealousy, which surprised her. When he started reading, however, she relaxed.

"'My Dearest Son. We praise God that you have been delivered, and hope you will return home to us soon.'"

He lowered the letter.

"I'll go," she said.

"No. Stay."

"You don't have to read it out loud."

"But I want to."

"'Mrs. Dehner has been so kind to mail your note. I pray that your hands are healing and that you will be able to write us soon. Your nurse swears that is the case.'"

Ryan stared at her, not a glare, but rather a bemused look. With a shrug, she grinned.

"'Ryan, God favors us. We have received word that young Sam Houston Jr. was not killed during that awful battle on the banks of the Tennessee River as was originally reported by Captain Ashbel Smith.'"

He let out a sigh of relief. "Sam's alive!" he shouted to Grace, and her smile came as genuine as Ryan McCalla's. She did not know who Sam Houston Jr. was, but she was happy that he had survived the bloodletting at Shiloh. McCalla kept reading.

"'Gravely injured he was, but he lives. He was sent to a prison camp in Chicago or some Northern city. A Union chaplain found young Sam on the battlefield, and Sam handed him his Bible and asked that it be sent to his home. Poor soul, he thought he was dying.

"'By God's grace, the kind chaplain saw Governor Sam Houston's name (I know, Ryan, that Houston no longer serves as our governor, but he shall always command my respect and honor, and while your father strongly disagrees with Houston's sentiments, I will never forget all that he has done for our family, and our state!). Well, as I was saying, the chaplain commanded a surgeon to assist, and Sam Jr. was saved.

"'He is recovering in the North, and, writes Governor Houston, he will be sent home as soon as he is able to travel.

"'It is our dearest wish that you too will be furloughed to return to Cedar Bayou and regain your health. In the meanwhile, your nurse has said that you would like your violin returned, so I ship it to you, with a warm kiss, and devout prayer that it reach you safely in Mississippi.

"'God be kind to you. He has been most kind to me for delivering you from battle.

"'How is Matt Bryson doing? We have received no word of him, and his father asked me to see what news you could relate back to us.'"

He folded the letter, unable to finish. Making himself smile, he looked at Grace and asked: "*Missus* Dehner?"

She didn't blush. "A married nurse, I figured, commands more respect."

"I see."

He didn't. Well, she didn't, either.

"How did you know about the violin?"

She grinned again. "You talked a lot ... you were so wracked with fever ... when you first arrived. When I figured you wouldn't die, I just decided ..." Another shrug. "Would you play?"

Ryan set the letter aside. He drew the case from the duck wrapping, his fingers trembling, then slowly unlatched the sides and opened the case.

"It's beautiful," she said, gasping.

His fingers plucked a string. "My father said it sounded like one made when Columbus was sailing for America." Shaking his head, he laughed. "Like he would know how a good musical instrument is supposed to sound. A guy named Miremont made it. He's French. Papa bought it at the New York Crystal Palace nine years ago." His arms shook as he withdrew the violin. He found the bow.

Grace's heart beat rapidly. Ryan McCalla had been her second patient. The first had died, and she swore that this young man would not. That had been a desperate struggle, his leg infected as it had been. One doctor, a cynical cad from New Orleans, had said Ryan should be sent to the hopeless ward. When another had suggested immediate amputation, the New Orleans man had scoffed and said: "Why bother?"

Dr. Landon, however, must have read something in Grace's face, seen the tears in her eyes, for he had stepped forward and announced: "Gentlemen, he is my patient, and I will see him walk out of this place on his own two legs."

A song came from across the hall, and she cringed. She didn't like that song, but every soldier around Corinth was singing it these days.

Tucking the violin under his chin, Ryan McCalla waited until they finished the verse. When they repeated the verse, he stretched the bow across the strings, and played.

*I'll put my knapsack on my back,*
*My rifle on my shoulder.*
*I'm goin' away to Shiloh,*
*And there I'll be a soldier.*

A legless man three cots over laughed. Another man joined in the song. Ryan's toes tapped as he played, and, no matter how much she disliked the song, Grace Dehner smiled. She could never figure out why every soldier in the South had to sing either a happy war song or a sad love song.

He stopped suddenly, although the men in the room and across the hall kept singing. Ryan lowered the fiddle, and stepped around Grace. "Hello, Sergeant."

"Corporal McCalla," came a gruff voice, and Grace turned, frowning.

She hadn't met one sergeant she cared for.

"This is my nurse," Ryan said excitedly. "Miss Grace, this is Sergeant Rutherford. Weren't for him, I'd be buried up in Tennessee."

Well, maybe she'd make an exception for this barrel-chested, bearded man.

Sergeant Rutherford grunted something that might have been a hello, and Grace realized she had better go.

"Sergeant! Hey!" Ryan McCalla sounded like an excited twelve-year-old on his birthday. "Hey, Little Sam isn't dead. I got a letter from my mother, and she says …"

Grace walked out, down the stairs, leaving the noise of that song behind her. A clock began to chime, telling her it was time to go home. She stepped outside into the blast furnace, and made her way from the Corona Female College.

Dust blew in her eyes. More than a month ago, the streets of Corinth had been a mud bog; now water was scarce. Eighty thousand Confederates had crammed into the city, and most of them were sick. Those who had been fortunate enough to escape the carnage at Shiloh were now being felled by dysentery. Even those who were well looked broken-hearted.

It was a matter of time, people kept saying, before the Yankees resumed the fight. Before General Grant, or whoever was commanding the Northern troops, turned Corinth into a Shiloh.

Locomotives belched smoke at the depot, and Southern officers belted out orders, sending white men and slaves running around like ants.

She stopped at the Waldron Street Christian Church to pray, and to get the wretched smell of death, of disease, of the stink of stagnant water from Dismal Swamp out of her nostrils. Afterward, she hurried home.

* * * * *

Thursday morning found her throwing up in the privy, wiping her mouth, then walking back to the college over her parents' protests.

"Grace," her mother called, "we must pack! We are leaving today. General Hardee insists ..."

The words meant nothing to her. She didn't answer; she had to go to the hospital. Hospital. Not college.

Town surprised her. Men frantically escorted their wives to the depot. Slaves, already sweating in the miserable heat, carried trunks. Children cried. It wasn't just civilians at the railroad station, either. A train pulled out carrying cheering Confederate soldiers. She didn't understand any of this, and hoped she'd never understand war.

Once inside the college, she changed into a frock, put a bonnet over her hair, and hurried upstairs, hoping to hear fiddle music. Or was it a violin? She'd have to ask Dr. Landon.

In the geography room, she stopped at the door, and gasped, bringing her hand to her mouth, thinking she might throw up again. The bedroll was empty.

"No," she choked out, but quickly lowered her hand.

Ryan McCalla wasn't dead. She spotted the case on his bedroll, and sat down beside it, picking up the note.

"He left late last night, young lady," the legless man said. His voice broke into sobs. "And if them blue devils hadn't taken away my limbs, I would have gone with him."

Grace unfolded the note, feeling tears stream down her cheeks.


Mrs. Grace:

We are pulling out. I must rejoin my regiment. I cannot thank you enough. I know I would be dead were it not for your kindness and compassion and that mule-head of yours. Ha. Ha. Please take care of the Miremont for me. I sha'n't have much use for it where I go.

Good luck. God's will be done, I might come back for it someday. Until then, I remain

Your obt servant,

Ryan McCalla

Corporal, Second Texas

Infantry, CSA

# CHAPTER
# TWENTY-THREE

JUNE 7, 1862
CORINTH, MISSISSIPPI

Colonel Miller was a prisoner of war. Captain Clark was dead, joining Folker, the Masterson cousins, countless others. No one knew what had happened to Rémy Ehrenreich, but they assumed he had been captured. A few men suggested that he had deserted, but Caleb Cole knew better. Rémy was on his way south with Madison Miller, and most survivors of what soldiers were calling the Hornet's Nest. Or, he, too, was dead.

A few weeks back, Caleb had overheard that Private Joseph von Arx, that kid so happy to show off the scratch in his arm, had died of blood poisoning somewhere in Illinois. Caleb thanked God that the cut on his hand had not become infected.

Three hundred Missourians from the Eighteenth had survived the bloodletting at what the Union Army called the Battle of Pittsburg Landing. Newspapers had other terms for it: NEAR-DISASTER ... A PERFECT SLAUGHTER ... THAT DRUNKARD'S FOLLY ... It hardly sounded like a hard-earned Northern victory.

General Henry Halleck had assumed command of Grant's forces, and had continued the drive south, slowly, methodically, with so much caution, Caleb figured, had Halleck been in charge at Pittsburg Landing, there would be no more army of the Tennessee.

For weeks after the battle, they would march a few hundred yards, then dig rifle pits, throw up earthen breastworks, wait, wait, wait.

Maybe all that caution had paid off. After all, here stood Caleb, in Corinth, Mississippi.

The Rebs had sneaked off. Maybe Halleck had wanted them to get away, so he wouldn't have to fight them. Most of the residents had gone, too, leaving behind only doctors, nurses, and the most grievously wounded Confederates.

The Eighteenth made camp on the grounds of something called the Corona Female College, and Caleb helped ease Seb Woolard onto his bedroll. There were no tents any more. The tents of the Eighteenth Missouri had been left back at Pittsburg Landing, filled with bullet holes, destroyed by artillery shells, or trampled in the muck. He used his own blanket to cover the shivering boy.

"Want some water?" Caleb asked, uncorking his canteen.

"I can't swallow." Seb struggled to speak those three words, and Caleb barely understood him. Seb squeezed his eyes shut, biting back pain. "My ears ache something fierce, Caleb." Caleb put the back of his hand against Seb's forehead. He was burning up.

"I'll get the surgeon." Caleb rose.

"No!"

Caleb heard that, all right. He squatted beside Seb again. He couldn't blame Seb for that. The Army had sent to the Eighteenth a contract surgeon to take care of the wounded. So far, the sawbones had procured all the morphine for himself and, now that the drug had worn off, was busy consuming all of the alcohol allocated for the Eighteenth Missouri's surgical needs.

"Just let me die, Caleb."

"You're not going to die," Caleb said. "You can't die." There was no one else left.

Behind him came the curse and sigh, and, as Caleb turned, he saw a ragged, long-legged girl—yes, a girl, who almost matched Caleb's height, and towered over just about anyone he'd ever known—stepping off the cobblestone path and approaching them. She set a black satchel into the burned-up grass, and pulled down the blanket Caleb had stretched over Seb. Leaning down, she let her long fingers work around Seb's throat.

"How long has this been going on?" she asked. Seb looked almost as shocked as Caleb must have. He tried to answer, but his voice was gone.

"Are you a doctor?" Caleb asked.

She turned, her face harder than anything Caleb had seen since Pittsburg Landing.

"I'm assistant to Doctor Kenton Landon, the finest surgeon ever to leave the Thames River and the greatest medical mind in Tishomingo County. Surely you've heard of him, or are all you Yankees ignorant?"

"Yes, ma'am." It was all Caleb could think to say.

She started to say something, but a smile cracked her façade, and she went back to examining Seb. Caleb realized what had made her grin. *Yes, I've heard of Doctor Landon*, or, *Yes, all of us Yankees are ignorant.*

"He has a high fever. Lost his voice. Suffering from chills, and his jaw and throat are tender. Can't swallow, can he?"

"No, ma'am."

"What else?"

Caleb thought. "He has complained of headaches, and his ears have been hurting him, too."

"That figures."

A minute passed. Then another.

"What is it that ails him?" Caleb asked as she reached into her satchel.

"Well, it isn't cholelithiasis."

"Oh." He blinked. *That must be good.*

"My guess is quinsy."

Which didn't sound as awful as cholelithiasis.

She snapped the satchel shut. She hadn't pulled anything out, and slowly rose. "Tonsils have swollen."

Caleb grimaced. "Will you have to cut them out?"

"Doctor Landon is likely too busy with more serious ailments, especially considering this boy's an armed invader in our home. I'd recommend gargling with chlorate of potassium, but we don't have that. No quinine. No morphine, either."

Caleb snorted in contempt. "We don't, either. Surgeon used it all for himself."

Her face changed, and the tension in her body was released. Shaking her head, she stretched out a long arm, and it took a moment for Caleb to realize she was asking him to help her to her feet. He moved quickly, awkwardly, and pulled her up.

She brushed the dead grass off her wrinkled skirt, pushed sweaty bangs off her forehead, and said, her voice softer now: "Take a flannel cloth, soak it in hot water, wring it out, put it on his throat. I'll ask Doctor Landon if he knows of a poultice that might help. Meanwhile, have him breathe in some steam."

"Steam?"

"You know how to boil water, don't you?" The edge returned.

"Yes, ma'am. Sorry, ma'am."

She picked up her bag, and started away. "He must be a good friend of yours."

The snigger escaped Caleb's throat before he could stop it, and that made her turn. Their eyes locked, and he shrugged, embarrassed. "I just don't want to see anyone else die."

He didn't know what he had said. Certainly he didn't mean to make her cry, but she was sobbing now, knees bending, sinking to the earth, lifting her head and letting out a piteous wail. Nearby Missourians turned to stare, and Caleb rushed to her. He hesitated, then reached out. He mouthed, "Ma'am," but couldn't say anything. Didn't want to upset her even more. At last he kneeled in front of her, and felt her lean into him, drenching his shoulder in tears and snot. She wrapped her arms around him, squeezed.

Behind him, he heard Corporal Vaughn say something rude, and Caleb vowed he'd make that Weston brigand eat those words. Just as suddenly as the dam had burst, the tears stopped, and she pushed him away, mumbling something, scrambling to her feet, wiping away the tears, leaving bits of dead grass on her cheeks.

"Just do what I say," she said, "and maybe your friend will be all right in a few days." She started running to the deserted town.

Caleb caught up with her before she was off the campus.

"You forgot your bag, ma'am."

"Stop calling me ma'am. I'm seventeen years old."

"I just turned seventeen myself." He tried to think of when.

"Good for you. I'll be eighteen in August."

"You want your bag, ma- ... uh ... well, what should I call you?"

"The name's Grace Dehner."

"I'm Caleb Cole."

"That's alliterate."

"No, ma'am," he said, angrily. "I'm not like Seb Woolard. I can read and write."

She stopped, turned, and laughed. "Are all you Yankees so dense?"

He tried to smile at her, and shrugged, realizing his misunderstanding of her Southern accent. He held up her black bag, and her eyes hardened once again, and she snatched it.

"Give me that!"

From inside came a strange sound. Not medicine bottles rattling, but rather an out-of-tune musical note.

"I was bringing it to you," he protested.

"Well, thanks."

It was his turn to get angry. "What riles you so? I was bringing you that grip. You left it behind. And I didn't ask you to look in on Seb. I didn't ask to be here. I was supposed to be keeping Missouri safe and in the Union. I didn't do anything to you, lady."

"Didn't you?" She pointed. "This was my home, Caleb Cole. Look at it now. My parents have gone. Miss Prudence even left. Doctor Landon now finds himself treating sick Yankees as well as dying Southern men. Look around you, Caleb Cole. This was a vibrant city, full of laughter. I used to race Johnny James down this street, and I beat him every time. Now he's gone off to fight. So don't tell me this is none of your doing. You're a Yankee."

"Like I said, Miss Dehner. I didn't ask to be here. I wish to Sam Hill I was slopping hogs back in Putnam County."

He had taken five steps when she called out his name. He turned, half expecting to find her pointing a Derringer at him, but, instead, she tilted her head toward town.

"Walk me home, Mister Cole?" Not an order, but a suggestion. That woman had more moods than she was tall.

* * * * *

"This is where you live?"

The brick two-story looked practically deserted. It took a moment before he realized it was a church.

"Where do you expect me to live? In that contraband camp?"

"How about a home?" He could be just as feisty.

"It burned down. When our Army was evacuating."

"I'm sorry." He meant it, too.

She climbed the steps, pushed open the door, and went inside, lighting a candle. Reluctantly he followed her, and, inside, she put the bag on a pew, unfastened it, and pulled out a ...

"Fiddle?" He shook his head.

"A Miremont," she corrected. She offered it to him.

"Ma'am, I can't even play a jew's-harp. Now, I can call pigs, but I can't carry a tune."

"It's all right. I just want you to see it, hold it."

He took it, his thumb accidentally striking one of the strings, the note echoing in the cavernous church.

"It's ..." He let out a breath. "It's beautiful."

"It is." Her voice sounded different. He looked at her. "It belongs to a corporal in the Second Texas Infantry. His name is Ryan McCalla. I just wanted you to see it, touch it, so the next time you find yourself in a battle, you think about that beautiful instrument, and you think about who you're fighting. Because he's no different than you, Caleb Cole. That's what I wanted you to see. Thanks for walking me home. I'll check on your friend tomorrow."

He handed her the violin, tipped his hat, and shook his head. "Miss Grace," he said, "your beau that plays that fiddle ..."

"He's not my beau, mister!"

"Sorry, ma'am ... uh ... Miss Grace. That fellow is different than me. Because if he can play that instrument, he's a better man that I am. Thanks for your hospitality. I'm sorry to have been a burden to you."

He was at the door when he stopped, slowly comprehending what the young woman had just told him. He turned so quickly, he startled her, and she was balling a fist, preparing for the worst.

Instead, Caleb asked meekly: "Ma'am, what did you say that Reb's name was?"

# CHAPTER
# TWENTY-FOUR

SEPTEMBER 3, 1862
TUPELO, MISSISSIPPI

The bugle sounded, as Ryan knew it would. All that night, he had been unable to sleep, but now glumly he tossed off his blanket, pulled on his boots and hat, and joined the silent procession.

His limp was gone, his thigh rarely even aching these days, but that was to be expected. Shiloh seemed like an eternity ago. On May 29, he had pulled out of Corinth with the rest of the Second Texas, moving forty miles south along the Mobile & Ohio Railway. With Colonel Moore promoted to general, William Rogers had assumed command of the Second, and Captain Ashbel Smith had been promoted to lieutenant colonel. After a corporal from Company B had painted SHILOH onto the regiment's battle flag, they had resumed those mundane drills, finally moving to Tupelo, and had sent Lieutenant Colonel Smith back to Texas in search of conscripts to fill a void.

And they had been branded cowards.

That irked everyone in the regiment. Matt Bryson and scores more had died. Little Sam Houston, Gibb Gideon, and many more were prisoners. Colonel Smith, Ryan, and just about anyone who had taken part in that battle now wore scars from those two days. They had given their all, and the only reason they had broken and run on that second awful day at Shiloh was because of stupid orders, coupled with a murderous spray of grapeshot, Minié balls, and canister. The Yanks had fresh troops. The Confederates had none, and Albert Sidney Johnston had been killed on the afternoon of the first day. Newspaper reports, however, labeled the Second a blight on the late General Johnston's glorious record. Newspaper reporters, Ryan thought with contempt, wrote from second- and third-hand reports from the comfort of their Houston offices seven hundred miles from the bloody banks of the Tennessee River. Colonel Rogers swore he would prove the Second Texas' bravery to the world.

The first step would be to execute a coward and a deserter.

It made Ryan sick, but he followed Sergeant Rutherford and the rest of the regiment to the open field, forming a square, the head open where a grave had already been dug and a post set in the ground. What was left of Company C faced Company A. For an eternity, they waited until a fife began playing a dirge, and a drum tapped out a solemn rhythm. Four men from Company D carried the coffin, the condemned prisoner, sobbing, marching behind it. Bringing up the rear came the chaplain, fifer and drummer, and then twelve men, their shouldered muskets capped and loaded.

When they reached the grave, the coffin was placed on the ground, and the prisoner sat on top of it. The preacher prayed, the lieutenant got the firing squad ready, while Colonel Rogers and the Second waited.

For thirty minutes.

"This isn't right, Sergeant," Ryan heard himself whispering bitterly, and, to his surprise, the sergeant answered: "No, it's not, McCalla."

Ryan pressed his luck. "He's not a coward."

"But he is a deserter."

He started to say more, but Ryan stopped. There was nothing he could do to save Harry Cravey, who had joined the Second—no, it wasn't even the Second when he had enlisted—with the understanding that he would stay in Texas, defend the Lone Star State against Yankee invaders. Baby Cravey had never dreamed he would be shipped off to Mississippi and ordered to fight in Tennessee.

Two weeks ago—five months after the Shiloh disaster—some of Bedford Forrest's scouts had found Cravey, half starved, sobbing, and wearing rags, hiding in a hayloft at a farm this side of Vicksburg.

At last, on Colonel Rogers' orders, Harry Cravey was told to stand, but his legs wouldn't work, so the chaplain, provost marshal, and fifer and drummer had to help him. His arms were bound behind the post. The provost marshal said something, the chaplain prayed again, and Colonel Rogers placed a blindfold over Cravey's eyes.

Cravey wailed.

"Ready."

Ryan closed his eyes.

"Aim."

He mouthed a prayer.

"Fire!"

Ryan's body jerked at the crash of the muskets, and, eyes squeezed shut, he heard Baby Cravey cry out: "Oh, oh, Lord, oh!"

When he looked up, he saw Cravey, head dropped, held upright by the ropes and the post, his white shirt stained crimson. Colonel Rogers had each company march past the dead boy on their way back to camp.

It was there that Ryan saw Gibb Gideon.

Dressed like some tatterdemalion, Gideon slapped a weathered, miserable rag for a hat against his thigh, and raced ahead. Sergeant Rutherford hugged him, then Ryan got to embrace the foul-smelling Texian, and the rest of Company C whooped and hollered and slapped the filthy Gideon on his back.

"You old coot!" Rutherford said. "I thought you were captured."

Corporal McGilloway tossed Gideon a brown clay jug.

"I was!" Gideon pulled the hat back on his head, and took a slug from the jug. "We got exchanged." He coughed as the liquor exploded, shook his head, grinned, and took another pull. "Took me forever to find you boys." He coughed again.

"Is Little Sam with you?" Ryan asked.

"No. Was he caught, too?"

Ryan nodded. "And wounded. They sent him to some place called Camp Douglas near Chicago. I guess Sam's back home with his folks in Huntsville now."

"I was in Alton, Illinois." Gideon stoppered the jug, and handed it back to Corporal McGilloway. "Least, that's what the Yanks told me. Never want to go back there again. They exchanged me and five other fellows in July, but I had the dickens of a time finding you boys."

"We're glad you did," Sergeant Rutherford said.

"Looks like I missed a good show." Gibb Gideon abruptly ended the joyous reunion. "What?" Gibb took a step back. "What did I say?"

Ryan knew he couldn't answer, and Rutherford struggled with the words. "It …" he began, but then Lieutenant Woodall was spitting out orders, and Ryan started reaching for his knapsack and musket.

"Thunderation," Gideon said, "I just got here."

Rutherford no longer showed any familiarity. He started growling at the remnants of Company C.

"You heard the lieutenant. Come on, you miserable petticoats. We're moving out."

# CHAPTER TWENTY-FIVE

Memphis had surrendered. The Confederates had abandoned Fort Pillow. Southern armies had retaken Baton Rouge, and whipped the Yankees at Manassas, Virginia, for a second time, but reports were trickling in of a slaughter of troops at some town in Maryland. No one seemed to know yet whether the Confederates or bluecoats had won the battle, and Grace Dehner really didn't care. Closer to home, less than a week ago, Grant's Army had driven back a Confederate attack at Iuka, a small railroad town on the Memphis & Chattanooga line just a few miles north.

Grace wondered if Ryan McCalla had taken part in the fight at Iuka. Wondered if he were still alive.

Standing on Waldron Street, she stared at what remained of the church she had called home since June. Yankees had dismantled the brick walls to build ovens for baking bread. All that remained of the church was a shell, and those wooden frames were slowly being torn down for firewood.

Yankees—at least those not sick from heat and disease—ate well. Grace was living off seed-tick coffee and dandyfunk, a stew of salt pork, molasses, and hardtack. She had to barter with the bluebelly webfeet, those infantry troopers like that Missourian named Caleb

Cole, for the hardtack and salt pork. Well, she never had to barter with Caleb. He wouldn't take anything. Not that she had much to offer.

The battle at Iuka had sparked the Yankees to stop lying around, sweating in the heat. Realizing the Rebels still had fight left in them, they had begun to erect fortifications, building earthen breastworks and redoubts. Slaves worked alongside the bluecoats, but even the former slaves, who had set up a contraband camp on the woods at the edge of town, had grown weary of the Yankee presence.

Tightly gripping the black satchel that held Ryan McCalla's precious violin, she turned away from the church and wandered down Waldron Street.

Most of the Southern wounded had either recovered and been sent to Northern prison camps or had died, but that would likely change. Dr. Landon had gone to Iuka with two other surgeons to care for Rebels and Yankees wounded there. She didn't know when he would return, even if he would return. Why would anybody return to this squalid place?

Corinth stank. The temperatures no longer topped one hundred degrees in the afternoon, but ninety degrees proved miserable enough, and the air remained thick with dirt and dust. She couldn't remember the last time it had rained. Creeks had turned into sand, and so had a number of wells. Mosquitoes, however, still thrived ... somehow. So did horseflies. One buzzed her neck as she made her way to the Corona Female College.

That had changed, too.

With most of the Southern wounded gone, Yankees had turned it into their hospital, treating the myriad felled by dysentery, diarrhea, and various swamp fevers.

From the campus, she could see one of the Union fortifications atop the hill to the south. The Yankees called it Battery Tanrath. It was three hundred yards west of Battery Lathrop. North of the college stood Battery Phillips, and beyond that the Yanks and slaves were constructing Battery Williams on a knoll south of the Memphis

and Charleston rails. Across those rails, maybe seven hundred yards
west of town, towered Battery Robinett. The Yanks were moving
in twenty-pound Parrott guns, siege cannon, or so she had heard
in passing. She knew the names, but not who Tanrath, Lathrop,
Phillips, Williams, and Robinett were. Dead soldiers, she figured.
Heroes to the Northern cause.

She stopped, the notes of a banjo coming to her, hearing a
Yankee version of a Southern song.

> *I'll put my knapsack on my back,*
> *My rifle on my shoulder.*
> *I'm going to Pittsburg Landing,*
> *And there I'll be a soldier.*

"Miss Grace!"

She turned, smiling as Caleb Cole ran toward her, hat in hand.
He stopped, out of breath, and nodded.

"Mister Cole," she said.

"I've been … looking for you."

"You found me."

After he put on his hat, he reached inside his blouse and pulled
out several items. "We're pulling out, ma'am. I was hoping you
might … keep these … for me."

She set the satchel at her feet, and awkwardly accepted his
offerings. "Where are you …?"

"Oh, like as not we'll just be repairing train tracks the Rebs keep
tearing up. It's not like they'll ever let the Eighteenth Missouri fight
any more. General Roscrans seems to have forgotten all about us.
But, well, after Iuka …" He swallowed. "I'd just be obliged if you'd
keep these for me."

She saw a letter addressed to a Miss Maryanne Corneilison,
another addressed to Mrs. Ethel Cole. She fought back a tear,
remembering walking around the depot back in April with a wicker

basket, accepting letters from Rebel soldiers about to march north to the Tennessee River. She saw a Bible underneath the letters.

"Caleb," she began.

"It's not a family Bible," he said. "A sky pilot gave it to me in Saint Louis. Mama wanted me to take our Bible with me, but I told her I couldn't do that, that I'd get one. But … well … it's just this feeling I got."

"You want me to mail these letters."

His face froze. His Adam's apple bobbed. She knew before he tried to explain. "Not right yet, ma'am. Only …" He smiled.

"I understand." The words took all the effort she could muster.

Almost devoutly she opened the satchel, and put Bible and letters beside the Miremont's case. There was another item, and she held it up, shooting Caleb a quizzical stare.

"Oh, that." Grinning, he reached down and took it from her. "That was a gift. I reckon I'd best keep it."

"I didn't know you chewed tobacco, Caleb Cole."

He stuffed the plug back inside his coat pocket. "I'll be back, Miss Grace. God's will be done, I'll …"

She came to her feet and kissed him before he could finish. The fool Yankee would never know how much he and Ryan McCalla were alike. He staggered back, and before he could return her kiss, she had turned, grabbed the satchel, and hurried back toward town.

# CHAPTER TWENTY-SIX

OCTOBER 3, 1862
CORINTH, MISSISSIPPI

For days, since settling into rifle pits they had dug two miles north of Corinth, they had been expecting a fight. Scouts and couriers galloped through the thickly wooded hills. Trains had all but stopped running. Officers kept reminding the soldiers to "Keep a sharp look-out," or "Fortify your position." All that night, Caleb Cole had clutched his rifle, listening to his heartbeat, his stomach growl. It had been so quiet he could have sworn he could have heard his own sweat dripping off his chin.

The silence was awful.

It ended at dawn.

Cannon blasted in rapid succession, shattering the stillness. Caleb shot to his feet, pulling back the hammer of his rifle, hearing Seb Woolard do the same.

They waited for orders, which never came.

Rebels pored through the woods, engaging Federal troops. Cheers ran up and down the rifle pits, but no shots were fired. The boys in blue stopped the gray assault, but not for long. Too many more Rebs came forward, piercing the woods with that terrifying scream. Union soldiers blew up the bridge over Cane Creek, yet even that couldn't stop the Rebs.

"Sergeant Master—" Seb Woolard stopped. "Oh …" His voice trailed off as he remembered Sergeant Masterson had died months ago at Pittsburg Landing. "Caleb, what do we do?"

Caleb could answer only with a sigh.

Finally Jake Ault began barking orders. "Come on, Missouri lads. We're pulling back."

It wasn't the order the Eighteenth expected.

"Dang, Capt'n!" someone cried. "Them Secesh will just shoot us in the back!"

Seb was already moving, and Caleb followed, half expecting a bullet to pierce his heart. He could hear lead balls slamming into trees, could make out a few prayers. They reached Corinth, stopping only to let teams of mules pulling cannon and caisson pass, then let a platoon of cheering Wisconsin recruits hurry to try to thwart the Confederate tide.

Pass Battery Robinett, finally pausing briefly at the Memphis & Charleston rails. Officers yelled at other officers. Enlisted men stood, sweating, shaking. Caleb stared across the street. A house was burning, and no one tried to put it out. A shell burst in the woods a quarter mile from the depot. He found himself looking for a tall girl in the streets only to see soldiers in blue running pell-mell in various directions.

"Heaven help us."

The voice caused Caleb to turn. Seb Woolard caught his breath, and Caleb took a step back to let litter bearers rush the wounded through, their screams piercing his already pricked nerves.

"Eighteenth Missouri!" came the command. "Follow me, boys."

Double-quick time, they hurried. A shell exploded, flinging Caleb to the ground, peppering him with dirt and twigs. For a moment his ears rang, and he sat up, shaking his head, spitting out sand. A moment later, he heard the wails of his fellow Missourians. He smelled blood, manure, death.

A hand pulled him to his feet. "Come on, Caleb!" Seb Woolard said, and Caleb, legs still wobbly, somehow managed to follow Woolard through the smoke up a ridge, finally dropping into rifle pits.

"What do we do?" Seb yelled at a passing sergeant, who did not stop to answer.

"You keep your head down," came a weary reply from a dirty Wisconsin private. "If you want to live."

* * * * *

Hugging the earthen walls, listening to Minié balls pass overhead, they waited. Behind them, Union artillery answered Confederate charges, shaking the ground, loosening the dirt above Caleb's head.

An hour passed. Then two. Caleb moved only his legs to keep them from going to sleep. Two Missourians had gotten overly curious, and dared to peek over the rifle pits. Uncle Bill Smith had caught a bullet in his mouth. Harley Greene had been shot through his left eye. Their bodies remained where they had fallen.

At 3:00 p.m. new orders came, and Caleb pushed himself to his feet, keeping his head down below the dirt fortification. "We're moving back," came a whispered command.

Someone answered the order with a barrage of profanity. "Is that all we get to do? Run away?"

Caleb understood that feeling. Lowering the hammer on his rifle, he realized he had not fired one shot all day.

"Let's go, Missouri!" came a cry, and they climbed out of the pits, started running toward Battery Robinett.

He couldn't see the sun. Wasn't sure if it was sinking behind the forests or just obscured by smoke. Lead sang over his head. Then he heard those sounds.

*Thud. Thud.*

*Thud.*

A corporal next to him pitched into the dirt. Seb Woolard

swore. He leaped over a dead body. Another.

*Thud.*

*Thud.*

Grapeshot tore through the ranks. The Rebs had gotten that close. Men screamed. Caleb spotted flashes from the siege guns inside Battery Robinett, felt the ground trembling like an earthquake.

*Thud.*

"Caleb!"

He stopped, turned, let a bloody Missourian stumble on, then ran to Seb Woolard. As Caleb dropped his rifle, a Rebel ball tore off his hat. He reached forward, rolled Seb Woolard on his back.

"Oh, Lordy, just look at me." Seb bent his head, shook it, lay down, and spit out a mist of pink froth. "My shirt's ruint, Caleb. Oh, Lordy, if I could just have a clean shirt. I'd feel a mite better if only I had on a clean shirt."

Seb Woolard, farmer, thief, and coward, had likely never owned a clean shirt.

A bullet plowed through the dirt that separated Caleb and Seb. He slung off his knapsack. Rummaging, dropping socks into the dirt, tin plate and cup, razor (which he had never used), he finally located the muslin shirt rolled into a ball. He moved closer to Seb.

"Here you go," he started, but Seb Woolard couldn't hear him.

Anguish roared out of his mouth. Groping, he found his rifle, turned, cocking it as he brought the stock to his shoulder. He felt the kick, smelled the smoke. Dropped the rifle, picked up Seb's, and left him in the dirt, a muslin shirt atop his cold face like a shroud.

Nightmarish memories flashed before him. Hiding in that pigpen, swearing how he would never hide again. Faces of Sergeant Masterson, Boone Masterson, Captain Clark, Uncle Bill Smith, Folker, the Ehrenreich twins, Seb Woolard, all those others dead, wounded, captured. Seb Woolard's rifle boomed. Caleb stopped, reloaded, backing up, trying to remember all those commands and drills. He might die today, figured he would, but he sure wouldn't catch a bullet through his shoulder blades running from a bunch of Secesh.

He was climbing up Battery Robinett, saw an artillery major reaching down to help him up the last few steps. Their hands locked. He stood on the top.

And felt the bullet slam into his chest.

# CHAPTER TWENTY-SEVEN

She awoke freezing and shaking to the deafening roar of Yankee and Confederate cannon. Yesterday had been like stepping inside a blast furnace, but the predawn hours of Saturday had turned bitterly cold. Grace Dehner had slept in her clothes. She pulled a blanket off the bed and draped it over her shivering body. After lighting a candle, she moved out of the bedroom and descended the stairs of Miss Prudence Caxton's house on Fillmore Street.

Musketry began accenting the roaring artillery. Her hand slid across the balustrade, and she caught a breath as her pathetic little candle illuminated the first floor of the home. Most of Miss Prudence's stained-glass windows had been shattered, probably from the concussions of artillery rather than Minié balls. Another match flared, lighting another wick. Then another as the guests in Miss Prudence's abandoned home began to stir. She had to be careful where she stepped, maneuvering around the forms of sleeping slave children before she slid into the family parlor.

There familiar smells greeted her. Alcohol and quinine, blood and bourbon, vomit and human waste.

The Yankee surgeon—she hadn't caught his name, or had already forgotten it—lay asleep on Miss Prudence's divan. She used her candle to light a lamp, and moved to the parlor sofa, kneeling to check on the Ohio teen who had been shot in the stomach.

"Mister Benson?" she asked quietly, but he did not stir. Lowering the candle, she found the broken piece of mirror, and held it underneath his nostrils, although she already guessed that he was dead.

The doctor's boots plopped on the hardwood floor, and he snorted, cursed, and moved wearily. Grace bit her trembling lip.

"He dead?" the doctor asked.

She could only nod.

"Hey!" His shout caused her to jump. "A couple of you darkies come haul this body out of here." The Yankee fired up a cigar. "We'll have need of this bed before too long, I warrant."

Grace had moved to another wounded Yankee, busying herself by removing his foul-smelling bandage. Behind her, she heard an old slave's timid voice: "Where we put this boy, Capt'n?"

"Stack him on the porch," came the answer, "with the others."

*  *  *  *  *

All that morning she worked, as she had all yesterday, never stopping to relieve her bladder, fill her stomach, or even wonder what Miss Prudence Caxton would think if she could see her beautiful home today.

Black children sat in the winter kitchen, singing spirituals with their grandmothers. Mothers and fathers helped bring in the wounded, or carry out the dead to the porch.

The grandfather clock had stopped chiming. Musketry sounded closer. The front door burst open, and a bluecoat captain screamed something Grace couldn't understand. A nearby slave's eyes widened in fear. As the officer turned, stepping through the threshold, his head exploded, and he crashed into the foyer. More window panes shattered. A white-haired slave cried out, clutching his shoulder, dropping to his knees. A bullet thudded into the portrait of Andrew

Jackson Caxton above the mantle. The songs had stopped in the kitchen, replaced by terrified screams. Another bullet smashed another window.

"Get down!" The Yankee surgeon pushed Grace behind the staircase landing.

"My God," he said, softer now, dropping a bloody metacarpal saw onto the rug. "The Rebs have burst through."

Through the broken windows and front door blocked open by the dead captain's body, she made out figures in butternut and gray moving down Fillmore, through the empty lot across the street, firing muskets, pistols, cutting loose with Rebel yells.

A raw-boned figure appeared in the doorway, stepped over the Yankee officer's corpse, and Grace saw his horrible face, blackened by powder, blood, dirt, grime, his grim eyes locked on her like death.

The bluecoat surgeon blocked the black-bearded figure.

"This is a hospital, you cur, so …"

The musket the Confederate held roared, and Grace shrieked as the surgeon fell atop her. She kept screaming. Couldn't shut up. Refused to open her eyes. Yelled and cried until she could no longer hear the sobbing children, the din of battle, the howls of dying men.

"Stop it! *STOP IT!*"

Something popped, and her cheek stung. Her eyes opened, focusing on the hollow face of a Negress. Blinking, Grace tentatively touched her cheek. The slave glared at her without fear, even though she had just struck a white woman. In Corinth, Mississippi.

"You gots to be strong, missy," the slave was saying. "That doctor, he be dead. You's all these boys got left. You gots to get your strength from the Lord."

Grace was moving now, retrieving the metacarpal saw, although she had no idea how to use it. She thought about Dr. Landon, wondered if he remained in Iuka, if he were dead. She looked through the door. A shell exploded in the street, sending gray soldiers in every direction.

The ringing left her ears. She peeked inside the parlor, then stepped over the dead captain and onto the porch. A man held his right arm in his left, blood spurting from the empty socket. Waving a saber over his head, a Confederate officer screamed at him, and she caught a few words: "... not hurt bad ... keep goin' ..." The wounded soldier stumbled forward, carrying his right arm, and collapsed a few yards later.

"Come on!" Dropping the surgical saw, Grace hurried down the steps, through the white gate torn off its hinges. She reached a Confederate soldier crawling through blood and body parts. Her mouth trembled.

"Ryan."

The soldier looked up, blood trickling through split lips. She let out a breath.

*It's not Ryan McCalla.*

Looking back toward Miss Prudence's house, she shouted: "Come on! Help me get these men inside! Come on!"

She reached down, gripping the wounded Confederate's shell jacket, jerked him forward. "Come on!"

The slave who had slapped her came out first, helping Grace with the wounded Confederate, yelling in some language Grace couldn't comprehend. The slave who had been shot in the shoulder staggered out, taking the burden from Grace. She ran back to the street, and this time several black men and women came with her, to help gather up the wounded.

She stooped to roll over another Confederate. Two slaves, maybe her age, stopped to help. "Leave him," she snapped. "He's dead."

Moving to another. And another.

"This one!" she barked. She grabbed the Confederate's legs. A husky slave with a bald head took his shoulders. As they moved toward the house, a musket ball buzzed her ear. She didn't flinch, but, as they stepped through the broken gate, she looked up the street.

The Confederates were coming back. Retreating.

Somewhere, a church bell began chiming.

It was only noon.

# CHAPTER TWENTY-EIGHT

OCTOBER 4, 1862
CORINTH, MISSISSIPPI

Hell came with dawn.

Federals unleashed their wrath from the myriad batteries erected around Corinth, and Ryan McCalla pressed his face closer to the earth. Beside him, he heard Sergeant Rutherford whisper: "Fool officers. We never should've stopped last night. Would have the Yanks whipped by now."

"Just like Shiloh." Gibb Gideon chuckled.

The night had been spent in misery, the temperature dropping. No fires. Not even to light pipes or cigars. No songs, unless you counted the wails and groans of the wounded Rebels and Yankees who lay scattered across the battlefield like autumn leaves.

Rolling onto his belly, Ryan dared to lift his head. Solid shot roared, the hot air rushing maybe a foot above his hat. He thought he could make out that three-story college building for females, where that kind, tall nurse had cared for him just a few months back.

"String Bean," he said, and lowered his head before another Yankee shell took it off.

"You say something?" Gideon asked.

Instead of answering, Ryan chanced another look. One of those murderous redoubts lay four hundred, maybe five hundred yards ahead. A Parrott roared, blowing off the tops of trees a half mile behind him. Rifles sang out from pits and redoubts, from trees and rosebushes. One of the Germans from Company F sat up, swatting his chest as if stung by a bee, then toppled over.

*Thud.*

*Thud.*

*Thud.*

"Lieutenant!" Sergeant Rutherford roared. "We stay here, we'll all be dead in an hour!"

They had charged yesterday toward the massive battery with Texians from the Sixth and Ninth regiments, alongside some Mississippi boys from the Thirty-Fifth and the Forty-Second Alabama. Now, an Alabama captain rose to his feet, waving his kepi, motioning his men forward.

"Forward Alabamans!" he shouted. "Texians sha'n't beat us to those breastworks."

His troops answered with Confederate yells, and they started surging ahead.

"Come on, Texas!" Colonel Rogers rode forward on a bay horse. "Mississippians, let's give them …"

Ryan couldn't hear anything else now, for he was yelling, too, charging alongside Sergeant Rutherford and Gibb Gideon. A Texas soldier fell, dropping the colors, but Gibb Gideon picked up the flag, kept going. Glancing to his left, Ryan saw an endless stream of Confederates racing, firing, dying, yelling, breaking through.

He leaped over two dead men, almost lost his footing. Lead spit up bark, and he found himself weaving between the tree trunks that lined the field like tombstones in a cemetery. Round shot decapitated a lieutenant. Ryan ground his teeth.

What was left of a patch of woods slowed their progress, and by the time they had cleared the remnants of trees, the Yanks had switched to grapeshot. Buckshot cut down Mississippians, Alabamans, and Texians by the dozens. A bullet pierced his canteen, but it had been empty since yesterday afternoon. It reminded him, however, of how thirsty he was. Then another memory flashed through his brain: Shiloh, his canteen also pierced by Union lead.

"Boys, give them a volley!"

He almost stopped to fire, only to realize the order had come from a Yankee. They were that close now.

Shots rang out. Grapeshot ripped through the ranks. His eyes burned with sweat. The frigid morning was now an ancient blur.

He spotted the colors on the ground, and slowed. Gibb Gideon was crawling away, holding a bloody left leg. "Go on, Ryan!" he yelled. "Don't you pick up that flag!"

Ryan shifted his Enfield to his left hand, but Colonel Rogers beat him to it. He rode forward, leaning in the saddle, picking up the colors, then stood in the stirrups, waving that Lone Star flag, yelling something Ryan couldn't hear, daring the Yankees to try to kill him.

"Hurrah!" Gibb Gideon was yelling. "Hurrah for Texas. Hurrah for Colonel Rogers!"

"Keep your head down, Gibb!" Ryan yelled as he raced past his friend.

They were leaping into the ditch now at the bottom of the battery. Colonel Rogers swung from the saddle, leaped over the ditch, planted the flagpole into the dirt on the side of the battery.

A bullet killed his horse. Another tore off his hat.

"Come on, you Texas devils!" Rogers started climbing up the earth.

Ryan followed, yelling, too ashamed not to follow his commander, his friends. No one would ever accuse the Second Texas of cowardice again. Not after this day.

Onward, upward. His feet slipped. He stumbled, climbed back up, pushing his way forward, using the dead and wounded as steps.

A grenade landed at his feet, fuse smoking. He knelt, picked it up, tossed it over the top, heard the explosion a second later. Other explosions echoed. He stopped, grabbed another grenade, heaved it over the wall.

He came up, inside the battery now, ducked a bayonet thrust. Instead of firing, he rammed the Enfield's stock into the Yank's face. A ball grazed his neck. He clubbed a Union officer. Another Yank struck him like a bull, wrapping massive arms around Ryan's chest and back, squeezing. Air exploded from Ryan's lungs. He tried to butt the soldier's head, but couldn't, then, through blurring vision, made out Sergeant Rutherford thrusting his bayonet through the big bluecoat's back.

Like dead weight, the Yank fell against Ryan. It took a moment for Ryan to regain enough strength to push the corpse away. He grabbed his Enfield, stopped, fired.

There was no time to reload. He clubbed one man, stopped, and jerked a revolver out of the unconscious officer's holster.

"Our boys are in town!"

"Billy Yank's on the run, fellas!"

Ryan moved forward, firing the pistol twice. Leaped over a dead bluebelly. Another. Pulled the trigger again. A hand reached out, caught his right foot, sent him falling headfirst. He landed, tasting blood in his mouth, rolled over, cocking the revolver, finger tightening on the trigger as he found the bluecoat's face.

His finger relaxed, and he lowered the pistol, letting it fall into the dirt.

"Missouri," he said.

"Texas." Caleb Cole grinned.

The Yank was bleeding from his left shoulder, but his left hand pressed tightly against his ribcage. Ryan rose, walking on his knees, hands reaching down, grabbing Caleb Cole under his arms. He inched his way back toward one of the abandoned Parrotts, dragging the wounded Yankee behind him.

A Mississippi sergeant stopped, stared, began to lunge with his bayonet.

"Get out of here!" Ryan snapped. "Go kill a Yank who's trying to kill you!"

That, somehow, stopped the sergeant. The hard-faced man in butternut swore, spit, and moved away.

After a minute, Ryan stopped, biting back pain, and eased Caleb Cole against an empty box of shot.

"See you around, Yank," he said, and took off, forgetting that he had no weapon.

They had the Yanks driven out of the battery. Almost. Suddenly ten Rebs in front of him cried out, falling into heaps. A bullet parted his hair. Ryan slid to a stop, pried a Mississippi Rifle from a dead Texian's hands. He opened the cartridge box, rammed home a load, looked around him. Blue and gray and butternut lying together. Blood and blood and blood.

"Boys!"

Shots.

"Boys!"

*Thud.*

*Thud.*

*Thud.*

He coughed from the thick smoke. Had to use the rifle to push himself up.

"Hold your fire, Texas!" Above the din, he recognized Colonel Rogers' voice. Somehow, he made out a white flag.

"NO!" Ryan stopped.

Muskets roared. The Yankees answered. Colonel Rogers, dropping the handkerchief he had been waving over his head, pitched backward.

Yanks streamed into the battery. Fresh troops or ornery soldiers who refused to yield to the Confederates—Ryan couldn't tell. What did it matter? Ryan fired. Tossed away the empty rifle, tried to find another gun. All around him he heard Southern accents. "Hold your fire." "Surrender!" "Save yourselves!"

"McCalla!"

Sergeant Rutherford pointed as he ran past Ryan. Back toward the breastworks, the Parrotts, and cannon, the dead and dying, the colors of the Second Texas.

He swore, fighting back tears, and staggered away.

"McCalla."

Another voice stopped Ryan. A ball raced over his head, and he ducked, looking behind him as he veered toward the wounded Missourian.

Caleb Cole held out a canteen, and Ryan took it, gulped down tepid, wretched water, and tossed the blue-woolen-wrapped container back to the Yank.

"You hurt bad?" Ryan asked.

Cole smiled. "Busted a rib or two. And took a ball." His left hand moved away from his ribs, and disappeared inside his blouse. Confederates raced past Ryan, but no one stopped.

"Be seeing you, Yank," Ryan said. He had to get out of here. Else get killed or be captured.

"Wait."

Looking back, Ryan saw the Missouri boy's hand reappear, holding a brown plug of tobacco. Ryan could just make out a flattened piece of gray lead in the center of the quid Governor Sam Houston had given him before the Second left Houston. Vaguely Ryan remembered handing this Yankee that plug at that pond back at Shiloh.

"Best take this, McCalla," the Missouri kid said. He laughed, more from fever and pain than humor. "I don't chew."

Ryan took the quid, ramming it into his pants pocket. He rose, and began helping a limping Alabaman out of the battery.

Before disappearing in the smoke, he shot Caleb Cole a glance and a smile.

"Neither do I," he said.

# EPILOGUE

"Friends of the South," General Prentiss began, "particularly American citizens, I came, I saw, and I was conquered." When the crowd's laughter died, the aging bluecoat general went on. "We came here to go to Corinth, but Corinth came to us."

Ryan McCalla moved his way through the throng as the Yankee general continued his history of the Battle of Shiloh. At least that was a Southern victory, an Alabaman had said yesterday. Yankees had called the battle "Pittsburg Landing," but it was the Confederate name, "Shiloh," that had stuck.

By any name, Ryan didn't need to hear a bluecoat general's version of the battle. For two days, he had lived it. Reporters and historians took notes, and, finding daylight, Ryan walked along the path in what was now a park, starting toward the cemetery, then veering off. Not that he could find Matt Bryson's grave. The Yankees had given their dead proper burials, but most Confederates had been dumped unceremoniously in shallow pits, their bodies barely covered with mud.

That was probably why Shiloh National Military Park had been established back in December. Farmers had complained too much about their pigs rooting up the remains of dead soldiers.

Now, veterans of both Northern and Southern armies had returned to the battlefield. Yesterday, Ryan had approved a resolution the Confederate veterans had made:

Resolved, that we extend to the Union veterans a hearty and cordial greeting, and desire that this association be perpetuated so long as any of the survivors of the Shiloh battle be permitted to remain.

Today was sunny, not like those wet, miserable days thirty-three years ago. He could smell peach blossoms, yet this time the odor was not accented by malodorous stenches of gunpowder and death but wonderful aromas of brisket and coffee. He passed a campfire, saw a tall man wearing a Confederate artillery shell jacket talking to a silver-haired man in a blue dress uniform.

He kept walking, passing Southern ladies holding parasols and waving paper fans. He tipped his hat, and continued until at last he reached the place.

The park had posted a sign on a tall stump.

A split-rail fence ran through it near the woods. He didn't remember that from 1862, but most of the battlefield remained as it had been. The names veterans on both sides had given sections had taken root. The Hornet's Nest. The Sunken Road. The Peach Orchard. And this place. He looked again at the sign: Bloody Pond.

If he closed his eyes, he thought he could hear the moans of dying men pleading for water, begging for mercy, the occasional pop of a musket or the murderous explosion of an artillery shell fired from one of the Union gunboats. Instead, he heard the rippling of water, and the wind rustling through the trees. A frog croaked. A robin chirped. In the distance, he heard music, laughter, and a voice.

"Is your name McCalla?"

Ryan turned, pushing back his hat, watching the bald, pudgy

man in an ill-fitting coat—not a military blouse, but a plaid number—walk toward him.

Even after three decades, the name came to him instantly.

"Caleb Cole."

Caleb Cole set a black leather grip at his feet, and extended a ham-size hand. Briefly they shook.

"I was hoping you'd be here," Cole said. "Wasn't sure you were even alive. Spent all yesterday wandering through the Rebel camps, and most of this morning. I'd about given up." He turned his head, and spit a river of tobacco juice into the leaves.

Another memory flashed through Ryan's head. "I thought you didn't chew tobacco."

Cole wiped his mouth with the sleeve of his plaid coat. He winked mischievously. "My wife and daughters wish I'd never taken it up."

Wife and daughters. Ryan felt a tinge of regret. He had never married.

After Corinth, the Second had moved to Vicksburg and stayed there, half starved, burying Sergeant Rutherford from fever three weeks before they had surrendered on July 4, 1863. Ryan, Gibb Gideon, and the rest of the regiment had been furloughed back to Texas as paroled prisoners of war. Exchanged in November, they had returned to Camp Bee, and spent the rest of the war around Galveston.

Then Ryan had begun a career in wanderlust. Up the cattle trails to Kansas. Laying track for the railroad. Mining in Colorado. Working a jerkline in Wyoming. Running a faro layout in Montana. He had seen a lot of country. He remembered little of it.

He had no idea what had ever become of Gibb Gideon, or any of the other men with whom he had fought.

"You still in Missouri?" Ryan asked, just to be polite.

"Nah. Got home after the war and ..."

"You see much action after Corinth?" Ryan interrupted.

Cole shrugged. "Atlanta campaign. Kennesaw Mountain."

He frowned. "Well, we marched with Sherman through Georgia and the Carolinas."

"I see."

"Nothing I was proud of."

Ryan forced a smile. "War's over. I'm no unreconstructed Reb. It's good to see you."

Cole spit again. "Well, anyway, I got back to Putnam County once we were mustered out, but I just couldn't find any pleasure in slopping hogs after all I had seen and done. Got a job feeding railroad workers in Nebraska. In other words, I shot a mess of buffalo. Did that all the way to Cheyenne. Then quit, moved south. Shot buffalo for their hides for a spell. Worked on the railroad betwixt Dallas and Fort Worth down in Texas. Took to freighting in New Mexico Territory. Wound up in Bisbee, down in Arizona Territory, with a stage line, and now I own a mercantile in San Diego, California."

"You've done well."

"And you?"

Ryan laughed. "I have a twenty-dollar horse and a sixty-dollar saddle."

"That'd make most Texans I know jealous."

This time Ryan's laugh was genuine. He gestured toward the pond. "I don't know, Cole. Somehow, I thought it would be different. Or maybe I thought it would be the same. By jacks, I don't know what I thought."

"It's been thirty years, McCalla. We were kids when we first came here, dreaming of war and glory, seeing nothing but hell and privations."

Ryan nodded. "All that's left is wormwood and gall."

Laughter wafted through the trees. "No," Cole corrected. "Most of these folks came here remembering the glory, or what we thought was glory. I saw friends die."

Ryan frowned. "So did I."

"Yeah, but I don't remember the horrors. Oh, I did for the

longest while. But, gee willikins, it's been better than thirty years. These days, I remember a Reb I met at this pond. A Reb I saw again in Corinth. I remember humanity. That's why I came back here. Well, one reason, anyway."

Pushing his hat back, Ryan tried to think of something to add only quickly to determine there was nothing else to say. "Well, Cole, it's good to see you." Again, he pointed at the pond. "Thanks again, for pulling me out of that."

Cole rubbed his ribs. "Thanks for the plug of tobacco. It saved my life at Corinth."

Ryan had taken only a handful of steps before Cole called his name. Facing the Missourian, he saw him kneeling, opening the satchel.

"I have something for you, McCalla."

Ryan's mouth fell open, and his heart seemed to stop. He knew what it was, and could not stop the tears welling in his eyes as Caleb Cole respectfully brought over the Miremont case.

"Where did you …?" He almost dropped the case.

"When I heard about the reunion …," Cole began. Tears flowed down his cheeks, too. "I came out here early. Wanted to see … I guess … no, of course not. I knew her, too, McCalla. When we were stationed in Corinth that summer."

Their eyes locked. They said her name at the same moment. Ryan sank to his knees, and Caleb knelt beside him.

"Grace is dead?" Ryan didn't bother to wipe away his tears.

"Her daughter's name is Clarinda. Clarinda Atkinson. Married with a baby daughter of her own now. She's the spitting image of her mama, though, Clarinda, I mean. Even taller than me. Seems Grace married this English doctor …"

"I remember him."

"Way too old for her. Created quite the scandal in Corinth, especially when everyone learned she had been living in the doctor's place after her home was burned, and this church where she'd been staying was torn down by Union troops. They sang her praises in

Corinth, though, those who remembered her. Said she helped save many a life during that battle in October. Blue and gray. She had a good life, Ryan. She wouldn't want any tears. Died five years ago, Clarinda said, of influenza. Her husband had died … oh, I don't know … when Clarinda was just a baby. She went right on doctoring, Grace did. Went right on doctoring, and Clarinda says her funeral was the biggest ever in Holly Springs, Mississippi. That's where they moved after the war."

He pointed to the case. "She kept that all those years. Kept something for me, too." Caleb reached inside the bag and pulled out a Bible and two ancient envelopes, yellowed with age.

Wiping his eyes, Ryan opened the case. "When I left Texas," he said, his voice sounding ancient, "I thought I would die in battle."

"I thought the same thing. Definitely figured I was a goner when you Rebs came busting through Battery Robinett in Corinth."

Ryan hefted the violin. He had broken his mother's heart, never playing any type of instrument, not even singing in the church choir, after he was back in Texas. Once she had asked him if he had gotten the violin she had mailed to that nurse in Mississippi, but he had never answered.

His hands trembled. He hadn't touched a violin since … his head shook at the memory. Abilene, Kansas, 1871. In his cups, he had bet a Texas drover he could play, and the drover had paid up at the Bull's Head Saloon. He had played "Lorena." The drinking had stopped, and Texas cowboys and Kansas tinhorns, former Rebs and ex-Yankees, had shed tears over the haunting melody.

"Play it," Caleb said. "Grace would want that."

He started to shake his head, but at the same time found himself pulling out the bow. He plucked a cord, tightened the string, then another. Drew the bow over it again. He looked up, shaking his head, about to lower the Miremont.

"Wormwood and gall," he whispered.

"No, good memories." Cole smiled. "Good friends."

A group of veterans walked up, laughing. Ryan spotted them, some in Union blue, others in gray, most in denim, duck, or broadcloth. Old men, who had forgotten the savagery. Or maybe they had just learned to live with it.

"Hey, Reb," a bluecoat said, "play us something."

"Play 'Dixie'!" a Southerner cried out.

"Better not!" snapped a Yankee, and everyone laughed.

Ryan tested the strings again, twisted a knob, loosened another. He looked at Caleb Cole, and whispered: "She hated this song."

He played. On the second verse, the Rebs joined in. The Yanks slapped their thighs. One danced a little jig.

> *I'll put my knapsack on my back,*
> *My rifle on my shoulder.*
> *I'm goin' away to Shiloh,*
> *And there I'll be a soldier.*

A lifetime ago he had marched into these fields and woods. He remembered thinking he was going to die. Remembered how that feeling had evaporated sometime during the savage assault. Surrounded by death, by inhumanity, and, yet, humanity; he remembered never feeling so alive.

On a Saturday evening along the banks of Shiloh's Bloody Pond thirty-three years later, Ryan McCalla knew he was being reborn. Closing his eyes, he could see Grace Dehner smiling down upon him. And Matt Bryson, and Sam Houston Jr., Sergeant Rutherford, Gibb Gideon, his parents, Harry Cravey, Captain Ashbel Smith, Dr. Landon, the men he had killed in battle, the soldiers who had tried to kill him.

The war was over, and he felt so alive.

## THE END

# AUTHOR'S NOTE

Books consulted for this novel are too many to list, but the main sources were as follows: *The Eighteenth Missouri* by Leslie Anders (Bobbs-Merrill Company, 1968); *The Second Texas Infantry: From Shiloh to Vicksburg* by Joseph E. Chance (Eakin Press, 1984); *Ashbel Smith of Texas: Pioneer, Patriot, Statesman, 1805–1886* by Elizabeth Silverthorne (Texas A&M University Press, 1982); Ralph J. Smith's *Reminiscences of the Civil War and Other Sketches* (W. M. Morrison, 1911); *Shiloh—In Hell before Night* by James Lee McDonough (University of Tennessee Press, 1977); *Shiloh: The Battle that Changed the Civil War* by Larry J. Daniel (Simon & Schuster, 1997); *The Darkest Days of the War: The Battles of Iuka & Corinth* by Peter Cozzens (University of North Carolina Press, 1997); *"Co. Aytch": A Side Show of the Big Show* by Sam R. Watkins (Collier, 1962); and the anonymous *The Lost Account of the Battle of Corinth and the Court-Martial of Gen. Van Dorn*, edited by Monroe F. Cockrell (Broadfoot, 1991).

I should also thank Christopher A. Mekow and other rangers at Shiloh National Military Park and the staff of the Corinth Civil War Interpretive Center. Both are absolute musts for any history buff interested in the Civil War battles of Shiloh and Corinth.

Johnny D. Boggs
Santa Fe, New Mexico

# ABOUT THE AUTHOR

Johnny D. Boggs has worked cattle, shot rapids in a canoe, hiked across mountains and deserts, traipsed around ghost towns, and spent hours poring over microfilm in library archives—all in the name of finding a good story. He's also one of the few Western writers to have won four Spur Awards from Western Writers of America (for his novels, *Camp Ford*, in 2006, *Doubtful Cañon*, in 2008, and *Hard Winter* in 2010, and his short story, "A Piano at Dead Man's Crossing," in 2002) and the Western Heritage Wrangler Award from the National Cowboy and Western Heritage Museum (for his novel, *Spark on the Prairie: The Trial of the Kiowa Chiefs*, in 2004). A native of South Carolina, Boggs spent almost fifteen years in Texas as a journalist at the *Dallas Times Herald* and *Fort Worth Star-Telegram* before moving to New Mexico in 1998 to concentrate full-time on his novels. Author of dozens of published short stories, he has also written for more than fifty newspapers and magazines, and is a frequent contributor to *Boys' Life*, *New Mexico* magazine, *Persimmon Hill*, and *True West*. His Western novels cover a wide range. *The Lonesome Chisholm Trail* (Five Star Westerns, 2000) is an authentic cattle-drive story, while *Lonely Trumpet* (Five Star Westerns, 2002) is an historical novel about the first black graduate of West Point. *The Despoilers* (Five Star Westerns, 2002) and *Ghost Legion* (Five Star Westerns, 2005) are set in the Carolina backcountry during the Revolutionary War. *The Big Fifty* (Five Star Westerns, 2003) chronicles the slaughter of buffalo on the southern plains in the 1870s, while *East of the Border* (Five Star Westerns, 2004) is a comedy about the theatrical offerings of Buffalo Bill Cody, Wild Bill Hickok, and Texas Jack Omohundro, and *Camp Ford* (Five Star Westerns, 2005) tells about a Civil War baseball game between Union prisoners of war and Confederate guards. "Boggs' narrative voice captures the old-fashioned style of the past," *Publishers Weekly* said, and *Booklist* called him "among the best Western writers at work today." Boggs lives with his wife Lisa and son Jack in Santa Fe. His website is www.JohnnyDBoggs.com.